Praise for The Dancer from the Dance

…the urbane and witty language of the narrator is a delight to read…
Glasgow Herald

Her style has the precision of John Updike's and the charm of Conan Doyle's … and her novel contains some of the most dazzling bits of description I have come across..
The New York Times Book Review

Stanford Powers must be one of the most unusual Americans in Paris in fiction … this is an extremely intelligent book, unusual for its creation of an outstanding three-dimensional Iago.
Punch

THE DANCER FROM THE DANCE

fiction by the same author

Descend Again (1960)
The Dancer from the Dance (1965)
Eyes (1966)
The Buzzards (1969)
Raw Silk (1977)
Opening Nights (1985)
Cutting Stone (1992)
Bridge of Sand (2009)
Simone in Pieces (2025)

THE DANCER FROM THE DANCE

by

JANET BURROWAY

with an introductory note by
ROBERT OLEN BUTLER

SANDNESS
MICHAEL WALMER
2024

The Dancer from the Dance first published 1965
© Janet Burroway 1965

Introductory note first published in this edition
© Robert Olen Butler 2024

This edition published 2024 by

Michael Walmer
Little Pradies
13a Melby
Sandness
Shetland ZE2 9PL

ISBN 978-1-7635656-1-6 paperback

INTRODUCTORY NOTE

How is it that works of manifest literary artistry in the modern era can be published and vanish while readers who have keen aesthetic receptors never discover them? As Walmer Modern Classics admirably revives Janet Burroway's splendid and shamefully overlooked *The Dancer from the Dance,* we all should consider the gatekeepers. The review community. Reviewers have a serious occupational hazard. They must pick a book from an ever-renewing pile on their desk and read that book on a deadline and describe it in semi-summary and explain it in condensed evaluative terms. And so what sort of readers are they of a work of literary art full of nuance and subtext and even currents of dramatic irony from an unreliable narrator?

They are too often *unfit* readers. Made so by the felt necessities of their job. They read too fast, unable to hear the narrative voice in their head, and with the question inevitably roiling within them: What am I going to say? And the way they find an answer all too often drives them out of their aesthetic sensibility and into their analytical mind.

In other words, it cripples their very ability to judge a work of art. The genuine reader of a work of literature is not meant to experience it thematically or abstractly or ideationally. The reader is meant to thrum to a work of literary art, like the string vibrating on a stringed instrument. A genuine reader is never intended to separate the dancer from the dance.

But alas, most of the early reviewers of Janet Burroway's second novel fell victim to their occupational hazard. They did not experience the book. They pondered the manufacturer of the pointe shoes; they named the bones of the dancer's port de bras. And as early faulty reviews too often do, they then put off potential later reviewers who might otherwise have taken the book from their pile and read it and actually thrummed to it.

The reviewers of *The Dancer from the Dance* largely failed to thrum to the complexity of its unreliable narrator, a diplomat in Paris who — like most of the great central figures of literature; indeed, like all of us — yearns to seek an answer to the eternal question: Who am I? He is doing so — often self-deceptively — in a circle of eccentric friends and in a central, complex relationship with a young American woman whose youth makes her a perceived blank canvas upon which he creates an ultimately flawed portrait of himself. He is full of the strivings and successes and failures of our shared humanity.

Now. Read this book. But slowly. You must always hear the voice of the narrator in real time. You must hear in him what he cannot ultimately hear in himself.

This is a book of great and subtle worth.

ROBERT OLEN BUTLER

Lamont, October 2024

For my parents

The characters in this book are fictitious, and the institutions fictionalized. Some of the buildings are real. I have felt it permissible to organize the AERO office of UNICEF for the convenience of my narrative, so that it bears only a vague resemblance to my memory of it, and probably none at all to the place itself.

J. B.

PART ONE

*A Sixty-year-old
Smiling Public Man*

*T*HEY are tearing down the little house at Parc Fasse-ville. Mme de Verbois warned me some months ago that they would do so. They had come to her, she said, only a week or two after Prytania's departure, kindly informed her that the house had been for a third time condemned, and requested to know whether, for a third time, she wished to appeal. Madame had said no, that the house was past its usefulness to her, and hoped that the land might be of some use to the city. She pointed out to me the appropriateness of the city's timing, in a voice of unusual gentleness, even for her.

I walked down the boulevard Wagram toward it the other day, in one of those impetuous Paris summer winds that catches now at a lapel, now at your hat, now warm and full in the face, now chilly at the nape of your neck. It promises to be an indifferent summer, unlike last year's, when already by this time there were optimistic speculations for the quality of the wine. I had brought an umbrella against an early morning cloud, and by that clear hour of the afternoon felt a little conspicuous and feeble with it, as if my caution were a sign of my age. I believe there was a time when I carried an umbrella as a sign of youth and promise.

The house stands at the northeast flatiron extreme of the park, where there is no entrance, but a spiked fence easy enough to climb if you are agile and so inclined. The alternate access is round about through the main gate at some two blocks' distance. I took the latter way. The Parc Fasseville is really a children's park, not very large or very dense; not thickly wooded enough, and closed at too early an hour, to be of much use to lovers. It has neither a fountain nor a pond, and one is not allowed on the grass, but it is richly planted in vibrant colors, here and there a statue commemorates an abduction or a general, there are scattered sandboxes and teeter-totters, there are wide graveled walks lined with canvas chairs at thirty centimes the afternoon. On a summer's day nearly all of these chairs will be filled with placid mothers in cotton dresses, chatting with their faces turned to the sun and fanning their necks with slow, limber gestures of their hands. The children play mostly on the gravel, guarding possessions, searching for treasures at the edge of the grass, skinning knees, quarreling over slights and stumbling in quest of maternal consolation and justice. I walked this gentle gauntlet slowly, now and again returning a childish stare, retrieving an errant ball, and almost reluctantly turning on to the little side path toward the house. It is nearly hidden from this junction by a screen of chestnut trees and a sharp granite boulder, so that the path is neither conspicuous nor particularly inviting. The boulder once skirted, however, one approaches from the back, toward a small porch with four columns, a miniature two-story structure of graying clapboard with a green shingled hip roof. It is old-fashioned without being venerably antique; charming in its way, but built without much care, and never properly cared for. It faces rather ridiculously toward the iron fence, and through that commands a view of high apartment buildings and shops, heavy traffic and a distant corner of the Arc de Triomphe. The effect of standing in this sheltered spot is startling. It is as if the gingerbread house of Hansel and Gretel were set down in the Chicago Loop: to the back and sides, the musical shivering of sunlit leaves and the sharp call of sparrows; to the front the rushing roar and grind of Paris traffic, bearing down head-on until it splits just at your doorstep and careens to either side.

This afternoon the incongruity of noises was augmented by the whine of straining wood, as half a dozen workmen crawled over the roof, pulling at nails and tossing shingles at random into the yard. I noted with satisfaction that this innocent little edifice, which had escaped the ax so many times before, was putting up enough of a final battle to make six strong men sweat. I had it half in mind to speak to one of them, saying something like, "Look here, my good fellow, take care when you get near the porch roof. There's a serious leak there, and it's probably rotten." In fact I knew of no such leak, but I had the unmistakable impression that I should gain authority over them by displaying my familiarity with the place, and it should have given me great pleasure to see them making themselves ridiculous with caution over the porch roof.

But I didn't say anything. I believe I feared some extravagant downfall — as if the hugest of the workmen would annihilate my claim by jumping up and down on the shingles with a diabolical whoop. Instead I sat on a rock, hung my hat on my umbrella handle and watched, thinking of the history of the tough little house, and adding my will to its will to survive.

The little house at Parc Fasseville was originally built as a gatekeeper's cottage when there was a gatekeeper to justify it. That petty official had long since been replaced by a series of patrolmen on daily beats when the city decided to condemn it, not on grounds of its decay but because the corner might be considered a valuable one, and the park would not seriously suffer from having this triangular reach lopped off. But M. Auguste de Verbois, who was at that time a member of the Parks Commission, intervened. M. de Verbois was partner in a pharmaceutical company, and was engaged on the side in some obscure botanical research. The house, he said, situated as it was in the very middle of native Parisian vegetation, made an ideal laboratory. He entreated them to lend it to him.

M. de Verbois' reasoning has always seemed highly specious to me — none of his findings were, to my knowledge, ever published, and at his death Mme de Verbois found very little in the nature of laboratory equipment to dispose of — but he was a formidable figure in what were labeled "public" affairs. He made eloquent use of his conviction (which I have no doubt was his real motive) that it was an outrage to fell such a charming spot for another gray hotel. And there being on the Paris Parks Commission, as on any parks commission in the world, several who were per se opposed to relinquishing a square yard of wooded ground, M. de Verbois' request was granted. The Commission forgot the house, M. de Verbois either did or did not study there, then he died and the keys fell into Mme de Verbois' hands. It was not many months later when, in her volunteer work at the Hôpital des Étrangers,

Madame encountered a Mr. Riebenstahl, the survivor of an automobile accident which had killed his wife. Riebenstahl was eventually discharged, his minor wounds past danger, but abandoned by such relatives as there were, and in a seriously disturbed state of mind. Madame installed him in the little house, and when the Parks Commission sent a representative to inquire about him, she told one of the few lies of her veracious life. She said that Herr Doktor Riebenstahl (who was not German, and had never been graduated from an English public school, let alone a university) was carrying on her husband's work, and that it had been her husband's will that he should inherit the use of the laboratory. She was mildly astonished when they dropped the matter once again.

Now Riebenstahl is also dead, and . . .

. . . and I found that my mind would not just then get past this stumbling block of Riebenstahl's death. I rose and restored my hat to my head, advancing cautiously toward the house and its parasites. The squirrels were scolding them shrilly, and the trees shaking grains of light on them like giant salt cellars. They had taken out the glass panes first and dismantled the window and door frames, which lay heaped on the ground like a pile of flung jackstraws. Two of the workmen — I was certain that they called themselves "destruction engineers" — had advanced by now almost to the porch roof, and knelt there in perfect safety prying the shingles loose in three deft motions, flinging them forward into the yard. My courage suddenly left me, and my sense that the house was putting up a fight. As for sweating, these fellows probably sweated in their sleep. A fragment of poetry came to me from somewhere: "The way they chewed unchallenged, just like flies/Into an animal already dead." I poked at a rotten step-rise with my umbrella, and indeed, the wood gave dangerously and a row of irritated ants circumvented the crack that I had made. One of the men on the roof saw me and called out that I was standing too close, that they had work to do, that it was a dangerous place, and that I had no business. I hooked my umbrella handle over my arm with a gesture of great dignity and, disdaining to answer, retraced my steps toward the main entrance, through the children and their indolent mothers.

It struck me as I walked that when I think of the beginning of the thing, the three of them — old Riebenstahl, his house, and the girl — come to mind in the same picture, as if they had been part of each other from the outset. Of course this is simply enough because I met them, by chance, on the same afternoon. But in retrospect I have taken the chance out of it; they seem very properly to have materialized in the same hour because their lives were linked, and indeed I think of that afternoon as a beginning, as precise a beginning as this sight of the little demolition is a precise ending.

Whereas in fact I first heard of the existence — though not the name — of Prytania Scott Obée through my son-in-law; an unlikely enough source in itself.

Harold is an English military careerist. That definition will damn him very neatly, but I should like to say by way of his defense that I myself am a man of un-American reserve, and have devoted my own life to that humdrum compromise of soul, the State. Indeed, I am tempted to admire Harold's vices of inward and outward orderliness, and would have no cause to dislike him if I didn't feel that he is devoted to his career. He takes frank delight in the implements of destruction, and is not prone to call them weapons of defense; I believe it never caused him any anguish to accept that evil is more interesting than good.

He is a big man, blunderingly honest; florid, and with the largest moustache I have ever seen in civilized society. In the right mood, and over the right wines, he can be a catalyst to any gathering of a boisterously gay sort; he is generous, just, and honorable beyond belief. All the more astonishing that he should tell his father-in-law about a waif he picked up in Frankfurt!

The only explanation is the one that presented itself even before he began: that it was very much on his mind. Harold so infrequently attempts subtlety that he has never acquired the knack, and if the occasion arises for any but military subterfuge, he looks rather as if he were trying to sort beads with gloves on. So when he said after dinner one night, "Well, old fellow, this is nice. Good to be home. Perhaps we should have a cigar together — in your study, what? A regular man-to-man"; when he began in this way I decided, though he had never done so before, that he was going to ask for money.

Harold was stationed in Paris at the time, and had met and married our Lucie some two years before. It had been agreed that they would live with us until Harold was returned to England. I think none of us minimized the dangers of that sort of *ménage-à-quatre;* we spent some pains not to intrude upon each other. Our evening routine was a kind of minuet in which we beamed and bowed as we exchanged our partners. It began with Luce and Laura in the kitchen, myself and Harold over sherry in the parlor; the four of us came to the table together, and as the meal ended split again, Harold to his sitting room, I to my study, the ladies to the kitchen; from whence, when all was in order, they finally rejoined their mates. Luce had imparted to Harold by some feminine means a conviction that my study was a holy place: I had never contradicted this impression, and it was therefore unusual in the extreme that he should alter the steps of the dance by forcing himself upon me.

As I led the way he said again, rather loudly, "It *is* good to be home again," and I supplied the appropriate banality, "It's good to have you back," though the fact is, God knows, that Harold enjoyed a good deal of self-importance when he was sent away on a military errand, and that I played at having a daughter again.

Harold offered me a Dutch cigar he had purchased in Germany, one of those Schimmelpennincks of the absurd length and skinniness called "con mil amores." He wandered about the room, lighting his darker cigar and surveying my books as if it were a great pleasure to see them. I sat down to wait him out.

It is difficult to describe a room both familiar and ordinary. I suppose there is something in my study very revealing of my personality, but I have no idea what it is. The furniture is the usual old-fashioned leather stuff, of good quality but rather the worse for wear; there's a sideboard with four decanters containing sherry, port, Courvoisier and apricot brandy, respectively from left to right; a large desk with a symmetrically arranged surface and untidy drawers. The walls are not what is properly called "book-lined," but there are a couple of floor-to-ceiling cases, holding mainly historical and political volumes. The older of these are well thumbed and smudged and contain the copious, literal-minded notes of my early years in government, while those from the past ten years or so look hardly opened and stand out brashly in their modern covers. This displeases me, but I could not say just why. The other walls have maps of various sections of the world, with small red-headed pins to mark our various UNICEF offices. A very ordinary room.

Even Harold had exhausted its evident delights, and after throwing a bogus smile or two out the window he dropped into the chair opposite me and said, "You know, the funniest thing happened to me in Frankfurt."

Good God, I thought, he's going to tell after-dinner jokes. I should have liked to have asked quite calmly, "How much do you need?" But it has never been my way to be precipitously frank, nor to require it of others; certainly not of my son-in-law.

"Yes, you see . . . quite touching, really. That is, absurd, I suppose you'd say. Actually, I feel a little responsible."

"What happened?" I asked, not really wanting to know, but relieved that it wasn't to be a shaggy dog.

"Well, I met this little girl, you see. . . ."

The father-in-law in me waked with a ferocious start. Harold felt responsible for a little girl he had met in Frankfurt. The "little" did not mislead me. I'd be damned if he'd get a penny.

"Perhaps you'd better start at the beginning," I said, rather sternly it must have been, because even Harold caught my inference, flushed and blustered.

"Oh, good God, sir! Upon my honor. Nothing like that! It's a trifle. You know me better than that, sir."

Indeed I did. It was very stupid of me. Harold's modicum of passion is spent entirely upon his honor, and I had often for my daughter's sake wished otherwise. Still, the notion did not instantly abate; even as I said, "Sorry. Go on," I shifted uneasily in my chair.

"Well, I'd gone out for something, you know. Can't remember the devil what. And I was crossing the Opernplatz when the bus from the station pulled up, and out of it got one of these touristy little American pieces, with her free map and her notebook. Nothing the least extraordinary about her; that is, she was pretty enough, but you know what they are."

"Yes," I said, still vaguely apprehensive, but confident at least of knowing what "they" are.

"That is, I assumed she was American at the time. Now I'm not at all sure. But she was wearing one of those bloody coats."

I raised my eyebrows.

"You know the sort: Americans buy them in Scotland for tartans, which they're not in the least. Very flashy, and quite absurd colors, purple and olive green and so forth."

I still didn't recognize the sort of coat, but I recognized that if Harold were ever to make an observation about clothing, that's the sort *it* would be.

"She looked all about, studied her map and cocked her little blank face on one side, and then as I came up to her she stopped me. I suppose she recognized the uniform. She looked at me very seriously — don't know that I've ever seen such a serious face. Not only that but it was almost . . . Oriental. Very peculiar. Didn't look American close up, and then she said in that most peculiar accent, that I couldn't place anywhere, 'Could you point me toward the Opera? And do you know what's playing there tonight?' Well now, really, that annoyed me quite a bit. You know what these blasted tourists are: they come to a place, don't know anything about it, don't know there's been a war, they get off the train and go to the opera and get back on the train and go on to somewhere else. And still don't know anything about it. Well, you can see my being put out."

"Certainly." Although I couldn't, quite. The question seemed innocent enough.

"So I just said, rather roughly, I'm afraid, 'It's over there,' and passed on. I suppose really it was a little brutal, if I'd thought about it."

"Why? Wasn't it where you said?"

"Oh, yes, in plain sight. Actually, it looks quite magnificent from there."

"So?"

"So I went on and ran my errand, damned if I know what it was, and came back across past the Opera House. And then I noticed a most peculiar little group of people standing about, Germans all of them, looking, well, *abashed,* I think I should say. Perhaps about fifteen of them or so, all staring at this girl, who obviously didn't know she was being looked at, not an idea of it in the world. And there she was looking at the Opera House, and a couple of actual *tears* running down her face. Bloody sentimental, eh?"

All this with the most frequent possible hesitations, interruptions, clearings of the throat. I wondered how he had proposed to Luce — "Well, dash it, the fact is, you know, I've gone and fallen in love with you." Poor Luce. It must have given her such a sense of power to upset the equilibrium of that bluff giant, like startling a moose. Harold was nearly always awkward, but I had never seen him conscious of it before.

"I don't quite follow you, I'm afraid," I said.

"Well, you've been to Frankfurt since the war."

"No, I haven't."

"Oh. Well, you know, the Opera House — it was bombed, of course. I'd forgotten the impression it could

make, and this girl, you see, can't have been more than
seventeen or so. The thing is quite intact. They haven't
done anything but put up a fence around it, and from
the front all you can see is that magnificent heavy-
handed architecture. I shouldn't wonder you could
stand there for ten minutes wondering how to get inside
that blinking fence before you realized that the thing is
entirely gutted. An absolute shell, very pompous and
solid, and inside nothing but rubble and ashes, and the
pillars shattered and thrown about all over the place.
The windows are blasted in, and the damn chandeliers
are still hanging there, swinging in the wind and creak-
ing like an absolute haunted house. You can see right
through to the frescoes, and a few of those are all right,
you know, and the rest are black and blistered up like
skin. Well, of course you can't afford to be sentimental
about that sort of thing, but this girl was just about
seventeen or so. You see?"

I saw, and saw why Harold felt responsible for the
couple of actual *tears*, but I also saw that it was not the
sort of responsibility Harold is generally prone to
assume. "What did you do?" I asked.

"The peculiar thing is, I felt very up to it, extraordi-
narily *awake*, somehow. I could even see what she was
thinking, I swear it. She had her dictionary open to the
W's. There's an inscription across the whole thing: *Dem
Waren Schoenen Guten* — 'For the Preservation of the
Good and Beautiful.' "

"Yes, I remember that now," I said.

"I must say it had never struck me just that way
before — 'Preservation,' you know . . . but then quite
suddenly the girl looked up and saw us all staring at
her — she looked absolutely terrified! But as I say, I
wasn't in any muddle about the right thing to do. I just

stepped in and put a hand under her elbow and steered her away. She didn't seem in the least surprised; didn't resist or anything of that sort, just let me lead her off down the street to a coffee shop and order her a cup of coffee — these American girls never want tea — and then she said, 'Thank you,' as if it were the most natural thing in the world."

"And she said nothing more about it?"

"Not a thing. So I offered to take her back to her family, or whoever. And then she said, 'No, thank you,' and that looked like the end of our conversation."

"Are you sure she was American? Maybe that's all the English she knew."

"Oh, she knew English all right. After a while she said, very guarded and prim, you know, as if she didn't want me to get any ideas, 'I'm alone.' Well, naturally when I didn't lunge — I mean, I took it all very matter-of-factly — she loosed up a little. Appears she's traveling all over Europe by herself. Been to Switzerland, Vienna, Venice, the lot. She wasn't very communicative about her background . . . but damn it, man, she wasn't any little tramp! And all I learned besides was that she planned to travel 'indefinitely.' And when she finished her coffee she thanked me again and up and left."

"Oh, if she was an American schoolgirl, 'indefinitely' probably meant until daddy's allowance ran out."

"Just what I thought, exactly, and I thought when daddy's money does run out, she'll be quite stranded, and won't have the least idea what to do."

"I wouldn't be too sure of that," I said, soothingly for some reason. "That sort can usually make it to the nearest American Express to wire home collect."

"Yes, but well, the point is, you see, she wasn't really 'that sort.' She wasn't really any sort, and you never can tell, can you?" Harold had reached his capacity for evasion. He thrust his hands together between his knees as if he were about to take a sitting dive. "So to tell the truth, the actual fact is, I gave her your card."

"*My* card?"

"Well, damn it, it would have been indelicate to give her mine, you know — she'd never have taken it. But I could say, 'This is my father-in-law's address, if you're ever in Paris, or in need of any help.' You see, and she could take it quite for what it was."

"Yes, I see, that was very thoughtful of you."

"Do you think so? You don't mind?"

"No, of course not. I don't expect she'll write for a million francs, and if she does she won't get it — I've no objection."

Harold sighed back with relief. He has such an unconscionable fear of doing the wrong thing. "Well. It's a bloody trifle, isn't it?"

"Not at all," I said, "it's a very nice story," and our talk passed on to other things. It was a very nice story, but it was also a trifle, and my own relief was so great that had Harold been able to understand the gesture I should have offered him a check. And yet, I thought, there must have been some very remarkable quality about the Oriental American girl in the fake Scotch coat with the unplaceable accent, to make my stolid son-in-law sit there drumming his big fingers on the chair arm and dropping his cigar ash on my spotless carpet.

That was early October. Harold was ordered back to England before Christmas. We danced the dance to the end, all of us; took cheerful leave of each other, and the children had been gone for some fifty minutes before Laura broke into a flood of tears. Assuming that she wished to be alone, I took my book to the study and forced myself to read until I was sure she slept. After that we had several days of that sort of strain marked by exaggerated *politesse*. It did not end, but wore away. Our life with Luce and Harold had been extremely regular, and comfortably dull. Now Laura could not have enough of young people, or of old people who felt young, and though I should never myself have initiated her round of "evenings," I could see that they were in general good for us, like a pleasure cruise one takes for health's sake, preferring to be home in bed. We relaxed, and Laura would plant her absent-minded kisses on my high hairline as she passed.

Our particular friends, most of them Parisian-Americans in diplomacy or business, were for the time being somewhat neglected. Instead we saw a great deal of the irascible Yves Adam (which is the only name I intend to drop; and even so, it is ironic enough that my one famous acquaintance should be not an orator, but a mime), and of Adam's protégé Jean-Claude Bastien, and of Jean-Claude's Spanish wife Elena. Laura renewed her friendships with several of Luce's teachers from the Cité Universitaire, and through them, in her efficient way, soon made our apartment a kind of Union for foreign students. Of these, the English-speaking, and particularly the English, seemed to enjoy us most and to return most often, and this fact was for me the one lapse in all that therapeutic gaiety. I hope I may be permitted to say, without appearing pitiful, that our suddenly assembled collection of young foreigners put me for the first time in my life in an ambassadorial position. I had made special studies of Pakistan and Thailand, and prided myself on an understanding of the Eastern peoples; I made dignified if loquacious overtures of friendship to the several Orientals among our guests, ardently wishing them to understand that UNICEF was not a missionary, and that it was our constant goal to work within the framework of a given culture, promoting progress without Westernization. They listened to me with gratifying deference, and even when they dropped away one by one it took me some time, and cost me some effort, to admit that they had perhaps not after all wanted to discuss methods of teaching birth control, nor the organization of health education centers for peasant mothers.

Soon, however, I developed a sincere affection for Mme de Verbois' English nephew (a distant and complex relationship, but "nephew" will do), Kenneth Stoddard, who was studying medicine on a scholarship at the Cité. He was an open-faced, extraordinarily blond boy of the kind that one is disposed to call a "lad," with the lanky height that looks like adolescence even when it has ceased to be. He wore light lamb's-wool sweaters and tweed coats, which, new or old, had gray suède patches at the elbows. He could be recognized by these at great distances, and even more by his loose-boned walk, his body putting itself to motion with much superfluous angling of his elbows, knees and ankles. He had something about him of Harold's solidity and "honor," but refined and softened. He was practical without being cynical, and he struck me as particularly unlikely to be disappointed by life, or ever disillusioned by anything that mattered to him. Kenneth, at least, was interested in UNICEF's medical progress in India, and flattered me by toying with the idea of offering a few years at our center in Calcutta when he should have finished his studies.

One afternoon Mme de Verbois asked the two of us to

visit old Riebenstahl. Madame herself was growing increasingly rheumatic in her left leg, and she had not been to see him for several weeks. This being mid-January — January seventeenth, it was — she was concerned both for his health and at the fact that he had been left alone through the holidays. Also, it was the general opinion of the patrolman and mothers at Parc Fasseville that Riebenstahl was mad, and Madame needed to satisfy herself at regular intervals that their opinion had not found its way to him, to disturb his peace of mind.

So she said, and that he was not mad she insisted with vivacious indignation, wagging her lined round face from side to side.

"Simply, he has wounded himself, like most men, and he knows it, which most men do not." And she repeated his story clearly that I might not embarrass myself on this first meeting with him.

"Herr Doktor Riebenstahl" was a tool and die maker from Putney. He was something of a genius in his own field, as was attested to by the fact that when he was fifty-two his company had awarded him a bonus of five hundred pounds, in recognition of a number of inventions which had, over the years, saved them several millions. To the Riebenstahls, who had reared five sons and seven daughters on the perpetual promise of next week's paycheck, the idea of saving such a sum "for their old age" never occurred. Instead they spent a hundred pounds on an old touring car, and Riebenstahl took a two-month leave from the factory. They left Putney farther behind them than they had ever done before (a thing accomplished some fifty miles short of Dover) and crossed for France. Riebenstahl was impatiently anxious for Paris, and consequently driving rather faster than he was wont to do. Just outside Calais he met a careless *camion* that had taken the middle of the road on a hilltop turn. Riebenstahl's recollection of the situation was of the utmost clarity: the road was not wide enough to pass on either side, and he had not time to stop. He did have time to turn the wheel, and time to decide between colliding on the left or on the right. That the choice presented itself in this way the old man was quite certain: the left or the right, himself or his wife. Mrs. Riebenstahl had died before the ambulance arrived.

Madame's suggestion that it was instinctive to take to the right, and that had his English sedan not had its steering wheel so *unnaturally* on the right he himself would have borne the brunt of the collision, made no impression on Riebenstahl's professionally logical mind.

"No, Madame," he would say, "you yourself point out that I am English, eh? By the same token, it is *my* instinct to go to the left. No, no; I made a choice of instinct, but I know very well what kind."

It is perhaps strange that I had never seen Riebenstahl before. He had lived in Paris for a little over four years, and I had known Madame since my early student days. The fact is that the story rather disturbed me. I had never met anyone who could be certain, and would say, that he had failed in a crisis; and being myself the sort who considers that when the ship sinks or the theater catches fire, *he* will lead the chorus, I rather shrank from such blatant realism. Moreover, I knew that Riebenstahl lived by building scale models of the Eiffel Tower and selling them to tourists, and that he spent most of his living in the secondhand *boutiques* along the Seine: I had a vivid impression of what such an old man's personal habits would be, and I am particularly sensitive to odors.

Nonetheless, Madame had asked, and it was a very small measure of what Kenneth and I should have done to ease her mind. So on the afternoon of January seventeenth the English lad came to meet me at the old mansion in Neuilly which houses UNICEF's offices. I collected the used matches from all the ashtrays in the Shipping Division, cut short the file clerk Papadeneau (who was indulging in one of his endless tales of unrequited love), and we set off in a light snow toward Parc Fasseville.

I haven't the slightest desire to evoke the atmosphere of Paris in these pages: those who know Paris can evoke it themselves, and those who don't would do better to borrow the fresher impressions of travelers. Still, I must say the charm of Parisian bystreets has never failed me. I still look at the monuments and enjoy their grandeur, but I do look *at* them. Walking through the maze of bourgeois streets I feel myself a fitting part of their solidity; a resident, in short — something that a resident alien is always glad to feel. The sidewalks of the seventeenth *arrondissement* are very wide in winter with the tables stacked inside, and the *charcuteries* around the Place Malsherbes offer the alluring displays year round that those of the Place de l'Opéra assume only in the summer season. O grace! O symmetry! I say, because this is the travelogue part of my story: here is good taste expressed to the limit of both its meanings! The proprietor of the wide-windowed Coin des Clèves would never conceive of shaping his coleslaw into a turtle or a steamship, but he knows how to set it off with a ring of Spanish olives and a cross-hatched roof of mayonnaise.

Was ever a succulent *rôti de porc* so shown to advantage as in this cradle of *laitue Romaine,* plugged with cloves and crowned with mushroom caps?

Kenneth, I must say, was not so tempted as I to linger before these culinary delights, but he evidently shared my contented sense of residence. He swung along beside me gaily, long-armed, his straight blond shock bouncing in and out of his eyes, his English cheeks the color of rare roast beef. It was very satisfactory to have for companion a member of the younger generation who did not mind a twenty-minute walk in the snow.

When we turned in at the Parc Fasseville, however, we became a little nervous. The single gendarme at the stone rotunda eyed us suspiciously over the fist he was warming at his mouth. The two or three brave mothers out with waddling, overpadded children took protective half-steps toward their charges. Kenneth and I concurred in vague misgivings. Our visit was not expected; there was no assurance that Riebenstahl would know, or believe, who we were; it was quite likely that he had not seen anyone at all for a couple of months, and that if the man was insane he would behave very differently to two male strangers than to his benefactress. We were certainly not afraid of him, but we should have waxed cowardly if we had had to report an ugly failure to Madame.

Our fears were entirely unfounded. The path to the little house had been recently swept and a bird shelter on the front porch was hung with mutton fat so fresh that it still steamed in the clear, snowy air. The door opened almost immediately; we were greeted by a slight old gentleman in clean, though unironed, work shirt and trousers, suspenders and a bright wool scarf. His wizened face, at the sound of our names, broke into a beam of recognition and pleasure.

"Mr. Powers, Stanford Powers, the ambassador, is it? And the medical student, the nephew? By God, this is good of you, don't stand in the cold, what a surprise, where's Marraine?" (Everyone except me refers to Mme de Verbois as "godmother.") "Wipe your feet there, will you? Afraid it's a bit cold, can't be helped, it's a pleasure to see you, put your things off there."

I started to explain that I was not actually an ambassador, but he plunged on, "Your Excellency, you'll excuse me if I turn my attention to this young fellow for an instant. Kenneth, isn't it? I've been meaning to have Marraine ask you, Kenneth, do you fellows do autopsies up at the University?"

The interrogator was five feet and a few inches tall, with shoulders hung forward over a concave chest. Two prominent purple veins on his temples crossed at angles with the ear-bars of rimless glasses and disappeared into a sparse fringe of pale hair; on his pate half a dozen longer strands fluttered back and forth. There was enormous energy in his shrill voice, his narrow eyes, and the knobbly hands that wandered over his person and nearby objects as he talked. Much more energy, I dare say, than in my voice, eyes or hands; yet I started at the thought that this shrunken creature was three years younger than I. At fifty-six he was — my God! — *spry*. I tried to steal a glance in the vestibule mirror, but Kenneth entirely blocked it, concentrating on the hanging of his Burberry and murmuring, "Not autopsies. We dissect, of course."

"Dissections, yes! That's what I meant. Well," he thumped his emaciated chest. "What do you think of that? Would it be any use to you?"

"Oh, sir," Kenneth said.

"When I'm dead, of course. Nothing morbid. I've been thinking of giving my body to science. Would it be any use?"

Kenneth had recovered himself and tried to match the tone. "You'd be more use if you'd got a rare disease, of course. There's nothing interesting wrong with you, is there?"

"Oh, quite, quite wrong," the fellow cackled, "but I doubt it'd show up in an autopsy — a dissection. I killed my wife, y'know. I s'pose Marraine told you that."

"She told us that you thought so," I offered tactfully.

"Oh, yes, she's too good for this world, isn't she?" he replied — very sanely, I thought — and turned back to Kenneth. "You can tell me how to go about it, can't you? I know you can't put it in a will, these lawyers are so slow they'll have you six foot under before they unseal the testament. Haha!"

Kenneth gave him instructions for the donation, and I in turn glued my eyes on the coat rack. A man three years my junior was disposing of his body, and so urgently that he had not asked us to sit down.

Not until he had scribbled a pageful of names, addresses and precautions did he usher us into the long, narrow sitting room, and without any such phrase as "perhaps you'd like to see my house" or "you'll have to forgive the mess in here" he proceeded to take us on a tour of his *bizarrerie,* exactly as if he were a museum guide and we had come for the exhibition. I must say to his credit that the kitchen we passed offered a different prospect than I had imagined: there were not more than two or three meals' worth of unwashed dishes, there was a drying line of well-bleached underwear, and the only unpleasant odor was a suggestion of formaldehyde. The sitting room was cluttered in the extreme, but tidily arranged, and beyond a doubt recently dusted.

"Where's Marraine?" he asked again, stopping before a table lined with old maps, manuscripts, mechanical apparatuses and a microscope. "Not ill, I hope."

I explained her difficulty and her concern over his having spent the holidays alone.

"Holidays! Dear Heaven, what are holidays to me? I like to have her come, you know, but as for holidays! I'm a busy fellow. Now you might not think it," he flipped through the pages of a battered volume, "but this is Chinese. I'm learning Chinese, ha! Not too bad at it."

I expressed my genuine astonishment, and his eyes lit again with that curious, sterile intensity. "Your Excellency! Now here's a thing you could do for an old fellow: you ought to know some Chinamen in your line of work; could you get a Chinaman over here to me? To practice on?"

I explained that I did not have many direct dealings with the Chinese "in my line of work," but that I might be able to send him a student or two from the Cité. He nodded several times, his sparse hair shivering, and returned to the exhibition.

"My volume of poetry — in verse. Untitled up to now. I'm thinking of calling it *Manuscripture,* what d'you think of that, ha! No! it isn't up to much, it's accurate but sounds a bit religious, what d'you think?"

"I'd be inclined to think so," I agree.

"These here tomes are arranged from philosophy to electronics, and I'll let you in on a secret. They're the same thing! mark my words. Wait till I turn this on."

He was referring to a kind of machine, a structure of about three feet by four, and of a most amazing complexity. Every conceivable household nail, nut, wire, gear, ball bearing, spool, blade, and brush had been utilized in its construction. The switch operated a doorbell wire which, vibrating, set in motion a small pulley that turned a gear that in turn revolved a kind of tin windmill that knocked a small lead ball into a socket that activated another switch revolving another gear — and so on for five minutes until the thing had run full cycle, and a small rubber hammer tapped the doorbell wire, and it began all over again. We followed its intricate course for some time in fascination. Kenneth cleared his throat.

"What does it do?" he innocently asked, and Riebenstahl, who had evidently been waiting for this, wheeled on him with a look of fierce triumph.

"Nothing!" he almost shouted. "Nothing! That is, it does what you see it do, but it's got no ulterior motives for it, it don't claim a product, ha!"

I became all at once genuinely interested to know how sane he was. Did he, for instance, mean with this demonstration to show that philosophy and electronics were alike in intricately doing nothing?

"Now this here is how I make my living." He turned to a small table set aside from the rest, which held a nearly completed model of the Eiffel Tower, about four feet tall. "You wouldn't believe what Americans will pay for one of those. Handmade, you see. Compare it with the plans if you like, it's quite exact. Those people over at the library told me they hadn't got plans of the thing. People never know what they've got and what they haven't. Told me I couldn't get in without a card, too. But I got in. This is my two-dozenth model. What do you think of that, eh? Not bad, ha!"

What does one say regarding a matchstick reproduction of the Eiffel Tower? We agreed that it appeared to be very exact, and I produced my handful of used matches, feeling that the gesture had become condescending. He accepted them eagerly, however, scrutinizing them one by one, rolling each one back and forth between crooked fingers to spy out any crookedness, separating them into two piles on the edge of the table. This accomplished, he returned the rejects to me and pocketed the others, saying, "That's thoughtful of you."

Kenneth had meanwhile been examining the skeleton of a hand, singularly large and white, which was mounted on a velvet-draped lectern. "This is a fine specimen," he said. "Did you find it in Paris?"

The old man nodded, cackled, "I think that's my graven image," and passed back into the kitchen with a wave toward the sofa. We sat smiling noncommittally at each other, neither willing to venture the first opinion.

He returned in a short time with three battered cups and a pot of jasmine tea.

"All this talk of the reason and the power of love and God-knows-what-all," he said, as if continuing an unbroken train of thought. "Power of love, by God! Ever had that put to the test, have you?" He poured the tea with a hand that seemed to shake rather from intensity than frailty.

"I'm not sure that I have," I said.

"No, but I have. Ha! You might not think it, but I gave myself thirty-six years faithful to one woman. I did that! — sacrificed the earth for her, yes. Came to the test and I killed that woman. That's the power of love."

His insistence was, of course, embarrassing in the extreme, but he hurried on.

"Reason, then. Now here you are, I've got a fine

machine." He punched at the air. "Did I make it with my reason?" he demanded.

"Oh, surely . . ." I began, and Riebenstahl burst forth with a "Ha!" wagging his twiglike finger.

"There you are, what a notion! It's the hands make the difference, I tell you, the brain came after the hands. Suppose the apes were smart enough to think of the lever but hadn't got the dexterity to make one. Do you suppose for an instant they would have got on to the wheel?" His arm had fallen on the lectern, and he was holding hands with the skeleton now, toying affectionately at the finger joints.

"Every animal on this globe, down to the amoeba, has got hands enough for its survival. Man is the only one with hands enough for more than that — hands to make what he doesn't need, as much as what he does. And it isn't until you've got six times what's necessary you begin muddling your mind what *is* necessary, and why, and how it's come by. A man upsets the jungle order with a half a dozen trinkets that've got no use, and then — *then,* mind you, not before — it strikes him that there is an order to things, and he's got to make it out. Only, make it out in such a way that he can keep his trinkets. Oh, your Jesus fought a losing battle there. I know a dozen fellows in England; pride of the cult of mind, they are; they'd rather see the moons of Jupiter go sailing out of orbit than admit their Louis Quinze snuffboxes hadn't got a rightful place in the hierarchy of the universe. Ha!"

I wondered how, and whether, Riebenstahl had become acquainted with the pride of the cult of mind, but I followed now sufficiently well to find fault with his argument.

"How do you come out on the side of hands, then? If

28

things are as you say, shouldn't we give up the lever and the wheel, along with the trinkets, and live in the trees?"

"I never said a man wasn't a man, you know, I just want no nonsense about what he is, that's what I'm after. No. I beg your pardon, Your Excellency, but you'll forgive an old man: you political fellows, don't you go into your line of work so as to fit people into your own machine, and get 'em to run like gears without their knowing it? Isn't that your pleasure? *Manipulation?*"

"Actually," I said stiffly, "I'm with the UN Children's Fund. It isn't political in that sense."

"No, well, you wouldn't say so. Here then: don't you think you've devoted yourself to peace and brotherhood etcetera?"

"I try to think that."

"Good! a good answer. You see any more peace and brotherhood about than when you started?"

"It's difficult to judge."

"Ha! What is there more of? Some threshing machines in China, isn't that it? I gave up newspapers four years ago, but I've got a clipping about that somewheres. And pasteurized powdered milk at the equator, isn't that it?"

I looked at Riebenstahl's ceiling, which was of that kind of paint-covered pressed tin so popular among the Victorians of all nations, and I admitted that that was it.

"Just so." He turned on Kenneth. "Now you, young man. Why did you go into this business, muddling about with the intestines instead of taking pure and simple science?"

Kenneth blushed. "Not by any philosophical route. I think partly because I'm impatient. It's not in my nature to wait for twenty years to find out if those years have been wasted."

"Just so!" the voice cracked triumphantly. "It's your hands give you more satisfaction than your head."

Kenneth made a start of protest that that was not what he had said, but Riebenstahl stopped him.

"You're right. You've got extraordinarily beautiful hands."

Kenneth blushed again, which irritated me. He does have extraordinarily beautiful hands: long, pale, slender, and yet strong. I was annoyed that he could not admit it, and that a talented young man should redden twice in the space of six not very embarrassing sentences. But Riebenstahl continued. "I should like to peel your skin back and have a peep at *that* skeleton on my stand."

I winced, and if I had been given to blushing, this time I should have blushed; from squeamishness, and the inappropriateness of a crumbling old man's coveting a strong young man's bare bones. Whereas Kenneth, his equilibrium restored by the blunt remark, nodded and said, "I've often wished I could take a look at it myself."

I was suddenly very tired of the petty reactions and retreats that hamper human intercourse. I felt old, not with Riebenstahl's urgent spryness, but with the age of incalculable accumulated trifles. I wanted to be home, perusing reports of pasteurized powdered milk at the equator, and with Laura bringing my evening Bristol Cream.

Nonetheless our talk continued in the same vein for a little time before we took our leave, with warm assurance that we would return, and touching entreaties on the old man's part. We did not discuss Riebenstahl on the Métro to Port Royal, and when we alighted Kenneth said only, "Well, he's more interesting than any question of whether he's got his wits or not," which substantially expressed my sentiments, and we left the matter there.

But my depression had not lifted. I was trying to pinpoint its source. It was more than the spectacle of premature wizening, though that too still affected me, and I occasionally passed my fingers over my temples (which were, however, quite smooth and soft) feeling for a protruding vein. What was it Riebenstahl had touched in me? For a man who proved himself inept to win elected office in his thirties, the charge of manipulation cannot hit home. To a man comfortably settled in uncontroversial public service, the static state of brotherhood is no surprise.

So I suppose I envied him. Surrounded with paraphernalia, and preaching the gospel of manufacture, he was an ascetic of sorts. I might have summed up his remarks as the doctrine of disinterested doing, as pure in its way as a doctrine of disinterested love. It must be very comfortable to cut the soul from under you, to begin with things and tasks and believe in those until you have made a religion out of them. What has a man to lose who can proceed in such a way?

I was not hungry, and I wanted to be alone. Nevertheless it would have been rude to send Kenneth off to the Cité without a bite of supper, so I offered the invitation, and as I did so I had one of those involuntary and unjust forebodings, of how little I wished to rehash the afternoon for Laura, and how difficult her logical questions would be to answer.

Rebounding from the impulse, I stopped at the corner stall and bought a bunch of winter chrysanthemums. Then Kenneth and I had to haggle over who was to pay for them, and I mounted the steps more wearily than ever, the keys like so many icicles in my hand.

"Laura," I called as we hung our coats in the vestibule. "Laura, my dear, we're home!"

From the dining room came a blurry, unfamiliar voice, "She's in the kitchen." It was a young voice, too: another student, I thought; and reprimanding myself for the dread I felt at the prospect of an "evening," I followed Kenneth into the dining room.

We have one of those round claw-footed dining tables, and slung over the back of the chair nearest us, spilling on to the floor, was a bulky coat of many colors. With all due respect to Harold, I must insist that it was not "flashy." It was vivid, luxurious, and very badly wrinkled. I doubt that even an American tourist would take it for a tartan.

The coat was by so much the brightest object in the room that it took me a few seconds to adjust my focus on the girl across the table; once I had done so, that brilliance faded into proportion. She was, as my son-in-law had discreetly conceded, pretty enough! She had straight black hair which hung forward onto the table-cloth, and dark translucent skin laid over bones of uncanny regularity; the features of a skillfully made wax doll. It was the sort of face that one calls inexpressive, but had a quality that I can only describe as tactile. Like apricots or wax Italian matches, or certain minia-ture dictionaries that yield to the shape of the palm, it invited touch. The skin was malleability in repose, as if it would retain the imprint of a thumb.

She had a body like a young boy's, of medium height, and just now all her attitude conveyed was an insup-portable weariness. Her shoulders, and an expansive pair of eyelids, drooped down and forward like her hair, and she regarded us with solemn attention.

"She's making me a cup of coffee. She'll be back in a minute," the girl said.

Her voice did have an extraordinary quality, though once more I must disagree with Harold. The accent was unplaceable because it was not an accent at all. It was instead the blurring of perpetual contact with accents; a shadowy quality which, I imagined, pronounced her as "not native" anywhere. Her vowels were slow and broad, but whether with English affectation or Southern indolence wasn't clear. She half-suppressed certain consonants, the labials made with full lips not quite touching.

"You're Harold's girl from the Opera House," I said, to which she replied "Yes" without any surprise.

"Stanford Powers," I introduced myself, knowing full well that she knew who I was, and then introduced Kenneth, who stuck out his hand in the most awkward manner possible. He was very stiff and, I noted with some exasperation, positively trembling.

"I'm very pleased to make your acquaintance," he said in a loud jovial voice. The eyelids raised a sixteenth of an inch — the result was a stare — and as they did so I realized that the droop was a permanent feature. The eyes were brilliantly dark and round, but the lids slouched at the corners in, yes, possibly an Oriental way; though even at the moment I was sharp enough to guess, more likely negroid. She made no move to take the hand, and Kenneth subsided with a foolish grin.

"Prytania Scott Obée," the girl mumbled.

"I beg your pardon?" I inclined toward her, and she replied with more effort, "My name is Prytania Scott Obée."

Kenneth broke into a chorus of "Rule, Britannia!" but immediately stopped, blushing more fiercely than ever. On the girl's small face was the most effective look of disapproval I have ever seen. It was absolute expressionlessness. She was looking at him steadily, not "blankly," which implies some lack of understanding, but with a total absence of emotion or of interest. All that her dark features expressed was symmetry.

"Spelled with a *P*," she said in a tone to match the face; informative, not unkind, but quite mechanical. "I was named after a street in the Garden District of New Orleans, where my mother would have liked to live, but never could, because she was poor, and a quadroon." This information should certainly have alienated me had I seen any martyrdom in it, but the child might have been reading a newspaper.

"I should like to be called that, please," she continued, "and not Prytie, or Tania." On the pronunciation of these two unacceptable appellations one wrinkle appeared on the bridge of her nose, which amounted to a face of the most violent disgust. I quite agreed with her about the nicknames — no one, not even my wife, has ever called me Stan — and I laughed aloud. Kenneth, however, was choking on his tongue, and I offered him escape by suggesting that he help Laura. He literally ran to the kitchen.

Since she had parted with this much information, I assumed that Prytania Scott Obée was ready to explain herself, so I sat down in the next chair but one and folded my hands in my lap. After several moments of waiting for her, although there was no strain in our silence on either side, I decided that I had best fill in the story myself.

"You're out of money," I began. It was really rather

peculiar of me, because I had been unwilling to say the same thing to my son-in-law. She nodded, and I continued. "Let's see. Your parents are separated. Your mother has none, and you don't feel free to ask your father for any more."

The corners of her mouth tucked briefly inward toward her teeth — I learned that it was her form of spontaneous smile. "Very good," she said, and the compliment was richer than her confidence would have been. I should perhaps mention that I am the perpetual victim of confidences. Naturally reticent people, I believe, often are.

"So you'd like," I continued, emboldened, "a minor loan on your next allowance."

I had missed. Without changing, her features emanated indignation.

"I'm looking for a job."

"Oh, that's much worse. There's hardly any such thing as temporary work in Paris."

"A permanent job."

I must have looked skeptical — as I was. She flipped a hand beneath her hair and lifted a tunnel of air around her neck. "I've turned eighteen," she announced. "Of age," she added, and after a few seconds, patiently, "There won't be another allowance."

"Surely," I scoffed in a parental tone, "your father will send enough to pay your fare."

"Well, I don't think so," Prytania said, the image of quiescence. "He sent me to school in England four years ago. I don't think he'd take it kindly if I came back."

This intelligence, or rather the flatness of its delivery, disconcerted me a little, and I suppose Prytania thought I didn't understand it. For she added, still reading from that newspaper, "He lives on Prytania Street."

"Just so" — noticing that it was a favorite expression of Riebenstahl's. "At any rate, you've been looking for work, but you find that you must have a permit and that you can't get one." She nodded; I was on safe ground again. "But someone told you that you don't need a permit to work in an international agency."

"The American Embassy."

"And although you had no intention of using it, you just happen to have the card of a venerable member of the UNICEF staff."

Quite without warning she began to cry, out of eyes scarcely narrowed, as startling as rain in sunlight.

"I didn't mean to keep it," she said. "I don't know why I did. But I couldn't afford another night in the hotel. Your wife said . . . that you had a spare bed here, just till I find something."

She caught her breath once and the tears abruptly stopped. She had remarkable control for such a child. I was uncomfortable, and said in a voice as loud and jovial as Kenneth's, "Well, well, do you type?"

"Do I have to take a test?" she returned timidly, by way, I suppose, of a reply.

I sighed and then, apprehensive of more tears, attempted a laugh. "What am I going to do with you?" I asked, and she replied, "I don't know," in a manner which left no doubt, however, that it was entirely my problem.

Kenneth, heavily cautious, followed the coffee tray at arm's length toward us, the china rattling like cold teeth.

Laura came behind, laden with cozies, slotted spoons and superfluous sandwiches. Laura is always *carrying* things: suitcases and bundles of pamphlets and portable whatevers. She carries more brown-paper parcels into the house than the neighbors believe two people can eat or wear, and she carries them out again wrapped in green twine, to confound the schedule of the trash collectors. If she ever goes into the woods for a walk with free hands, she returns with burgeoning armfuls of shedding fern and dicotyledons whose names she cannot remember. Of all her burdens, she carries her head most precisely, a perfection of white and ivory waves on a brittle frame. She was capable of many and varied expressions in her youth, but a lifetime's demands on her universal sympathy have considerably narrowed her range, and her face now has its choice of amazement, pity or attention.

She gathered up my chrysanthemums and made a distracted inventory of the vases in the room.

"You've introduced yourselves?" she demanded brightly. "The most amazing thing, dear! Prytania met *Harold* in Frankfurt, and he gave her *your* card. Isn't that extraordinary?"

"I know."

"What do you know? Oh, Prytania's already told you."

"No, I knew about it before. Harold told me."

A conch vase juggled under the plate, Laura faced around to me. "You *knew?* Well but, for heaven's sake, why didn't you tell me?"

"I rather thought Harold preferred me not to," I said. There was no reason for me to be so malicious. Laura's fears were roused exactly as mine had been, and she confusedly emptied her arms and began pouring the coffee.

"Well now. There now, Prytania, that should warm you up. How was your afternoon? Prytania's has been ghastly. You know what it's like in those *préfectures* trying to convince them you've got as much right as the natives to earn your keep. It's really shocking."

It isn't shocking at all, of course. In a city with as much unemployment as Paris, the government has every right to think of its citizens first, and Laura well knows this, but she was encouraging the girl. And Prytania was apparently encouraged.

"I'm really pretty good at getting around by myself," she said, "but I've never had to think about not having any place to spend the night before."

"Look here," Kenneth put in, in that unnatural voice. "It's a real shame to spend your first three days in Paris in employment offices. I guess you haven't seen anything."

"I guess not."

"Well, look, you'll be taken care of all right now. How would you like me to show you around a bit? I mean, not the tourist places. I can take you some places the tourists never see."

"That's very kind of you."

"Do you like the theater?" he pursued.

I was glad for Kenneth's sake that at this suggestion she seemed to soften toward him. "Oh, yes," she said gravely.

"I think I can get some tickets for the Opéra-Comique. I'm sure I can. How about Saturday?"

I thought the Opéra-Comique a singularly unfortunate choice, especially as an example of places the tourists never see, but Prytania accepted gratefully, and Kenneth sat back in utter content for the rest of the coffee drinking.

When the girl had drained her cup Laura led her off to Luce's old room — I dare say tucked her in — and for the rest of the evening, through a cold-cut supper,

Laura and Kenneth exchanged excited remarks about the little stranger. When Kenneth went he remarked in an offhand way that he might return tomorrow.

And then Laura, braiding her hair for bed, set aside her company smile and turned to me.

"Dear . . . why do you suppose Harold didn't want you to tell me? About the card. Do you think there was anything . . . ?"

"He only saw her for an hour, Laura. He didn't even know her name."

"Oh. Well, then why did he . . . ?"

"He was sorry for her, because she seemed too young to be alone. He didn't want to give her his own card, because he thought she might suspect an improper advance."

"Why, wasn't that thoughtful of him. That's rather subtle for Harold."

"Very," I agreed.

"Oh, well, then that's all right. Darling, listen! I'm sure Prytania can type, and you know she wouldn't need a permit in your office. You're always saying you're shorthanded. She's young, but I was thinking that if you managed Schlutzburg right . . ."

And then I did it again. I was really very irrational and unjust that day. I was buttoning my pajamas before the mirror and looking at my hands, powerful yet and not a bit like Riebenstahl's, but still rather aged in their fleshy way. And I said, "Yes, my dear, we all know about your marvelous managerial talents, but I was capable of figuring that one out for myself."

Which Laura, of course, did not in the least deserve.

On the following morning, I "managed Schlutzburg" in the only possible way. I arrived a good forty-five minutes late (which is not my habit) and even then delayed my entrance, lounging against the pillars of the old mansion in full view of the personnel office window, idly counting the bleak chestnut trees. When I was fairly certain I had been seen, I shoved my hat back on my head, tracked mud through the double oak doors and swung into Schlutzburg's office without knocking.

"Say, Schlutzburg," I said loudly (the personnel manager distinctly dislikes being addressed without a titular prefix in the presence of his secretary), "where'd you pick up that girl you sent me, what's her name, Arienne?"

Schlutzburg swung his head in such a way as to leave his stiff collar facing directly front and turned on me the full wattage of his beady blue eyes.

"Miss Recheuse?" he asked menacingly. "Miss Recheuse comes with the highest references."

I rolled my eyes heavenward, a thing I seldom do, and which was rather painful in the upper muscles.

"I have had," he glowered, "most superlative reports of her from all the members of your division."

I laughed. "Don't doubt that. She's a saucy little number." (Miss Recheuse has buck teeth and wears thick-heeled shoes.)

"From the women as well!"

"Oh, well," I half-closed the door and then reinserted my head. "Say, by the way, my wife is sending in some little American piece this afternoon. I'm sure she's a half-wit. Sorry to trouble you with it, but you know how Laura is."

"I'll be the judge of that," he snapped.

"Oh, there's not much to judge," I pursued. "You know the kind, can't do her work and distracts everybody else from theirs."

Schlutzburg's secretary is the prettiest in the building, and he jumped to her defense with a dagger look.

"It is a most outdated prejudice that an attractive woman cannot be an efficient secretary." I shrugged, and he took up his pencil, rapping its eraser on his nose as if calling his thoughts to order.

"Can she type?"

"She's been doing some correspondence for Laura," I lied. "Laura says she's a wonder, but women can never judge these things. This one looks about twelve years old. Hopeless."

"I'll be the judge of that," he snapped again. "You're always complaining of being shorthanded."

"Oh, lord! Don't send her to me," I said, added, "I think she's part Negro," registered the outrage in Schlutzburg's eye, and swiftly closed the door. The personnel manager is technically my inferior in the agency scale, but very conscious of his actual power, and singularly protective of the evidences of his judgment. Aero division secretaries are seldom fired.

I don't remember exactly what I first turned my attention to that morning, but the routine seldom varies. On my desk, waiting for the stamp of my approval, is a shipment requisition and accompanying report for, say, one rubber date stamp and four red rubber desk rings (an item used to prevent ink spillage) for our shipping office in Cambodia.

Out of habit — no, not habit, but a concession to my youthful enthusiasm for government — I hesitate with my stamp above the report, typed in sixteen copies, and run over the arguments for the necessity of my action.

The items requested, from our wholesale supplier in Troy, New York, total eighty-seven cents in cost. They are heavy for their size, and the shipping fee is two dollars and nineteen cents from Troy to Cambodia. The estimated cost of a requisition and fifteen carbons is fourteen dollars in labor, paper and postage.

Now, I myself have a rubber date stamp; my secretaries protect their laps with red rubber ink rings: I can hardly ask my colleague in Cambodia to do without, nor would it be economical, considering the time it takes to write a date or mop up a bottle of ink. Decidedly I cannot expect him to go out and buy his own, supposing such things are available in Cambodia. Neither can I authorize a petty-cash office supply fund in each of our several hundred offices the world over, which would require at a minimum five hundred thousand cash dollars per annum, necessitate yet another set of secretarial records, and invite petty embezzling at the lowest levels. Our official supplier of rubber office apparatuses in Troy may well be at the farthest distance from Cambodia of any supplier of rubber office apparatuses in the world. Considering the postage, a retail stationery store in, say, Bangkok might well be cheaper. But to locate and deal with, to familiarize with our requisitional code, and to negotiate separately for each item with the dealer nearest each of our offices, would require two extra full-time secretaries in the AERO central office for date stamps alone.

My hand falls: approved: one rubber date stamp and four red rubber desk rings for Cambodia, sailing on the *King of Thailand.* Cost: seventeen dollars and six cents.

I do remember that, as usual, I had accomplished just so much that morning when the door scraped open. The door is very well planed and hung, and how Papadeneau should be able to make it scrape I have no idea, but there it is. It scraped, and Papadeneau scraped in after it. He is one of those fellows who always walks as if he is limping, though God knows each of his legs is as sound as the other.

When Papadeneau first came to us I put him down as in his middle forties. That had been six years before, and he was no older now. His age was not so much indeterminate as shifting; he slipped from adolescent to ancient and back again. Even his hair, both stiff and thin, was sometimes ashen, at other times ash-blond.

"Good morning," the file clerk said with one of his obsequious half-bows. "I have heard there is to be a new *secrétaire*." English is the predominant language in the agency, and Papadeneau is not to be outdone. I sighed, wishing fervently that an international agency need not bear so much resemblance to a rural town.

"Already?"

"Figure to yourself, you are very late this morning, boss. Already has Miss Antoine brought up the coffee."

Miss Antoine is Schlutzburg's secretary. "I didn't get mine," I grumbled, hoping to head him off.

"It comes instantly. How is she, this new one?"

"I know very little about her, Papadeneau. And nobody knows whether she's going to be hired or not, so we'll just have to wait and see."

"Miss Antoine thinks yes. She is pretty, beautiful?"

"I believe she is supposed to be attractive."

"Ah, yes, but *américaine*, isn't it? Not so pretty like my Tofine."

"Papadeneau, will you file this stack here? I'm a little behind this morning."

"Instantly. It is because you are come so late this morning. I have told about Tofine?"

"You've told me all about her. I'm very sorry."

"Yes. Figure to yourself, last night I met this gigolo. He is no more than this high!" He made a gesture at the level of his knees. "But I am not so without the brains. He has got my Tofine, but I have got from him something valued, and very cheap!"

I could see the poor fellow's paycheck following all the rest, and he badly needed a new shirt. I suppose I should long ago have managed Schlutzburg into firing him, but I could never quite bring myself to try it.

"What have you done?" I asked.

"I have purchased from him very cheap ten shares in a hotel."

"A hotel? In Paris?"

"In Paris, pooh!" He quivered with excitement. "On the moon! Imagine to yourself the crowds there will be a few years from today. Another gold rush, without doubt." He beamed with self-satisfaction at his display of American history.

"Oh, Papadeneau, you're a newborn babe. How much did you pay for them?"

"Excuse me, boss. In France this question is not polite. Very cheap, I tell you."

I groaned, and Papadeneau spat an indignant "paugh," managing all the while to retain his obsequious air.

"You think they will not get to the moon, you! But I will have the laugh. So it was with Christopher Columboss."

I thought there was very little to be gained by explaining the fine distinction between thinking that "they" would get to the moon, and thinking that Papadeneau would ever enjoy the profits of a hotel there, so I merely tapped the stack of folders and turned back to my work. Papadeneau picked up the reports, lingering at the door.

"Consider besides, Tofine is not the only fish in the

sea. I have discovered several, just by opening my eyes on the Métro this morning. Decidedly I have been blind. And there is this new one coming." He disappeared, scraping. Papadeneau prides himself on knowing just how far he can push me.

I dictated a few letters to the thick-heeled Miss Recheuse, who was more discreet, and more suspicious, in her reference to the "new one," and completed the morning's trivia in a fog of misgiving. Prytania was sure to exasperate the secretaries with her youth, and though I thought it unlikely that she should fall prey to any advances of Papadeneau's, he was quite as unlikely to realize this. Intramural emotions never improve efficiency. Perhaps I had described her quite accurately to Schlutzburg.

Shortly before noon I shoved the very small stack of my morning's accomplishments into the OUT basket and set off on foot to Mme de Verbois'. It was a brisk day, and I took its cue, not even pausing at the Coin des Clèves, and turning into the little courtyard on the rue Cardinet just as the clocks echoed half-past twelve all up and down the Seine.

Chez Madame! What white-and-golden, leather-and-crystal, fir-and-fur those words once sounded through my mind! And here, a lank cat foraging in an overturned pail, thin shafts of winter sun on broken blinds, the white-haired concierge in the door, her skirt hanging down to her ankles in front and up to her knees behind, her fingers pressing on a little giggle at the sight of me; not because I am interesting, a pleasure, or a scandal to her, but because my passing through the gate is all that has stirred the air in her court this day.

"O, M'sieur hehehe, pour M'dame d'V'bois, n'est-ce pas? Au troisième à gauche, M'sieur. O, heh!"

Forty years ago (five years ago, for that matter, but I met her forty years ago) Madame herself lived in Neuilly, in an ivory-colonnaded home very like our present office. Her husband Auguste was the sort that never grays beyond the temples, and he carried his upper middle-class rank with ceremony that would have adorned a duchy. I never saw him roll his tongue along his lower lip, preparatory to delineating the qualities of a wine, that I did not imagine him thus in his pharmaceutical laboratory, sipping from a vial and admonishing his assistant, "It lacks just that vitality and bouquet of pentasulphate."

Madame adored this cough-syrup magnate indulgently. She deferred to him with an air that said there was nothing in the scope of her ambition save the impeccable conducting of his *salon*. But it was Madame that we came to see. We were commissioners, ambassadors, shy clerks and passionate students. The incongruous company was made harmonious, and the pretensions of Monsieur made endearing, by that warm coverlet, the presence of Madame.

I had come to study international law, from a Chicago of which I now have an indifferent memory, and no personal impression. I cannot think that I was then aware either of crime circuits or of circulating opium, though having since learned of these I cannot separate them from a certain harshness that had characterized my life there, nor from the women I had known, who seem in retrospect to have been constructed of fringe on bone. Nor do I remember how I was first introduced to the circle of Madame, and it does not matter: I felt that I had fallen effortlessly into another century, where

46

statesmen weighed their words in the scales of justice, and women spread soft hands in softer gestures. Madame was witty, interested, sensitive. She was — benevolent — a quality fallen into disrespect these days, through the heavy handling of efficient public women. No one was ever more private than Madame, nor ever spread the privacy of her sincere compassion to so many.

It may be inferred that she was beautiful. Indeed it is today inferred by those few who meet her and, feeling the fine soft quickness of her eyes, say, "She must have been very beautiful once." They overlook the fact that age conceals all faces in the same impartial folds. At thirty-two, when I was twenty, Madame had been over-dressed by nature, with features too large for her frame to justify. Her cheeks, nose, chin, jaw, forehead all protruded as if worked in bas-relief on a marble plane. She was overweight ("A Rubens," the men and women alike would hasten to say), and her arms hung down absurdly long until she lifted them in gentle gesture, and whatever word had last been thrust upon the air became defined. She was a homely woman; a homely woman with many suitors. And when men spoke of her, they used to say, "Ah, Cécilie!"

It is saddening to see such a woman as Madame in reduced circumstances but it is not, thank God, embarrassing. When M. de Verbois died it was discovered that he had made no written agreement with his partner, and that fair-weather devil had calmly pronounced himself sole owner of the pharmaceutical works. If his conduct had done violence to Madame's conception of human nature, she had never so expressed herself in public. She as calmly hired a lawyer and when, a year later, he finally pronounced it hopeless, she sold the house to pay its mortgage and his fee.

"Well, well," she would say if someone tried to commiserate, "isn't it absurd, such a small woman in a house that size? Regard my apartment — a little doll's house, is it not? I'm storing up for my second childhood."

She lived on her pension, weekly batches of envelopes that she addressed by hand for an advertising firm, and the occasional renting of her third — what she called "extra" — room. At sixty-eight she learned to cook.

"*Mon Dieu,* whoever should have guessed that I'm so talented?" (And indeed, her cuisine was admirable.) "If Auguste had known his own wife could make such a *soufflé* he would have lived on a while to try it."

It was characteristic of Madame that, although she would lie to preserve it for someone else, she never considered moving into the little house at Parc Fasseville, to live on the charity of the state. For herself, she merely kept her favorite bits of furniture and a vast supply of china, crystal, linen. The kitchen pipes from the floor above sometimes leaked into her water closet and when they did so she would place a delicate silver bowl on the toilet seat to catch the drip.

This apartment, these cubicles stuffed like packing cases with opulent mahogany, seemed to me like a pattern of Madame herself. Her body aged rapidly in the unaccustomed inclemency of the old building; she became, what she by rights should long have been, a little old woman, confined by rheumatism and having for companionship only the cronies of her floor. She took on that faded scent of age, like dried petals in a tin, while her voice broke like an adolescent boy's. In these "reduced circumstances" the durable real Madame survived: solid as walnut, the sympathy of Armagnac, wit like a chandelier (not like a pickle fork — why is it that old ladies are perceived to be alert only when they have blunt manners and sharp tongues?). And woe to him who measured her thoughts by her surroundings! I once heard a student politely interrupt his own remarks to explain that Tennessee Williams, then under discussion, was "a decadent American playwright."

"Do you think so truly?" Madame replied. "I have always thought of him as a romantic. Perhaps it is the same."

And to those who deferred to her age she would declare, "It is very rude to be so polite!" and fall to laughing.

I perceive myself in great danger of painting one of those portraits which is all magnificence and praise, and yet leaves a sense of general distaste. Nothing is further from my intention. If I could endear Madame with the enumeration of some few foibles, or assure her humanity with a streak of viciousness, I should do so without hesitation. Simply, she is the one person of whom I can find no evil to speak. Her kindness is not cloying, her graciousness does not fall into hauteur nor her simplicity into affectation. The worst that I can say of her is that she has now grown old, and were it given to the rest of mankind to grow old in such a way, then age would soon take the honors from youth's hands.

Madame assumed that I had come to report on Riebenstahl, and she ushered me in with expressions of gratitude.

"He does weigh on my mind. He is such an affectionate old gentleman. I am afraid someday he will discover it."

So we spoke of Riebenstahl for a little time. I told of our afternoon in light and slightly caustic terms, imitating his "Your Excellency," dwelling with bogus abhorrence on his collection of paraphernalia. Madame was reassured for him. She began by laughing at my account, then ended by watching me rather closely. She still wore black skirts of an unfashionable length and big-sleeved blouses with some ruffled stuff at the neck. She traced the lacy edge of this with a plump forefinger, as if following out some circuitous thought. When I summed up, "He looks a hundred and two, poor fellow, but he's got the mental energy of a schoolboy," Madame let a little silence fall.

"He has upset you, has he not. I suppose that does no real harm. You need to feel yourself upset, I think."

"He seems to be so lonely," I conceded.

"Ah! You are going to start your games with me at this date? You could scrape his loneliness together and hide it under your fingernail," with a slight emphasis on the "your."

"I don't think so," I persisted. "All this ferocious activity is a kind of cover."

"*Bien sûr!* But not for loneliness. On the contrary, for all the remorse he feels at enjoying his solitude. He is not an ambassador: he believes what he says, that he killed his wife."

"Well, whatever it is, he's admirably spry about it."

"Oh, spry! Really, *monsieur le diplomate,* you Americans! I should like to add a freedom to your list: freedom from discretion. You haven't eaten. An *omelette aux fines herbes?*"

Over this dish, light and delicately spiced, I somewhat sheepishly approached my mission.

"Superfluous discretion isn't a fault Americans are generally charged withal."

"Oh, and a man is always hanged for the wrong crimes; it is the root of all theology."

"Then I shall be as blunt as you please."

"Begin."

"I didn't come about Riebenstahl at all. I came to suggest that one of us should do the other a favor; I'm not sure which way around."

"Ah, much better!"

I let a sip of superb Chablis slide down my throat.

"Through a series of circumstances," I began, not wanting to bring Harold into it again, "Laura and I have come in contact with a penniless American girl who has come to live in Paris. I'm trying to get her a job at the agency, and we thought perhaps she could rent your room."

"So simple? She is a student?"

"No," I said.

"Oh, she is older. That makes me hesitate a little. I might have some bother adjusting myself to one of your independent women."

"She's eighteen. If she were independent I wouldn't be troubling you with her."

"You make her sound like a refugee. Has she shoes?"

"Oh, good lord! She's very expensively dressed."

"So? Well, tell me about her."

"Laura says that you'll adore her."

"Which means that you do not agree."

"Not at all. I only mention it because Laura is so much more discerning a judge of people than I am."

"And I am a better judge of you than you. Come, what is she like. Intelligent?"

"I have no evidence of that."

"Alert?"

"From what I gather she is quite without humor."

"A beautiful recommendation. Out with it, why should a rheumatic old widow adore her?"

I smiled at her impatience and lit my pipe. "She seems discreet."

"Father of God! She must be pretty."

"Very, yes. Like a dark wax doll."

"I have sufficient dolls of wax to keep me company. Does this one talk at least?"

"Very little, it appears."

"And I shall adore her."

"I think you will."

"*You* think it now! You wouldn't say so. All right, I make no promises. Send your silent, humorless, discreet wax doll to me."

Now Madame was at her game, but it might have spoiled her fun for me to point it out. Such a "no promise" from Madame was as good as her hand and seal. I rose, saying that I must get back, and at the mention of my office Madame inquired after Papadeneau. I described his latest exploit on the moon, concluding, "He's a fearsome waste of time, and I haven't discovered the trick of putting him off, but in a way I can't begrudge it."

Madame cocked her head with a distant, quizzical expression. "You express yourself always so mildly, one sometimes wonders whom you hate."

I recall that this much pleased me. I smiled at her and said, "Not you, at any rate."

"No. No, not me. Affection is more complicated than you admit or realize, but I do not think even you so devious as that."

The remark was all the more wounding for its obscurity. I was startled into saying the first thing that came to mind — a "choice of instinct" Riebenstahl would say. I had half-turned to go. I swung back, and demanded, "Mme de Verbois, did you love your husband?"

Madame first laughed — I suppose my question really did not follow — and then her eyes, the first time I had ever seen it happen, brimmed over.

"That fool? That imposter? That pompous charlatan? I adored him. I *adored* him! Go away now. I am not crying because he died, I am crying because I loved him. Go away. Send your American to me."

Madame has never recalled these last few moments of that conversation, and I think it possible she has forgotten them. It is my description of Prytania she mocks me with, laying a Napoleonic hand upon her bosom and intoning in a fake bass voice, "From what I gather she is quite without humor; she seems discreet."

She delivers this line as if it were meant to be laughed at, but she does not laugh at it. She says, "Yes, yes," and once she turned on me, suddenly laying her hand along my arm.

"My dear, you have inspired me to compose a little saying. Listen: the truth that a man tells is to the truth that he knows as the truth that he knows is to the truth. 'Not bad, eh?' our Riebenstahl would say. 'Not bad for an old fellow.' "

At the time, however, strolling back toward Neuilly, I considered that I had described Prytania with sufficient accuracy, and that it was no tactical misfortune to have painted a less attractive picture than I might. What did trouble me was the riddle of Madame's "even you so devious as that," and what troubled me more was my own incomprehensible outburst.

I wondered if other men — like Harold and Kenneth, who present façades so massive that one can't but consider them solid to the core — if men like Harold and Kenneth ever suffer from these confusing inconsistencies of character. I thought perhaps I had seen a hint of it in Kenneth just last night, and I had watched Harold shrinking his thick shoulders toward his knees. And yet these two, each in his way, seemed heading unimpeded toward his desire.

Whereas I, who always had the power of instilling confidence and turning other wills toward my own aim, had never enjoyed the fruits of such a skill. Something in me not at all myself, so that I never acknowledged it till too late, had always upset my balance when the game was as good as won, and I had thrown my advantage away exactly as I had just now come from doing with Madame. Just so had I once, having earned the report of political dignity beyond my years, risked it on a reference to "the Democratic ass," deliberately ambiguous about whether I meant my opponent or his party's symbol. A small thing, but one that astonished me as much as my well-wishers, and not even my opponents had ever guessed how often I denied my own character with extravagant impulses.

Take this. In very January, on the route to Neuilly from rue Cardinet, spring was insidiously at work in the spare urban trees. Nodes and twig-ends were as gray as tarnished money, but the gray was forming itself in little knobs; taut, ugly swellings, almost invisibly defiant. I smiled at them and walked more briskly. I am much given to such observations, yet they are as incompatible to my nature as boiled mutton to my tongue. I am in general a wintry sort of person, look better in smooth-faced tweeds than these flimsy "miracle" fabrics, work best in temperatures under seventy, would rather walk in atmospheric dampness than my own. I almost said "natural dampness," and that too is myself as I am — placing perspiration on the side of things unnatural. Yet why do I recognize these things? And why, when it matters, do I always recognize them too late?

Prytania found her way to my office about two-thirty, with a formal note from Schlutzburg saying that she was to be "accorded every respect." He had given her a scale rating of B, with a salary of one hundred seventy dollars a month, which was better than I had hoped, and certainly better than she deserved.

There was nothing in her that afternoon to contradict my first impressions. She was if possible more solemn and straight-faced than the night before, and as businesslike as an eighteen-year-old girl is ever likely to be. She had slept her weariness off and stood as if her spine were made of wire; she had pulled her hair severely back in a rubber band, with the sole effect of exposing twice as much of that radiant, child-smooth skin. The collar of her soft silk shirt was dingy, and over it she wore a wool pinafore sort of thing in a murky color, with a coffee stain on the hip.

She said good afternoon and sat, drawing from her handbag a notebook with green pages. Over this she poised a pencil of the ineffectual silver kind that are used by countesses, not secretaries. I noticed that her hands were incongruously large, and rather stubby, and my impulse to chuckle was so compelling that I frowned instead.

"He's given you a very high rating."

"Yes, sir."

"Can you take shorthand in French?"

"No, sir."

"Then you don't deserve that rating."

"No, sir."

"Did you realize that?"

"Yes, sir."

"Did you mention it to Mr. Schlutzburg?"

"No, sir."

"It's really my duty to mention it to him."

"I don't think he cares, sir."

"Indeed."

The corners of her mouth flicked in and out again with the speed of a camera shutter. "He didn't seem to think you wanted me hired, sir."

"Is that so."

"Yes, sir. He gave me a little speech about racial prejudice. I think it was directed at you. He said I was to tell him if I wasn't treated properly."

I was somewhat taken aback. Really, Schultzburg had gone too far! Prytania paused a moment and continued.

"Earl Long was good at getting jobs for people."

I neither understood nor was I flattered by the comparison.

"Once he got jobs for all the Negro nurses in New Orleans. Do you know how he did it?"

"No," I replied coldly.

"He raised a ruckus about white nurses waiting on the nigger patients."

Those who find life most congenial when it is taken at the value of its formalities will perhaps understand that my reaction to this perception of Prytania's was one of positive fright. It struck me for the first time that she might be very bright — a view I have since, incidentally, considerably modified. Had she been playing the Southern servant with that yessir nosir business? I felt myself a little challenged, but the girl herself appeared to drop the matter, and proceeded with exhausting thoroughness to inquire about her duties.

My title is a cumbersome phrase beginning with the words "Coordinator of . . ." and intended to imply that I make numerous and momentous decisions. In fact I am a sort of glorified filing cabinet, my importance resting in the number rather than the significance of negotiations under my eye. The position requires a monumental memory and a penchant for organization, and to this extent it is true when, promoting an underling beyond me, my superiors claim that I cannot be replaced.

Prytania asked quite seriously if I wished to be addressed as Mister Coordinator. It was uncanny how the girl could wound. I replied, and I have no idea what I wished to gain by it, that, "Just occasionally, I think I should like you to call me 'Your Imperial Highness.'" At which Prytania once more "smiled" — that enigmatic curling of the lips inward — smile enough to show that she understood a joke was intended, not smile enough to guarantee that she was amused.

I had expected Papadeneau to invent an errand in my office, and it was not many moments before he arrived with a broken pencil in his hand, a mere symbol of excuse, since he does not use a pencil in his work, and left with the thing still unsharpened.

Mechanically, I performed the formalities and prepared to wait out Papadeneau's attack. But curiously enough it was through Papadeneau that afternoon that I first had a glimpse of understanding into what up to now had been Prytania's inexplicable appeal. I myself had found her wary, not overwarm, disturbing. Papadeneau found her — this much I saw that day — an audience, predisposed to regard his own concerns with exactly the importance he assigned to them.

He acknowledged my introduction with a ceremonious obeisance. Then, being a man incapable of holding more than three thoughts in his head at one time, he shot a wounded look at me and announced, "Boss does not believe it, but yesterday night I have bought into a hotel on the moon."

Prytania considered this information seriously — there is no other possible interpretation of her aspect. Sitting very still, she drew a few deliberate lines in her green notebook and then deliberately rubbed them out.

"How many stories?" she finally asked.

Papadeneau expelled a breath. "Very many. A sky-scraper," he said.

"But how many rooms?"

"Two hundred," he replied. I noted that his answer betrayed an amateurishness in tactical improvisation. Had I been so challenged I should have answered, "One hundred twenty-seven doubles and eighty-four singles, each with adjoining bath." Prytania, however, assumed the baths.

"Do you think that's practical?" she asked.

"Practical, no! Practical! Was it practical to discover America?"

She seemed to weigh the practicality of discovering America. "I didn't mean that. I meant . . . I don't suppose you could get more than two bathtubs in a rocket ship. Isn't it going to be prohibitive" (four separate albeit slurred syllables) "to transport two hundred bathtubs?"

Papadeneau stared.

"There aren't any trees, you know. Or is it to be concrete?"

"Concrete," he stammered.

"You'll need several mixers, and they must weigh a ton. It won't be easy. But as you say" — he hadn't said it, in fact, but it was in every anxious muscle — "what's easy that's worthwhile?"

She parroted this phrase in the tone of one who has never felt the difficulty of a worthwhile thing, nor discovered how little a difficult thing may be worth. I felt that I had never seen such solemn innocence.

Papadeneau, though, signified his concurrence with a sharp rap of the pencil on my desk, and Prytania looked upon him with approval. "It'll take a hundred years or so, but your grandchildren will thank you for it."

From then on Papadeneau treated the youngest steno in the agency with a deference he had never accorded Secretary Haverill himself. Her inkpot never ran dry, her typing failures were spirited mysteriously from the wastebasket; he asked her advice, he even, when she wished, left her alone to work.

"Vai-ry practical," he said of her to me, with an inappropriate tap of his forefinger against his skull. "Vair-ry practical," as if practicality were the virtue he had always held above all others. The hotel on the moon was never mentioned again, although one morning when I complimented him on a new white shirt, he laid the finger on his temple and confided, "To celebrate a small transaction."

Nor were my apprehensions of the other secretaries better founded. Prytania was inefficient and original — a disastrous combination in a stenographer — but the others were more protective than disdainful. Although she needed to be told everything from what we were *for* to how to fill the stapler, they were impressed by the flat logic of her questions. To some of these I did not myself know the answer: "Why do we ship Canadian blankets out of New York and Minnesota milk from Canada?" "Why do we send the *Midwives' Monthly* to classes taught in Urdu?" "What's the point of putting the date in Roman numerals on the new Arabic school?"

In neither official nor private conversations could Prytania's questions have been called *kind;* indeed her curiosity was of the sort that cracks composure; the answer to most of her questions was adequately, "Why, because!" Yet she was universally accredited with kindness. It must have been because she was a tireless listener; not the sort who makes a background of murmurings, exclaims, "How interesting," and "You don't say!" and "I never heard the like!" But a child who listened with impassive scrutiny, and who conveyed the flattering impression of listening for her own purposes, because what you said was more important than you seemed to realize. Then her flat remarks (How many rocket ships do you need to get two hundred bathtubs to the moon?) would hint at some hidden understanding, and if her words touched a sore spot, it seemed because she was wise, not because she wished to wound.

Toward the end of the day I dictated my quarterly report on price increases, and Prytania took it down in a none-too-rapid shorthand which appeared to be of her own invention. At one point I inadvertently referred to "the post-world war." A good secretary would have, in the typing, automatically corrected the slip of my tongue. Prytania simply quit writing and let me run on for a sentence or two until I noticed that she had stopped. Then she said, "You mean the postwar world."

"Yes, yes," I replied in some impatience, but I turned away from her mild eyes, full of the dumb reproach of some forest animal for the inexplicable corruption of mankind.

I dined at La Perouse with a blanket salesman from Quebec. Although bids come through my division, I have no vote in the choice of a contractor. After the manner of Francis Bacon, I explain this with utmost care as I accept a manufacturer's invitation, which I do only when the restaurant suggested is out of the ordinary. Perhaps there is something shocking in the way I can enjoy a superb meal in bad company. This fellow was appalling, his mind entirely swathed in Orlon fleece, but the *ris de veau Lyonnaise* was of a subtlety! I lingered, taking indigestion pills, over a third glass of Armagnac.

When I let myself into the apartment there were voices coming from what Laura likes to call the *salle*. Rather, there was one voice, but in a strident tone that suggested an audience.

"There you are. There you have it. You say that I misunderstand what you are saying, but there you sit, and I understand from the way you hold your cigarette the secret of the century's whole steel-blue sterility."

Strange to think that most of the Western world knows Yves Adam without his voice. Knows him, indeed, as a man who does not have one, does not need one, probably does not want one; as Zitzio of the omnipresent elbows, the bumbling scoundrel of his famous mimes. His voice is an extraordinary organ, the only male voice I have ever heard that is at once high-pitched and resonant. He speaks seven languages, and all of them bulge with images and loudly mixed metaphors.

"I give you in answer a small apple of irrefutable truth: technique is not enough, technique is a goldfish bowl, very necessary to hold the water in, but hardly an ornament without the fish. Your generation is cold at the core; all the perfumes of Arabia will not conceal that fact."

A woman, amused. "Are you saying that the generation stinks, Yves?"

"Stink, my dear Elena, I do not mind. Stink I find inspiring. Only if you are going to portray to me stink, with your body, I do not wish to be told that this is done by placing the knees just so, and the hands palm forward two inches from the nose."

I had hung my coat, and entered. Jean-Claude Bastien was draped on a chair and footstool, and his master, a rigid column of indignation, was planted directly in front of him with his back to Laura on the couch. One would instinctively have said that Jean-Claude was the world-worn teacher, and Yves the rebellious student. The young man, tall, slender, but broad-shouldered, with sole-shaped eyes and an abundance of dark brown hair, lay languid in every muscle, his right hand dragging a cigarette near the carpet. Yves Adam, so small, so insignificant-looking offstage that it never failed to give me a start, might have been a schoolboy in a fit of temper. His trademark, the famous goatee that thrusts straight forward as if it were an extension of the horizontal rather than the vertical plane of his face, trembled like a mat of naked nerves.

In the alcove against the window, Elena Bastien was looking into the street. She acknowledged my entrance with a friendly elevation of thick lashes, continuing to stroke her black chignon in a slow rhythm.

"You're accusing me of wanting conventional gesture," Jean-Claude was saying, "whereas what I really want is to move another step beyond it."

Laura rose and came to me. "There you are — how can you be so late? Had you forgotten? Come and give us a judicious decision; the master and his protégé are at each other's throats."

"Nonsense," said Jean-Claude.

"Our humble home is honored with your quarrel," I

said, shaking hands with Yves, and although I spoke with the exaggeration of mockery, this was true. It was a sign of intimacy with us that Adam should have allowed a dispute to arise.

"This young . . . chemist of mine," Yves appealed to me, "wishes poetry to be written by a calculating machine."

Jean-Claude described a helpless arc with his cigarette. His hand, clumsy in repose, became a thing of liquid and expressive grace the moment he made a gesture. "Not at all. Dear Yves, you're so romantic."

"Good!" shouted Yves Adam.

"You're so afraid that someone is going to trample on the mystic sources of your inspiration that you simply don't listen to what I say. I do not want poetry written by calculating machines. But I dare say a poem could be written about one. What I'm really saying is that we might enrich the mime if we'd look at things scientifically for once instead of . . ."

"Scientifically!" Yves trumpeted, backing himself into the nearest chair. "Bless me, my children, I'm a microscope!" And for an instant as soon over as begun, he flexed his back and stared through the cylinder of his hands at the plate of his knees in an attitude so entertainingly suggestive of a microscope that, indeed, it did his argument more harm than good.

"Oh, Yves, are you so bent on misunderstanding me? All I want is, once, to try to make a mime that evokes a thing and an idea rather than a person and a mood. I want to make a mime that uses the human body as a medium but does not use the human being as a subject."

"Good good good good," Yves barked, bouncing in his chair. "You do that. You have yourself an idea, and

when you've done it and you want to know why you
haven't got a mime, you come to me and I'll tell you
who a mime is."

"I doubt you'll wait for that," Jean-Claude said, smiling, but hadn't finished saying it when Adam went on.
"A mime is a man who can make one sense do the work
of five. He can sting five senses into life by addressing
himself to one. And that's the lap of Lazarus to his
audience, who didn't even know their senses had died."

Jean-Claude sighed and stubbed out his cigarette with
one slow turn of his thumb.

"I have much more respect for the senses than you
seem to credit, Yves, but you'll never get me to admit
they should be treated with all this sloppy reverence and
romance."

"Ah!" Elena fixed her husband with a look of tender
irony. "The things one learns," she said.

From his languor, so effortlessly that one could not
have said at what moment he had begun to move, nor
which muscles had done the work, Jean-Claude rose and
crossed to his wife. He laid two fingers on her shoulder
and, quite deliberately and simply, drew them down
across her breast and belly to the edge of her leather
belt, where they hung for some seconds. The irony left
her smile, and its tenderness matched his own. No one
was embarrassed.

On the other hand, I was quite conscious that no one
was embarrassed, and found myself wondering how such
impudent indecorousness could be so transformed by,
well, an accident of birth, a facility of muscles, an
arbitrary endowment of high color and good skin.

Elena was taller than I, towering over Yves; built to
Jean-Claude's scale. Her skin was strikingly pale, and
was made more so by the brilliant blackness of her hair,

which she wore twisted in four thick locks ascending from the nape of her neck. She had the sort of figure that high fashion and literature, to their discredit, have ignored since the early years of this century. From whence came all those "high, small, firm, round" breasts of the thirties' heroines? Elena was slim-waisted and narrow-hipped, but with a wonderfully full-blown bosom, round arms, and a distinct rotundity of *derrière*. She was hot-tempered, gay, a flirt — though I had noticed that she flirted exclusively in her husband's presence.

Jean-Claude is more difficult to describe, for unlike Elena's, his beauty was not a subject for possible disagreement. His features were an exercise in proportion; one could not praise the arch of his eyes without slighting the angle of his nose, nor call the strength of his jaw more judicious than the plane of his ears. Yves entertained the fear that his protégé was applauded rather as an idol than an artist. Elena had once helped me recall her husband to a third party by saying, "Jean-Claude looks like a gigolo."

I had been deeply shocked at the time — it was not my idea of a wifely remark — but that was before I had seen them much together, and in time I came to regard it as an expression of twofold honesty. Honest because it was an accurate description, and honest because Elena's love was not fragile: she did not mind admitting an attraction to gigolos (which most women share, otherwise they could not be gigolos) or her pride at having got a man handsome enough to be one.

And so they stood at the window bay, his fingers on her belt, in pure unpremeditated sensuality as comfortable to look upon as a deferential bow. I wondered how Yves felt about it, Yves, who had spent his life pursuing women as others pursue virtue, neither for the pleasure of the thing itself nor for its reputation, but for the pleasant self-knowledge of virility. I wondered how the rest of them would have felt if I should have walked over to Laura, . . . but I could not even imagine it.

"If you want a subject for a *human* mime," Jean-Claude laughed to Yves, "how about the way a woman takes every remark as intended for herself?"

So instead I turned to Laura and asked, "Has Prytania been in?"

"Dear, yes. Hours ago. Kenneth came by about six, and when I told him she was at Marraine's, he suddenly remembered he hadn't been to see her in an age. Poor lamb, I've never known him to be so transparent. They came back about an hour later to get her luggage."

"Mme de Verbois took her, then?"

"On the spot. They were going to have dinner with her, and then Kenneth was going to show Prytania 'the places tourists never see.' He said something about Montmartre and the Bateau Mouche." She laughed and I joined her.

"To do the same thing as a modern painting," Jean-Claude was saying, "either a distortion or a pure design, so that the audience will understand that the reason this human body doesn't move like a human body — like a Picasso with two faces — is that we're trying to reveal something that a human body contains but doesn't ordinarily reveal."

Yves was marching in circles around the piano now. "How?" he asked less loudly.

"I told you, I don't know exactly. Everything I've come up with is cliché in just the way I want to avoid. But that doesn't mean the attempt's not valid."

66

"All right, then, Jean-Claude. Why?"

For the first time Jean-Claude sat up in his chair.

"Because," he said, "when an art form doesn't share in an artistic revolution, it doesn't survive it. It becomes a mummy, a museum piece."

He spoke gently. All of us knew that Yves had not many active years left, and that he lived in perpetual dread of the mime's decaying or being subsumed into the other arts. The master continued to pace, in a smaller circle about the coffee table.

"All right," he said, sighing and then frowning to deny that he had done so, "I hope I may never be accused of saying that any subject is not a fit subject for a mime. You can play a paper clip for all I care, but the first thing you need is some notion how it feels to be a paper clip. Have you ever noticed what those wolf-hounds say about you in the papers? 'A superb *study* in drowning.' I could put a tape recorder in the audience, and you know what you'd hear on it? 'How im-*pres*-sive, isn't his control mag-*ni*-fi-cent, how does he ever *do* it.' Nobody'd say, 'My God, I can't breathe.' "

Yves's voice had worked up to high wind and hail-storm; one would not have believed it could come from such a bland, abrupt little body. He used his hands like a symphony conductor, and punched his accented syllables as if to knock them flat.

"Nobody'd cry, nobody'd get a headache, Jean-Claude. And I tell you, whatever the theater's worth, it's worth because of one spoonful of sci-en-*ti*-fic fact: people can feel what they haven't experienced. Isn't that a miracle? Isn't that the cloven tongues of fire? Well, nobody will ever feel what you've experienced if you don't feel it yourself. They'll come, all right, they'll come, professor; they'll sit and say, 'That's what I call control!' But I suppose that's enough and plenty for you."

And he marched dramatically to the door as if leaving us forever, except that just short of it he turned and began pacing back. Jean-Claude also stood, also put his hands in his pockets, also paced.

"Yves, Yves. Why must you pretend to be the Stanislavsky of the mime? You don't mean a word of it, you don't care a damn. You can afford to slight technique because you take it for granted. Listen: I'll make you a bet. Right now, I'll mime three sensations — no, wait, I'll make it more difficult. Three smells. I'll improvise three smells, which you will recognize and to which you will react, and I won't once take my mind off my muscles. You'll only have my word for it that I've succeeded, but I'll be honest. All right?"

"I know exactly what you can do and what you can't," spat Yves, but he collapsed sideways into his chair like a marionette whose strings have been cast aside. He gave an abrupt little nod, and at the signal the two of them changed natures. Yves shed his tension as a duck sheds rain: he disappeared, became the background. Jean-Claude's features began for the first time that evening to display their mobility with a look of fierce concentration. His attitude of intense readiness made the last half-hour's performance look like the very mime of a lazy man.

"And a, *one,* two, three . . ." said Yves in one last short eruption of contempt.

Jean-Claude began. By the piano, at the corner farthest from our group of chairs, he slouched his shoulders and slung his weight forward on to his pelvis. From the depth of his hands in his pockets, we could tell that the pockets were empty. His shoes, which were fashionable and new, he made shabby by flexing his toes upward and out, so that we saw their soles. He took a couple of melancholy steps and stopped, blinking his lashes and rocking on his heels in comic brooding. Then his nostrils began to twitch. He rolled his eyes in a sidelong glance at the end table on his right, and a look of sentimental beatitude spread from his extended nostrils across his face, down to his bobbing Adam's apple and his shoulders, which he lifted almost to his ears.

With doddering tenderness he closed his fingers around an imaginary stem and pulled it to him from the table. He flexed his free hand, let the other slide up the stem, and nuzzled the bloom on his palm, letting his lip catch on the petals as he mouthed it again and again. Finally he leaned away with lowered lids and raised brows, in a paroxysm of ecstasy.

He remained thus for several seconds, as if afraid to draw another breath, no muscle of his torso moving, but his whole body swaying on its heels from side to side. Side to side. Side to side. All at once, at the angle farthest from the flower, his nostrils twitched again. He made a visible effort to return to the fragrance of the flower, but the act of drawing a breath drew him, reluctantly, back to the left. Eyes on the flower, he made a few stealthy shuffles to the left, a few surreptitious sniffs. He bestowed a tearful smile of apology on the flower, faced round to the left and let drop his jaw.

Laura, Elena and I laughed, and were awarded a sharp "Ssst!" from the master.

Jean-Claude sank several melancholy inches into the floor and his tongue lay dead out the corner of his mouth. He leaned on outstretched palms against the glass — it was obvious that there was a glass, because if there had not been he would of necessity have lost his balance — and was rapt once more, except that this time his nose kept jerking and his tongue turning over on its side.

At last he drew away, slowly, sadly; with monumental effort disengaged his eyes from the food and his hands from the glass, squared his shoulders and turned away. He took one more step of his walk. So unexpectedly that I heard myself gasp, a wave of shock ran through his body and he stopped again, rigid with loathing, his eyes riveted on the carpet two feet ahead of him. His nostrils distended, lengthened this time rather than widened, his mouth twisted itself down and out of shape, his chin drew doubling into his neck. It was wonderfully ugly; I felt myself mirroring his fear. With dreadful caution he advanced toward the thing on the carpet and nudged it with the side of his upturned toe. He tensed again, drew back his foot; his eyes ran in terror over the ground after the maggots that had issued from that decaying thing. He gagged. My own dinner made a few vicious turns.

"My God, please stop," said Laura.

Jean-Claude stopped and Yves, in comic deference to his hostess, seized an imaginary broom and swept the offending thing into a corner. We all relaxed, praising Jean-Claude. The master, however, returned to his seat and declared, "You cheated." We erupted in unanimous protest.

"I didn't!"

"Now, Yves. . . ."

"Bad loser!"

"Jean-Claude, supposing you tell me what those three things were."

"Come on, Yves. Anyone here could tell you."

"I should like you to tell me, please. The last one?"

"It was a dead alley cat, full of maggots and flies."

"Yes. Color?"

"Tiger."

"It had been dead how long?"

"At least three days. Run over."

"Good. Now the second one."

"Food, of course."

"Quite probably. And the first."

"A flower."

"What sort of flower?"

"Oh. Well. . . ."

"What sort of flower!"

Jean-Claude shrugged. "A rose."

Adam stroked his beard with the backs of his fingers. "No," he said, "it was not a rose."

Jean-Claude shrugged again. He had reassumed his indifference.

"It was not a rose. Because when you felt its stem you did so without looking, and with your fingers together. If it was a rose, you'd have got stuck, which you didn't. When you touched the bottom of it your hand was almost flat, hardly cupped. You can do that to a peony, but if a rose was that far open you'd knock it to pieces by breathing at it, let alone taking hold of it. You were hungry enough in the second, but we don't know if there was meat or ice cream behind that window, because you didn't either. But the last one, ah, Jean-Claude! That's where you cheated. You did not have your mind on your muscles. It was a tiger-colored alley cat which was run over at least three days ago and was full of maggots and flies. I stake my reputation on it, you have seen such a cat not long ago."

"Jean-Claude . . ." Elena said gently.

"On the way here," he admitted.

Yves spread his hands in pontifical absolution. "But my darlings, why do you look abashed? Is this a matter for shame? Such cheating is the staff of art. Depend on it, my heart is full of the Holy Ghost; if my own Jean-Claude can gag on a dead cat, perhaps he is made of flesh."

"But he didn't!" exclaimed Elena. "I did."

"Right," said Jean-Claude, rescued. "Plain observation, pure technique."

"Did I look so ugly?" from Elena, laughing.

"A draw!" cried Adam, lurching to his feet. He strode once more to the door, this time in genuine exit. "A draw! My friends, it's late. We've squandered half the night and part of morning, and we haven't brought up a bucketful of honest water. A draw! Let's leave before we take up the ax again."

A general check of watches, general astonishment at the hour. Jean-Claude and Laura followed to the vestibule. I stayed behind to help Elena with her coat.

"Do you think it's serious?" I asked.

She threw me a mocking glance over the fox-fur collar. "You mean the quarrel, don't you."

I said I did.

"Oh, everything is serious, my friend." Her eyes were blacker, brighter than the fur, and cast doubt on the seriousness of anything at all. She faced around and fastened her coat. Curiously beautiful, a woman's fingers deftly pushing a button through thick wool.

"But the quarrel? . . . will be forgotten till it is taken up again. Tomorrow they won't have any problem except the matinée."

"Do you think Jean-Claude will succeed in making his abstract mime?"

"I'll tell you," Elena answered with a contraction of her brow. "I hope not."

"What do you mean?"

"Oh, it's a little difficult." She flipped her gloves to smooth them out. "My husband is . . . Too much comes easily to Jean-Claude, and so he takes everything too easily. He is in need of needing something he can't have. Do you see?"

"I think I do."

"Yes, yes. No one but Yves has ever made him work. And so he is lazy about everything but his work. Lazy about his clothes, his face, his feelings and his marriage . . ."

"Elena!" I exclaimed. "I know Jean-Claude adores you!"

She dismissed the whole discussion with a peal of laughter.

"Of course!" She turned away with a teasing pout. "Do you think there's anything so difficult in that?"

PART TWO

Among
School Children

KENNETH was not stupid, however stupidly he may
have begun with Prytania. As a student, he was quick,
devoted, and well spiced with the prejudices we call con-
victions. That it was good to help people to delay their
dying he took to be an axiom. That it was necessary
toward that end to discover and record the patterns of
nature, he took on the authority of his superiors. He was
gifted at detecting patterns. Moreover, he was capable of
unbegrudged surrender, and if, in argument, he was
proved wrong, he enjoyed the proof for its own sake, or
as if it were his own.

It was not his fault if certain patterns are obscure, or
if he had not yet made it an axiom that women wish to
be presented terms, not asked for them. It was not his
fault if he did not recognize that much of the woman in
the girl Prytania. It was not to my credit that I could
have told him.

Had he dissected a frog for her on their first evening
out, she might have loved him. He took her instead for a
ride on the Bateau Mouche, and spent his real elation in
counterfeit poetry.

Had he not said, "She's a real lady," of Madame, Prytania might have guessed the depth of his affection. He repeated this phrase as if it were an epigram.

Had he taken her to Riebenstahl, she might have discovered that all his pleasures were not rooted in cliché. He cultivated an acquaintance with a rather ugly student of the theater at the Cité, and presented him as evidence of an interest in the arts. To this boy, who had a beard so untidy that it must have been trimmed so, Prytania listened with her usual absorption. But when he told her for the fourth time that we'd got to get the guts back in the drama, she inferred that he had nothing more to say. She disliked him, and liked Kenneth a little less.

Every young man goes through it once or twice, and I watched him feeling that, as with Chicago, I must have at some time known this chaos from inside. In London he had been a moderately successful student lover; his gangling ease was too near nonchalance not to prove a challenge. Now, suddenly, because he felt himself inadequate to a girl, he denied his qualities and found his interests insufficient. Instinctively he knew he wouldn't do, and so, instinctively, he floundered about to find some self that would. His failures never taught him, as they would have taught him in the lab, that he had begun with a faulty premise; only that he hadn't yet quite found the formula.

He should have explained the present state of the cotyledons; he predicted the color of crocuses in the spring. He should have taken her to scientific lectures and treated her to his knowledge of the skull. He took her to the Opéra-Comique. It did not strike Kenneth as dishonest, let alone as unendearing, that he implied familiarity with the place, nor that he declared it with conviction the best institution of its kind in the Western world. He wished it so for Prytania's sake, and if she had said so he would have believed it unconditionally.

So at first, at best, she tolerated him. She seemed to look at him with pleasure; his fairness, and the line of his lanky frame. She might have enjoyed just watching him, if he'd sometimes have done with talking, or with shifting from side to side while he looked for something else to say. If she asked about his work, he said it was technical and dry. If he thought so, Prytania asked, why then had he chosen it? Kenneth knowingly replied that men were peculiar creatures, and liked things technical and dry; and made some remarks about the beauty of the provinces, of which he had no very intimate knowledge. He was much more astonished than I when she rounded on him, "Kenneth, what *do* you care for?"

"You," he replied.

"Oh, Kenneth. How am I to know what that's worth if I don't know what you're like?"

He spoke of her as hot-tempered, to which Madame said, "So?" and Laura said, "Absurd!" I added the adjective to those collecting in my mind.

"What's Prytania like?" Laura asked one afternoon. I thought my ready-made reply would amuse her.

"She's a vai-ry practical hot-tempered Oriental American octoroon with an unplaceable accent in a fake Scotch coat."

"Cute. That's what I mean. Everyone seems to think she's *ravissante* some way or other. But no one quite agrees what way it is. I'm not at all sure she'll wear well; I'm beginning to tire of her. Don't you think she puts that blankness on a bit?"

I said, "You seem to have decided what she's like."

"No, not at all. I wondered if you thought so too; you

see so much more of her, I thought perhaps you'd
figured her out. What do you think? What *is* she?"

A flytrap, painstakingly digesting a mosquito.

A Blake proverb, masquerading as a Victorian cliché.

Blank paper, uncut crystal, virgin clay.

Disorder, locked behind dark-polished wooden doors.

The door ajar. What did it open on?

She was, to begin with, a young body, not yet perfect,
not yet perfectly unconscious of itself. Her deliberate
efforts at grace betrayed the comic concentration of a
colt first trying out its legs. Her office manner was a
singularly unsuccessful fraud. Her first few moments in
any crowded room, where she could not help but feel
the stir her entrance always caused, left her in a desperate isolation. Her hands, particularly, blunt and
large enough to have been borrowed from some other
body, or as if she had not yet grown into them, strayed
from each other to her hips to her hair and back again.

Yet her instinctive gestures had a breath-taking
beauty of pure tactile joy. She was, for instance, not
used to the daily wearing of her high-heeled shoes. I
caught her once alone in the outer office after lunch.
The shoes were hung by their heels on the rim of the
wastepaper basket and, sitting on one ankle, she held
the other in both hands, stretching her leg over the ditto
machine in a ballet *point*. She hadn't heard me enter,
and sat for a moment chanting *"Un, deux, trois, quatre;
un-deux-trois-quatre,"* as she flexed and stretched her
toes.

The concentration of her pleasure in herself, the dignity of it, unnerved me like the uncovering of a guilty
secret. I tried to leave as quietly as I had entered, but
stealth is noisy. Prytania turned, her ankle still in hand,
and slowly lowered her foot to the other knee.

"My feet hurt," she explained, without expression.

She was (are all the young to some degree? — I have forgotten) a resident alien in any neighborhood, any room. She was so used to being unused to her surroundings that I truly believe she had no joy of the familiar. She struck no roots, made no commitments by so much as a "See you soon." Yet as if it were necessary to establish an instant home because there was to be no permanence in it, by the end of the week she was known to every shopkeeper on rue Cardinet. The *patronne* of the Livres Malsherbes plied her with catalogues of English paperbacks, the *patisserie* put aside a *baguette* for her supper; she followed the progress of the druggist's newest nephew and talked astrology with Madame's concierge. She owned only one pair of the stiletto shoes which she apparently thought necessary to her job. When the heels ran down she left them in the repair shop after work and walked the half-block home in the slush in stockinged feet. *Pieds-nus,* they called her laughingly after that, but the second time she did it no one who lived there stopped to stare.

She was a superb acquaintance, a discovery at first meeting to Secretary Haverill, the UNICEF watchman, our Cité students, and to Laura. She seemed to know by shaking hands with people their theology and philosophy, and though her own might have made scant conversation, she knew how to feel where she was in sympathy and where in disagreement, and how to say so. Her questions went to the root and core, because nothing was too obvious for her to say. Where others would have shrugged or thrown up their hands in exasperation, she went ahead and explained the thing that was self-evident to everyone save yourself.

Yet she was an impossible friend, if friendship is

meant to engender ease. Her immediate entrance into one's concerns implied a promise, a complicity. When it went no further, she became a perpetual accusation. I mean, that once I had heard her handle Papadeneau, I felt her the one person to whom I might convey my annoyance and affection. I said, when he had interrupted us with some foolish recitation, "I think you're most aware of your own inadequacy when you come face to face with someone who really couldn't be better than he is."

"He might be taught to bathe, though," Prytania said.

I did not for an instant believe that she had misunderstood me, nor that she cared whether Papadeneau bathed or not. Her remark meant, "Spare me your inadequacy; please don't involve me in your compassion." I felt my own privacy invaded by the bluntness of the rebuke. I became myself more rigidly the employer, and treated her with that impersonal kindliness which, usually, I found so comfortable.

She was, in one instance only, apparently without reserve. As suddenly as she became a resident, she became a daughter for Madame; the daughter that, by one of those arbitrary cruelties of nature, *"Marraine"* had never had. Madame alone refused to indulge abstractions about Prytania, and to the contradictory generalizations she would reply without exception, "So?" It was a banality intended to express attention, but in time I heard it as the challenge, "So what?"

Madame herself supplied the vitality of which Prytania's actions were devoid. "Look, she has brought me flowers! Like the garden at Neuilly, are they not? Oh, it takes me outdoors again!" Why had I never thought of it? And Prytania took her literally outside.

On payday, which meant every other Friday, Prytania took a taxi from Neuilly, helped Madame down the stairs, and brought her to our house for dinner and the evening, taking her back again by cab. Such a simple, such an obvious thing to do, yet neither Kenneth nor I had ever considered such a move.

Prytania duly paid her rent, and supplemented it with extraordinary gifts (a plumber for the flat upstairs, to save the silver bowl — why hadn't I thought of it?) but the rent itself was put aside for pleasures they could share. Prytania bought Madame a secondhand phonograph, and Madame replied with records. They took particular pleasure in items both motherly and extravagant: Chantilly slips and volumes of classics bound in yellow silk.

One would have thought, in an atmosphere of so much mutual affection, that Prytania might elsewhere have relaxed her guard. But she changed not at all, and even at home with Madame, all the visible evidence of her warmth was in the vase of daffodils on the sill.

She was an enigma, yet slowly I began to see beneath and through her contradictions, no one of which was so startling as that there should be, under that placidity of mien, any contradiction at all. Her gravity, her calm, were the faces of distrust, and formlessness, and hunger. Her interest in other people's interests had all the sincerity of greed. She was waiting; she was assimilating; she was standing by. What I had taken for lack of humor was an innate disbelief in all simplicity. She failed to laugh not because she didn't get a joke, but because she refused to take it at face value. Mere foolishness annoyed her, and the object of wit, she considered, could not be laughter. The attitude was disconcerting to everyone, I think, except Madame, who found it superlatively congenial. For Madame never indulged a joke without a point, and Prytania never conceded that a joke was without one.

Nevertheless, in fact the girl could laugh. One afternoon I dictated in a requisition, "Eleven round mouth solid socket shovels; one sack thirty-six hickory pick shafts." Prytania lifted her minute stare. "Round mouth solid socket shovels; one sack thirty-six hickory pick shafts!" she repeated in my own officious tone. She choked and spluttered, she shook, she wept.

Once again, I came upon her in the garden, in the snow. The walks, freshly shoveled the day before, had been freshly thwarted before the staff arrived. Now human footsteps gingerly traced each other toward the door, while bird and squirrel tracks made mad circles equally in the paths and on the grounds. Prytania stood with her fists thrust in her plaid-coat pockets, laughing alone in a clear free ringing that set the icicles ashiver.

"Is it because we walk in lines, and the birds go where they please?" I asked, and she turned to face me, breaking off as if the idea alarmed her.

"I don't think so. The look of it strikes me, I don't know why." She went with me into the building, and added as if some apology was in order, "Miss Recheuse says I only laugh when things aren't funny."

Suddenly or slowly, I'm not sure which, I understood. Meanings did not amuse her; it was patterns. Like Catholics who best enjoy a joke with Jesus in it, Prytania laughed at arrangement and design, because in her own disunity these were all she really believed in, all she prized.

She had a great longing after order, though she had no talent in that direction, nor in any direction she had yet discovered. Her admiration for the acid Miss

Recheuse was genuine, and she practiced the secretary's splay-legged, chin-high pose. Had she known she was pretty and amusing thus, she would have been mortified. Her little notebook contained so many charts and graphs and lists that she could no longer sort them, and she fretted for days when she could not recall if a particular page of figures was meant to represent an office code or her own finances.

She was at eighteen the real embodiment of passivity, the vessel that accepts and comprehends, but has no means as yet to turn its contents to account. Yet because she neither looked nor behaved a nonentity, virtually no one recognized the quality. No one, I sometimes thought, except myself.

And if no one recognized her impotent passion to order and arrange, it was perhaps because her façade belied her in yet another way. That symmetry and subtlety of feature ought to have been reflected in her clothes. But her whole struggle of understanding and inaction lay in them: her garments were always in faultless taste, always in disrepair. Never old, always worn. Without ever appearing to raise her arm above the shoulder, she ripped her sleeves and tore her silken armholes. Her knees always found the grass in a new white frock, and she sweated shamelessly — never have I seen a slight girl sweat so — fading the cottons and matting the wools.

I should not go so far as to say her dishabille became her. She was not the sort who made a stranger say, "I wouldn't put a hair in place." Indeed, nearly everyone who met her wanted a hand in her perfecting. But to me there should have been profound distress in seeing her perfectly groomed. It was as if the surface of her ruse was one of her gracious admissions of defeat: Look how human I have to be after all. I can't touch a surface without ruffling it.

"What do you think? What is she?" Laura asked.

I said, "I haven't the remotest notion."

"But Goddammit, if she hates me, if I bore her, why doesn't she simply say, 'I'm busy'? It's dis*hon*est to go everywhere I ask her."

Two days in May particularly I remember, a nest of little tensions over which I sat, uncomfortably, in the rôle of mother bird. Kenneth had lost his charm as a companion. He had taken up smoking — Gitanes, for masculinity — and the stains on his fingers (which I believe he made no effort to remove) offended me like the repetition of an obscene remark. His interest in his work had fallen sharply, as if the aridity of it, which he had invented for Prytania's sake, had convinced him once for all. He walked less, talked more, said less, let an abstracted scowl disarrange his features, and answered me with a peremptory, "Yes, yes, interesting," if I attempted to resume our old topics of conversation.

He was sitting in the chair from which Harold had told me of Prytania, and like Harold, forgot to flick his ash. Now and again he would glide forward, limp as batter in a bowl, till his buttocks balanced on the very edge of the leather seat. Then, abruptly, with what looked like resolution, but was not, he would right himself with a whap! of his back against the chair, from thence to settle down again in his doughy lack of spirits.

"Except; there's just a possibility — don't you think there's just a possibility? — that she's one of these people who has to act the opposite of how she feels."

"I think that's an eminently workable hypothesis," I said.

"The fact is she treats me worse than she treats anyone else. (Whap!) So it's just possible that's meant to mean she likes me best. But all the same it's pretty difficult to handle. I never know what I'm supposed to say or do. I swear to God, I worry about whether my hair's combed properly!"

Viewed generously, it is the particular skill of Western statesmen to make old truisms sound as if they have never been true before. I had only one bit of advice that might have been any use to Kenneth. The message was, "Be yourself." I should like to have been capable of an apposite epigram, for to have baldly delivered those words would have been a betrayal of his confidence. Not that I had invited the confidence, or wanted it.

"Kenneth," I said, "as I see it, this is a practical problem, and not a complex one."

Kenneth let out a sound between a moan and a growl and slid to new depths, so that if his weight had not been wedged against his heels, he would have landed on the floor.

"No, listen to me. If you wanted to fall out of love with her, that might be complicated, but in fact you wish Prytania to become your wife. Or have I misunderstood you?"

"Good God, no! That's it." He protested with yet another sudden drawing of his body to upright angles. So uncannily like Harold was he behaving that I had a moment's wondering what he had done with his moustache.

"And you aren't the naïve sort who thinks that a girl has to be struck by lightning, or that a marriage will founder simply because it happens to be based on a few reasoned choices."

"That's the kind of marriage I think sound," he said, without conviction.

"Well, then. It's an essentially practical problem. You aren't asking for any miracles, but for a contract, an assent."

"Excuse me, sir, I appreciate your trying to help, but the fact is, all this is pretty far removed from the mess I'm in."

"Of course it is," I said.

I have an image of myself in these situations. I sit with my legs crossed at the knee — that attitude which symbolizes chastity in a woman, mere nonaggression in a man. My cigar is fire-end-up before my nose. Its smoke mingles with the fumes of brandy rising in my nostrils. It is the others, not myself, who have cast me in this rôle of Sancho Panza, Oenone, a Chorus of Argive Elders; but once in it I control the total gamut of companionship. I am the backboard, the brake, the bucker-up. The buttons of my worsted vest represent the rational world. My value lies in that I never return confidence for confidence; I do not advise by personal analogy; I present the image, but not the details, of past experience.

And I know the rules. A certain amount of brutality is permitted, even required, but it must be directed toward the means and not the end. I may say: You've bungled this horribly because your thinking's shoddy. But I may not say: Look, Kenneth, give it up, she can't be won. You'll never have her, and if you did, you'd love her in a labyrinth while she praised you for a good fellow, and her own mind would wander off down passages you aren't cut out to follow.

"Of course it is," I said. "That's because you're in a mess. A course of action is always an alien idea to emotional chaos. Did you want sympathy? Why didn't you go to my wife?"

"I'm sorry. Please go on."

"All right. What have you done that's failed?"

"Every move I make is wrong."

"Instances."

"Well, I took her to the theater last night . . ."

"The theater doesn't work. What then?"

"But, my God, Prytania loves the theater!"

"Things Prytania loves don't work. What else?"

"But, sir . . ."

"What else?"

"Oh, well . . . the worst débâcle was when I asked her for a kiss." He jerked the hand with the cigarette, coming perilously near to burning his chin.

"Kenneth," I asked with the requisite gentleness, "in four months, you haven't had so much as a kiss for your effort? That does seem hard."

"Oh, no, it isn't that. It was the asking. Christ, she's got so many ways of making me look a fool! I asked her, you see, and she said no, and flipped around up her staircase like I'd pinched her on the street or something. I'd got over it by the time I saw her again, and decided to play the gentleman. Well, we were standing in the middle of the Tuileries, end of February, not many people about, but all the same . . . She throws her arms around me and nearly knocks me off my feet. And then she said, 'Kenneth, never ask for what you can take. It's clumsy. I hate clumsiness. I'm sorry, I can't help it.' Great. She's sorry, but I'm clumsy. There's a hell of a chance that's going to make me *graceful*."

"I don't suppose you mentioned that to her."

"Good God, sir, it's suicide to take that tone with Prytania."

"You've tried it then."

"Of course not."

"Put it down as something you haven't tried."

Kenneth stubbed out a half-smoked cigarette. I felt, in an impersonal way, that it was going rather well. His enmity was transferring itself to me.

I let a little silence fall, and then asked archly, "Kenneth. What would you say are your finest qualities? What have you to commend yourself as a prospective husband?"

The blush, the squirm, the lighting of his last Gitane. At last he effected a squaring of the shoulders and a solemnity rather touching on his boyishly haggard face.

"Honesty and fidelity," he pronounced, self-consciously, but less so than at the mention of the kiss. I had been thinking about youth in those days, and Kenneth's manner struck me as a key. I know myself perhaps two hundred people to whom I could speak of kissing, not one to whom I could have said, "I am an honest man."

The line of argument his words suggested interested me less, but I followed it out, bemused at the eagerness with which Kenneth took my lead. I brought him deliberately toward discovering that he was being unfaithful to his work and representing himself dishonestly to Prytania. I had once watched Riebenstahl mounting matchsticks one on the other to build an Eiffel Tower, and I thought of it now as we proceeded by short question and short answer, none of them interesting in themselves, but falling agreeably into a pattern I had contrived. To the best of my remembrance, it was the first time that night that Riebenstahl had come to mind at all.

90

With a little laugh, "What should I do then? Take her to the lab?"

"It might be worth a try; you've nothing to lose."

"I couldn't, really. It isn't allowed."

"You could handle it indirectly."

"How?"

"Take her to Riebenstahl."

With some surprise, I realized that this was what I had been leading to all along. To this day, I have no idea why. I was callous to, even bored with, Kenneth's adolescent anguish. I really believed his failure with Prytania impossible to avoid by now. I had meant to prescribe, as counselor, a general course of action. Now it seemed that all along I had planned him a rendezvous.

"I'll meet you there, by accident, and see how it goes along," I said, making him accessory, I suppose, to the incongruity of my wanting to interfere.

It was one of Laura's evenings. As I ushered Kenneth into the hall, I saw Elena Bastien's emerald back disappearing toward a medley of glass and laughter. Yves, with his offstage awkwardness, was battling a hanger into his coat. Kenneth mumbled, "Supposed to pick them up at eight," snatched his macintosh, and ducked through the circle of new arrivals. Laura, staggering under wraps, passed me with an impersonal smile which meant, "Couldn't you give me a hand?" I returned the same sort of smile and shrugged toward Yves, who turned just then, peered furiously at me, and blared out, "I hope you haven't got a funny story to tell me!"

"I hadn't been planning on it," I replied. I always enjoy an exaggerated dignity when Yves is in his raving bantam mood. Laura shifted her load and passed out of sight.

"Because I can tell you I would trade the Paris press tonight for a fifteen-minute silence. If I could take all the words I have heard in the last four hours and roll them up in a little ball, like lint, and sweep them into the incinerator, I give you my golden pledge there would be no language left."

"Jean-Claude?" I suggested.

"Jean-Claude, Jean-Claude." Yves sent the hanger screeching along the bar. "Jean-Claude!" he concluded, bouncing on the balls of his feet, his elbows dangling about him as they do when he plays Zitzio.

"Still trying to dehumanize the mime, is he?"

"But no, my friend, that is just the point, he is not trying. He is talking, speculating, theorizing, postulating . . ."

"Are you saying that you *want* Jean-Claude to make an abstract mime?"

Yves blinked at me, then shook all ten of his fingers at me in a paroxysm of impatience.

"What other course is there?" he demanded. "Ionesco in the theater, Nicoll in the dance — by now Martha Graham is old-fashioned, and we are the horse and buggy in a laced corset. Spendid, let Jean-Claude streamline us. I am too old."

"But, Yves . . ." I was going to ask why he didn't simply say so to Jean-Claude, but he silenced me with a gesture and a pitiful lowering of the lids.

"Oh, yes, I am, I'm very fit, but I'm older than you think. The muscles are very amenable to exercise, but the arteries don't give a penny-damn. There's the fact, I haven't got long. I'll probably live to be ninety, that's the burden of being so blossoming fit, but I haven't got long on the boards."

As much as Yves could ever be said to whisper anything, he whispered this, and squeezed my forearm, enjoining me to silence. "Brandy, brandy," he added, and went weaving toward the living room. I straightened his coat on its hanger, smiled, and followed.

Large platters of small foods crowded every surface of the *salle*. A white-coated waiter dispensed martinis and champagne with an air which suggested that neither the liquor nor the drinkers of it came up to standard. He moved soundlessly through groups that were comprised of our more dignified student habitués and the gayer of our professional friends. These two categories remained religiously distinct, but a judicious scattering of saris and fezzes protested our cosmopolitanism.

An "evening" differs from a cocktail party in that it offers some more or less distracting point of focus. Laura had developed a vast acquaintance among the student and semiprofessional performers of the Right Bank, and one of them, a woman with a neck like a swan and a mouth that bore disconcerting resemblances to the same bird, stood by the keyboard of the grand, rendering (as opposed to singing) "La Traviata."

In spite of an insect-buzz of conversation, the piano was indeed the center of attention, and attention perceptible only in short, repeated glances and a slight inclination of every conversation cluster in the one direction. The soprano evidently sensed this interest, for, flushed with pleasure, she addressed herself directly to each group in turn, traveling left to right and back again like a revolving fan. Here and there she caught an eye, and was awarded an apologetic smile, as from someone too kindly to tell her that the credit belonged neither to her skill nor Verdi's.

Leaning on the arch of the piano box, Prytania looked more slender even than she was in a cotton dress

high at the neck and low at the waist, the color of
radishes still warm from garden ground. She was listening to Jean-Claude, and she was laughing. Her head was
tilted back so that her black hair fell on Madame's
shoulder, and the peal of her laughter, which was not
loud, was nonetheless so clear that it effected sharp
dissonances with the aria. Kenneth, beside Jean-Claude,
bore so ill-tempered a frown that he might have wished
to hear the song.

"Who is the dark beauty?" Elena greeted as she
joined us.

"*Messieurs?*" the waiter haughtily proffered his tray.
Yves directed a stare of microscopic intensity into the
nearest champagne glass.

"None of that party soup," he answered in English
with a Texas accent. "See if you can snitch me a bit of
the old man's brandy stores."

"Why doesn't someone tell her not to wear a long-
waisted dress?"

"What? What are you saying, Elena?"

"The *gamine*. She should have fullness in the torso."

"Jean-Claude is saying something senseless," I
observed.

Elena interrupted her appraisal to make a face at me.
"What a gracious host you are."

"I happen to be certain of it, because Prytania only
laughs when things aren't funny."

"You know her?"

"It's my party!"

"No, it isn't. And anyway, it's usually your wife who
picks up the strays."

This remark would have seemed unkind but that
Elena herself was one of my wife's "strays." Jean-
Claude's marriage, Yves' bantering affection for the

Spanish girl, our own acquaintance with the master and his protégé, all were the result of Laura's having bought a particularly unsatisfactory crepe suit-blouse in Madrid. Maria Elena de la Iglesia was the shop's assistant buyer. Laura had got a new blouse and Elena had got a longed-for trip to Paris. My wife had arranged for an interview with an American export shop; the rest of it, including Jean-Claude Bastien, Elena had managed for herself, but there remained between Laura and Elena the sort of affection which does not require understanding because it is based on kindness.

"You only stand by with the pocketbook trying to look benevolent."

"That's an unnecessarily nasty thing to say."

Elena giggled at me and slipped her arm through mine. "I've had my share of champagne," she said.

"You are a bit free," snarled Yves. "Hey-on, there!" He was jostled from the side by Frau Blaumgarten, and a second time by Herr Blaumgarten in her tow. The Blaumgartens were, both of them, in beer; they had married some twenty years before at the same size, and he had grown steadily smaller as his wife, who seemed to thrive on the Blaumgarten product, simply grew.

"So pardons," she flashed her upper plate back over her husband's head. "Such a love-link party. The *gnä-dige* Laura *ist* so . . ." The rest of her remark was lost in the direction of the soprano, who had by now finished her aria and was acknowledging applause by displaying the uncovered part of the rat in her chignon.

"Vonderful!" Frau Blaumgarten averred loudly. "My husband hast always" — her tone was meant to imply "until now" — "found the opera boring."

"Boring? How interesting!" twittered the soprano.

Yves cursed and snatched his snifter from the returning waiter. Elena and I accepted champagne and toasted each other merrily; for my part, feeling rather that I might with some effort become merry than that I was.

"Yoo-hoo!" A long female forearm flapped itself toward Elena, and a gaunt creature detached herself from a little group at the other end of the room.

"Oh, please, let's join Jean-Claude," Elena whispered. "I don't remember her name, and I remember she's interested in foundations."

So we drifted toward the group at the piano, Yves keeping pace with us, and only taking the trouble to remark, *"I've* had enough of Jean-Claude today."

Prytania by now had done with laughing, but there was about her expression a kind of feverish fragility, like a china teapot that may burst at any moment from the weight and heat of what it holds.

"What foolishness has Jean-Claude been spinning for our Prytania?" I asked Madame, and shook her hand.

"As a matter of fact, I've been imitating Yves," Jean-Claude replied easily. "Miss Obée has been to the Opéra-Comique, and not to the Poche Adam! You don't look properly after your employees."

"That was my fault," Kenneth put in, a little too politely.

The rhythm of our chatter broke for just so long as to be noticeable, and then Prytania turned to Yves.

"M. Bastien tells me you speak seven languages. How can that be? I always thought that mimes were mute."

As usual, she had scored. It was anything but an original thought, and many had implied as much in their surprise at his skill, but no one had ever challenged Yves with it in just the way he preferred.

"All the others are," he returned, looking at her for the first time. "My assistant, for instance, has only twenty-two words in his vocabulary. But I have taught him to conceal it very deftly."

"How clever!" Elena spattered a few drops of champagne. "Imagine you keeping it from your wife, Jean-Claude — is that fair? I wonder what those words would be? I know: the first one is work, and the second one is . . . talk."

"And all the others are Elena," Jean-Claude said, steadying her with his arm and neatly managing to shut her up as well.

"After all," said Yves, "perhaps it is wishful thinking. Small ideas sometimes wear great words."

Jean-Claude raised his arms with an "Yves, Yves, Yves!" of appeal, and Elena went gently rolling off into the crowd, where she was instantly seized upon by the woman interested in foundations.

"Beloved master, can't we let it rest? Who got us into this, anyway? The blunt American tongue, as always."

It was unlike Jean-Claude to take up banter, and I decided that he had matched his wife's champagne consumption. He narrowed his eyes at Prytania, but this time Prytania did not laugh.

"Mme de Verbois thinks Americans are too discreet," I said, and smiled at that lady, who lifted a brow as if to say, "Do you still remember that?"

"What an idea, Marraine!" Kenneth dismissed it shortly.

Jean-Claude stared at Madame. "Surely you can't have meant that. The Americans chrome-plate their deformities."

"I call that discretion," replied Madame. "Perhaps it is just a way of using words."

"Words again!" blared Adam, and raised his glass to Kenneth. "Young man, you seem very inarticulate, and

rather sullen. I like you. Escape with me, I'll treat you
to a private store of brandy."

Struck off balance, Kenneth allowed himself to be
propelled off toward the study.

"Never mind," I said to Jean-Claude. "He'll regret it
when he discovers Kenneth is a scientist."

"Doesn't he care for scientists?" from Prytania.

"Ah, no." Jean-Claude put on a solemn face. "He
thinks they're overemotional."

"I think so myself," Prytania said with a quick depression of her nostrils.

We laughed, and Jean-Claude clapped his hands.
"Voilà, Madame! In your way of using words, do you
call *this* American discretion?"

Her eyes half-hidden in crinkles of pleasure, Madame
put her plump palms forward to shield herself and
laughed, "If I am to answer a challenge, I really must
have a chair."

We vied with each other in our apologies and dis-
persed in three directions for an empty chair, Madame
protesting after us, "But no, it is a compliment to me.
Please, I have felt most well."

There was not a seat to be had. Older couples sat in
stolid guard over the sofas, and long-legged girls, their
backs to them, perched on the arms, speaking of
Nietszche to bepimpled young men, or of the young
men to each other. Frau Blaumgarten, quite alone, with
an air of taking in several conversations at once, though
in fact she was isolated from any of them, had possession
of the only really portable chair in sight, Laura's most
fragile Louis Quinze, over which the good Frau's thighs
extended like a head of beer on a brim.

As I hesitated, wondering whether I might acquire
the chair without the Frau, I noticed that the window

seat in the alcove, nearly hidden by its curtains, had not yet been discovered. I shouldered my way back to Madame and signaled the others. "Port in a storm," I said, with as genuine a sense of revelation as if it were not my own window seat, which I knew to be hard and narrow.

I had raised my hand to pull the curtain aside when there erupted from the corner concealed by it a series of breathy explosions like the strangled howls of a frightened dog, and La Traviata burst through the curtains, chin high, neck red, her well-trained diaphragm never to recover from such agitation. She shot past without seeing us, sending the curtains flying; and my hand, poised as it was to close on the edge of the fringe, simply did so, exposing a heated Herr Blaumgarten regaining his balance on the window seat.

The good gentleman pulled himself up and pretended to be brushing his trouser knees, giving us a dapper smile and nodding. "Do come please and zit. It is delightful here, so breezy."

We had no choice but to do so. In the same instant I had a stab of resentment against Herr Blaumgarten for trapping us into saving his face, and a pang of conscience for the poor Frau Blaumgarten whom I had been so pleased to leave by herself. But Laura, I thought, whose instincts for the forlorn and the displaced seldom err, no doubt had compassion and to spare for both of us.

The strains of "Liebestraum," played with precocious fervor by an adolescent from the Alliance, came dripping through the party sounds like jam through cheesecloth, and we listened for a moment with studied intentness. What had we been talking about? Oh, yes

. . . but it hardly seemed appropriate to continue an anatomy of discretion.

We spoke of beer. Rather, Herr Blaumgarten spoke of it; its subtleties, its temperament, its care and consumption; spoke just a little too earnestly, and rather longer than was absolutely necessary to prove his ease.

The French, he assured us, did not understand, had never understood, and would never understand beer. Beer to them was something to be consumed when the local wine was unpalatable or the pockets nearly empty. One could understand what this might do to the sensibilities of a man whose father's father had devoted his entire existence to the proper cultivation of the hops — could one not? So that if it hadn't been for the Nazis he should never have set foot on French soil. But how was he, a *true* German, to tolerate the Nazis? And could he have foreseen the occupation? — which was trouble enough when it came, with suspicion on both sides and no beer money anywhere. Oh, he had had his trials.

Prytania lay back against the sill at the corner farthest from Herr Blaumgarten, her hair lifting and splaying against the open panes. She might ordinarily have devoted her attention to, and challenged, Herr Blaumgarten in his tirade, but tonight she was preoccupied. A spare suggestion of emotion played around her mouth and eyes. Once she shivered in the brush of wind on her bare arm, but when I moved to close the window she shook her head and leaned farther into the breeze. A young bird struck against the sill just at her elbow, dipped and climbed again. She did not move, and when Herr Blaumgarten finally excused himself and backed through the curtains, she gave him a barely polite glance of acknowledgment.

The rest of us smiled at him and, when he had gone, smiled about him.

"One could pity his wife if only she weren't so fat," Jean-Claude said. "At least that takes care of German discretion," and he folded his hands, facing Madame, in an attitude of respectful patience. "Well? Americans do not get caught in corners, is that it?"

Madame said gently, "There is a little cruelty in you, Jean-Claude. Not of a vicious kind, not deliberate, but born of thoughtlessness, and self-assurance. You are not egocentric, are you? But you cannot very clearly imagine other people's misfortunes. I think you are aware of that."

"Yes, I am," Jean-Claude said, stung.

"But can you imagine yourself beginning an acquaintance by saying, 'There is a streak of thoughtless cruelty in me'?"

"Certainly not!"

"No, certainly not. One cannot say such things. It is your misfortune, for people know the worst about you only gradually, and then, because you are kind and beautiful and young, and all of these things show, people are slightly, only slightly, disappointed. But the Americans, you see, have evolved a clever mask for keeping us from finding them out."

"Utter nonsense," I said.

"What are the Americans' faults, Jean-Claude? — excepting present company."

"That they're indiscreet. You already know my view."

"Yes, and what is that? They are gauche? brash? simple and too talkative?"

"Something like that, yes, that'll do."

"Stop an American on the street, ask his name and how he fares, he will tell you, 'I am brash, gauche, simple and too talkative.' Now is this not superbly discreet? Who looks for viciousness in such a man?"

"Idle cleverness," Jean-Claude retorted with an easy laugh, but Prytania stopped him by raising her hand: that troublesome hand, in the way as always, which reached hard toward him, recoiled just short of his shoulder and took itself aimlessly down the side of her dress.

"Marraine is clever, but she isn't idle," Prytania said.

Jean-Claude turned at her urgency and fixed her with a look half-conciliatory, half-questioning. His eyes were a flat bright orange-brown, hers the color of dry oxblood ink: a brown that splintered into blue and violet when struck at this angle by the street light. She drew an uneven and uneasy breath, as if she had spoken out of turn, but did not offer any explanation.

"As an American, you don't believe this nonsense, Miss Obée?"

"I'm not *inclined* to believe it," Prytania answered, "but I have learned that when I don't believe Marraine, I'm usually holding false beliefs."

"The girl's bewitched," Jean-Claude judged matter-of-factly, and she drew another, sharper breath, of a tension so out of keeping with his words that for a moment they seemed to mean something else. Jean-Claude broke back to Madame.

"No doubt the great mass of Americans are professionally sincere, but you discount their geniuses, Madame, who make an art of indiscretion by carrying it right to the heart and core of things. You haven't read their recent books and plays."

"Yes, I have read a little," ironically smiling, as always, at the indirect reference to her age.

"The new Americans are full of cruel, brute reality."

"You mean, Jean-Claude, that their books are full of pimps and perverts, the deformed and the insane. Come, isn't that what you mean?"

"I'm willing to admit a certain fascination with the frankly ugly. No doubt you think that part of my cruelty."

"Not at all. I am capable of such a distinction."

"But I admire it in them. We have never faced it quite that way. We deal in the grotesque, no doubt, but we must make it funny as well, a fantasy, theatrical. I couldn't do it any other way myself, but I admire it in them; not that they face just cruelty, but cruelty and reality at once. Do you follow that distinction?"

"I follow it very well, but I think I am not for that required to agree with it. When reality wishes to be cruel, it leaves off being frankly ugly, Jean-Claude. It buries its ugliness in tolerance and perception; in forgiveness and self-knowledge."

"So this is where you have been hiding!" Elena stood at the drapes and drew them together beneath her chin. "The assemblage is beginning to ask for a mime, my love, and the master looks disgruntled and about to leave. You've been here nearly an hour."

"Which time you haven't wasted on sobering up, I see," Jean-Claude replied, and laid a forefinger on Elena's lower lip. She brushed it with the tip of her tongue and dropped the curtains.

"A man who wants a moderate wife should never marry a Spaniard."

"I must find Kenneth," Prytania murmured, rising. She pulled back the curtain and passed Elena with the greatest care not to jostle her.

"Oh, yes, is that his name? He's been wandering

about with an unlit cigarette in his hand. I thought he
was looking for a match, but it must have been for you."

When Jean-Claude emerged from the curtains the
gaunt foundation lady clapped hands and called, "Here
he is, everyone! A skit! A skit!" And the cry was taken
up.

"Skit indeed," Yves Adam said under his breath as I
came upon him. "When my ducks have drunk themselves under the piano, call them a cab and a nurse, will
you? And don't make a noise about my leaving, if you
please," and he was gone.

"Unfortunately, I have no costume," Jean-Claude was
saying. The uninitiated made noises of disappointment,
but those who knew Jean-Claude began to clap in
rhythm, prepared to insist for as long as he deemed
necessary, since they were certain of eventual success.

Jean-Claude was not past, perhaps would never be
past, that delight in an audience which made him willing
to capture one from any gathering. He was so appealing
that what might have been false humility in another
only prepared us to be entertained, and the coaxing
became part of the game.

"But, my friends, how can I make art in a tweed coat?
The thing is physically impossible."

"Jean-Claude, *voyons, assez!*"

The Blaumgartens, together (it rather looked as if
they were holding hands), were on the couch, and I
snatched the Louis Quinze chair for Madame. Kenneth
and Prytania stood nearby, he smiling joylessly, she
solemn-faced but flushed with excitement.

"Do you want my coat, Jean-Claude?"

"*Your* coat? My dear fellow, I've never seen anything
that bore less resemblance to a costume."

"Mine?" "Mine?"

"I tell you, there's not a costume in the room."

Suddenly with that rush, hesitation, rush again that bespeaks an unresolved courage, Prytania stepped forward into the little clearing around Jean-Claude. With gestures in which one could not separate the beauty from the awkwardness, she bowed a stiff page-boy bow, hand on stomach, toe on heel, and flourished an imaginary hat toward Jean-Claude by its brim.

"*Votre chapeau, Monsieur.*"

It was the only time I ever saw Prytania deliberately call attention to herself. She was passionately embarrassed and determined, which gave her action an altogether different tone than the cheerful heckling that had preceded it.

There was a silence, and Jean-Claude stepped sharply back, sensitive to the dramatic moment. He gave the hat a slow and stern appraisal, then plucked it from her hand, holding it gingerly between two fingers. He turned it this way and that, disdainfully fingering the fabric and flicking off specks of dust. Then, with a begrudging shrug, he placed it on his head. He swiveled it about with a doubtful eye for its fit, pulled on the brim and tapped its crown a full foot above his head. At last he gave a superior smile and a stiff nod of satisfaction. His audience cheered and scrambled for sitting space while he waited in aristocratic impatience, and it gradually became evident that he was wearing a monocle.

Prytania still stood beside him, and when the crowd was quiet he turned back to her and thrust out his hands. After only a second's stage fright, she produced two objects, which Jean-Claude accepted as a cane and gloves, waving her back to her seat.

At my elbow Madame watched Prytania's retreat and, chuckling wistfully, she said, "Yes, he is very beautiful."

Someone shouted, "What is it called, Jean-Claude?" and drew to himself a regard of scathing indifference from the character Jean-Claude had assumed. Already it was comic, the figure erect and still while the hands helped each other into the gloves with effeminate dexterity. He continued the rapid finger-smoothing ritual for some seconds, then tested the walking stick with a flex and twirl. The gestures were made with such conviction that a girl at his feet shied from the path of the nonexistent cane. There was a roar of abandoned laughter, and I saw Laura frown.

Jean-Claude walked over to where Madame sat, and offered her a military obeisance.

"The American," he announced in cultured tones. "For Mme de Verbois."

He entertained us for some fifteen minutes with an improvisation of obvious, even hackneyed, situations, raised to art by the perfection of his skill. He engaged himself in erudite conversation with a woman who appeared to be even taller than himself, and sat with incredible control upon a chair where there was no chair, crossing his legs and even at one point hanging an ankle on the rung. He found that he was sitting upon chewing gum, that he itched in a variety of unpublic places, that his nose dripped and he had no handkerchief; and each of these indignities he survived with bravado and surreptitious machinations of his hands, all the while continuing his sophisticated reactions and remarks to the dowager. His changes of attitude were so timed that the laughter was never allowed to die entirely away, but each burst came upon the heavy breathing of the last. Prytania sat in open-mouthed absorption, bursting now and again into that clear laughter, like the ring of warm money in summer pockets.

At last the American (the title must have been generally obscure) gave in to his discomfort and suggested a breath of fresh air. Her hand tucked under his elbow, his own giving it exploratory pats, they took a stately promenade around the piano. He made love to her, describing in gestures and grimaces the amplitude, magnitude, breadth and depth of his love. There was nothing now immediately incongruous except that a man so tall should be casting amorous glances above his head, and the laughter did gradually subside, giving way to a general expectation of how he should make himself ridiculous. The mime went on; she appeared to be giving in. Most delicately he kissed her hand and elbow, and most gracefully he slid to one knee before her.

A split second before it happened, I knew what Jean-Claude was up to, and a glance at Laura's disapproving face showed me that she knew too. The toe of his nether foot just touched the point in the pattern of the carpet where once before he had ended a mime. That thing was still there. The toe began groping for a better foothold, and gradually, with growing horror, the American and his audience realized that he had kneeled on a dead animal. Waves of nausea swept him as he tried to conclude his proposal, and his face distended and distorted as he concealed his gagging. He had worked on it, I realized wryly; no one mistook the maggots crawling up his leg nor the nature of the smell that tugged at his quivering nostrils. The proposal was thwarted, and the lady left, but it was not in the least funny, and we had been too well prepared to laugh. The room was heavy with discomfiture, and the elder women made faces of frank outrage.

Still Jean-Claude pushed us. With scarcely a glance at his retreating partner, he rose and turned and made terrified attempts to clean his trouser leg. He bent over the rotten carcass with strangely ugly fascination. None of the dignity was left now, nor any pretense of it, to make us think that we were meant to be amused. Instead the American was animal-like himself, crouching, spasmodically drawing forward, extending a claw-like hand.

"Don't touch it!" Prytania shrieked, her voice breaking with the volume of a gunshot into that strained silence. Then a general breathy murmur rose, and Jean-Claude relaxed and stood with his own good-natured smile, and an uncomfortable nod to indicate that he was done. Since the applause did not begin, he deliberately laughed, picked up the imaginary carrion by the tail, and tossed it in Prytania's lap. We might at that have been well prepared, and grateful, to pass it off and tell him that, my, it was terribly realistic, had not Prytania once more shrieked, clawed at her lap, and issued forth a string of terrified cries. She flung herself on Kenneth's chest and wept into his jacket.

"You bloody idiot!" Kenneth shouted then, and people on the outer fringes began collecting themselves to leave. Laura ushered them out with a face of terrible cordiality, and Elena ran in intoxicated anguish to Prytania. Jean-Claude stood helpless, defensive and distressed, murmuring apologies that no one heard.

Kenneth was at once glowering, cursing, fondling Prytania's hair. Madame pulled herself from her chair with a grasp of my forearm.

"Can nothing be done? Kenneth will hit him."

"Kenneth?" I patted her hand. "Don't deceive yourself, Madame. Kenneth is perfectly delighted."

She stared at me, and then at Kenneth, who — it couldn't be mistaken — was swollen with protective, righteous pride. We stood to the side and watched as Prytania regained control of herself and turned to calming Kenneth, half-laughing, half-crying, begging for forgiveness of her foolishness.

The *salle* had miraculously emptied, and only the Blaumgartens stood at the door, still protesting that the party was love-link, really, delightful, never another so. Kenneth half-dragged Prytania to her coat, shielding her with his arms from both the Bastiens, who trailed after, still apologizing.

"I wonder which is more difficult to learn," Madame said, sighing, "relinquishing childhood or accepting old age."

"I wouldn't know," I answered shortly. "I haven't experienced both."

"I know," she said, watching me strangely. "That is what I mean. Listen, my dear, has Kenneth told you?"

"Told me what?"

"That he is taking Prytania to meet M. Riebenstahl tomorrow."

"No, he didn't mention it. So what?"

Kenneth was holding her coat, waiting in the vestibule, and Madame hesitated whether to leave me.

"Don't you want him to?" I prompted, surprised that she should care.

"I don't know; perhaps I am foolish. If I wanted it, I think I should have sent her myself by now. Prytania is so young."

"Oh, I should think Prytania proof against old Riebenstahl."

"Yes, yes. That is not what I meant. It was for his

sake. I am not sure his is the sort of age that wants much youth around it."

She shook my hand and turned away, then turned again, apologetic and appealing. "Would you mind very much going along with them?"

Startled, I focused sharply on her eyes, expecting to see some mockery in them. There was only trouble, muted with self-depreciation.

"I should be glad to."

"I don't mean with them, well, but as an accident."

"I understand."

"Thank you so much."

She joined the young people, and smoothly scattering words of balm, she ushered them out from under the Bastiens' distress.

Elena and Jean-Claude were the last to leave. Laura kissed them both good-bye, and at the door I heard her say, "It's that imbecile *ingénue,* of course. She wasn't even invited."

This was the spring of our glorious summer, but the spring itself came mulish, like an undecided woman, giving itself by grudging bits. May was marked by days of a tepidness that declined into dewy chill before the dinner hour. The ground was too dry to blossom, the air too wet to warm. Low mists like yellow gauze would group and gather and disperse, coyly hovering at the brink of rain, but never raining. Only the false acacia, wearied of idle promises and threats, broke petulantly here and there into flower, burdening the air with its sickly sweetness.

I was a familiar of the Parc Fasseville by now. The afternoon patrolman touched his pillbox brim to me. One of the hardy mothers who had brought her daughter all through winter waved a fly in my direction. The daughter slapped her shovel in the dirt and produced a grunt of recognition.

Riebenstahl himself, when I came upon him, looked no higher than my shoes. He tapped his garden spade as the child had done, pointed with it toward the steps and said, "Good, good. Don't say a word, ha."

I sat. He was planting tomatoes in a fan-shaped plot by the porch, curling the spindly roots to fit them into the cylindrical holes he had made. Then with a series of aspirates he would coax them to stand up straight, dribbling the earth through a loosened fist, pressing it into place.

His greeting had not meant that I was not to bother him. I knew enough for that by now. It meant, "I'm glad to see you. Don't tell anybody I'm planting vegetables, I'm not sure I'm allowed." Nonetheless, I sat drowsily for a while, pleased enough to watch a skilled routine. He worked himself along the rows, squatting, with alternate slides of toe and heel. At the end of one row he came upon a cardboard box of sprouted onions, and he picked one up and broke it into three sections, displaying it to show how the sprouting had re-formed its core into three hard wedges.

"You see that now? You ever seen that before?"

"Of course," I said.

"But now, have you ever thought about that?" He raised a crooked index finger before his face. "Conception," he announced, "is an act of sudden joining. Birth is a process of slow separation. Yes, not bad. I thought of that. Eh? Ever think of that, Your Excellency?"

I had told him several times that I was not an ambassador, but the title seemed to please him, and he wouldn't give it up. I think that by transferring me to a position of which he knew the worth, he derived more satisfaction from the intimacy that he had, also, invented or assumed. Riebenstahl treated me with obsequious familiarity, not unlike Papadeneau, except that Riebenstahl's took me in. He had adopted me. There was never any question that he was the older man. He was my superior in experience, he seemed to say, I was his superior in health and rank, but for all that we were very much alike and understood each other perfectly.

If I hinted annoyance at his chatter, he would nod and say, "Ah, yes," as if annoyance also were an experience of which we were mutually aware. At such times I left in a minor temper, determined that I should simply neglect ever to call on him again. The irritation would persist until it was replaced by sheepishness that I should blame a poor half-mad old man for being — what? Presumptuous? Scatterbrained? I would go again, against my will, but full of forgiveness and dispassionate appreciation for his talents. "Your Excellency," he would greet me then, excusing my delay, "you must be a fearfully busy man. Don't say a word, I know what it is, not having the time to think your own thoughts out."

His own thoughts were, indeed, his only interest, and his tacit assumption of our similarity was partly an excuse to put them in the air between us. "Society is so constructed," he would tell me, wagging his folded glasses at me, "that when we fail to achieve the ambition of our youth, we can blame it on the great Machine. That is the sole purpose of society, yes, ha." He could never resist these little ha's, which were the sound of triumph rather than amusement. "Ha. Haven't you found that to be so, Your Excellency?"

I would answer to the effect that his generalization no doubt sometimes applied in part, and he would accept this as total affirmation, restoring his rimless glasses, which redoubled the intensity of his eyes. "Love. Love is a commodity for which the demand perpetually exceeds the supply, and the *family unit* is a factory for the production of a synthetic substitute. Do you like that?"

Nevertheless, he always assumed that I did, and he never allowed me sufficient time to discover whether he was contradicting himself or not, but would be off on another prepared maxim that had rather resemblance than relevance to his chosen theme.

He stood now from the last tomato plant, rubbing the small of his back with the handle of his spade, gloating over the garden plot. And indeed, it was very beautifully done, the rows set in interlocking curves to the edge of the fan, their pattern accentuated by stakes of copper pipe. It did not surprise me to find that Riebenstahl was a good gardener, though I knew he had spent the whole of his life in a grassless part of London. There was nothing he could not learn to do with his hands, and I had no doubt that had he been born in the Stone Age, civilization would have got along much faster.

"Onions'll wait," he said, which meant, "Come into the house and sit down."

It was dark to gloominess inside, and Riebenstahl's careful clutter loomed like the half-seen objects in a horror house. He had acquired, since I first knew him, a supply of human and bovine bones, a plaster reproduction of a brontosaurus, the internal working of a defunct Mercedes-Benz, a broken power saw, which was back in use, and a quantity of books which ranged from Restoration poetry to fission, and for which he had constructed a case on the principle of a Ferris wheel, allowing each shelf to be viewed at eye level with the flip of a switch. These, and a number of suggestively

draped pediments and pedestals like veiled statues, reduced the floor space to the size of a large table. I
carefully picked my way to the couch.

"Ah! Something special," Riebenstahl said, and from
under a dictionary stand, from the depths of an imitation jade spittoon, he produced a bottle of 1947 Grands-
Echézeaux, one of those heady wines from the Côte des
Nuits, which seems to produce its own light, and gives
off a scent of truffles. It was the last object I should have
hoped to find in Riebenstahl's spittoon. It was the
nature of the old man that one should never know
whether his successes came by accident or design. There
was certainly no reason that Riebenstahl should have a
taste for wines; but then there was no reason that he
should have a knack for Chinese, which a Taiwanese
student I had sent him "to practice on, like" emphati-
cally assured me that he did. From his smirk of pleasure
I expected him to wag a finger at me any moment, and
in fact he did say, "You won't refuse that, now, eh?" as
if Echézeaux were my special weakness, of which he had
personal knowledge.

To my further astonishment, for we usually drank tea
out of unmatched cast-off cups, Riebenstahl brought out
a pair of wine glasses of modern Swedish crystal, un-
adorned bells as sheer as silk on stems no thicker than a
picture nail. He held first one and then the other to the
window light, sententiously inspecting for dust. In his
cumbersome, knobbled hands, the glasses seemed vul-
nerably fragile, so that I was relieved for them when he
set them down and poured the wine.

It struck me as a pity that Echézeaux should be
uncorked and drunk in the same moment, and out of
stubborn purism I let it sit for a good while on the
coffee table, watching it where it caught and flung the

little light there was, like a candle in a scarlet globe. Riebenstahl sipped and chatted and prescribed for the ills of the world. I listened to little of it, but I remember that at one point, taking a bead on me through the glass, which I feared would splinter or disintegrate, he sharpened his tone to ask, "Well, now. People never know the worth of a thing, by God. What do you say? If you had to make a choice tomorrow, to deprive the world of wine or your wife, what d'ye suppose you'd do?"

Theoretical choices always annoy me. I mocked, "What book would you like on a desert island?" and Riebenstahl chuckled and cackled and wheezed. But whether this meant *touché* or "I knew you wouldn't say," I couldn't say.

He said, "Ah, yes, yes, yes, yes, yes."

By the time Prytania and Kenneth came, we were into our second glass. When Riebenstahl saw Kenneth he said, "Well, well, by God. We're drinking wine."

Kenneth looked undecided whether these were words of welcome or unwelcome, and saying very specifically, "Hello, sir," he drew Prytania into the room.

Prytania's face was so consistent that it was easy to ascribe its different lights to the clothes she wore; in this case an enormous white silk scarf, which must have been bought within the hour, for it was not so much as creased. I noticed for the first time that "olive skin" refers to a quality rather than a color. So sharply framed, her skin had that quality, of luster from beneath, as did the oval of black hair that shone between her brow and scarf. Echézeaux, had it been black, would have been the color of her hair.

Riebenstahl appraised her thoroughly, walking from

one side to the other, emitting little coughs of satisfaction and surprise. "Well, yes, now! Lovely, lovely, ha!" He shook her hand, and having done so, turned it over in his own, fingering the muscles as if he thought of buying them. "Ah, yes!" he said again to Kenneth, "strong in the hands, no drawback, ha!"

If these attentions should have been insulting to Prytania, she did not seem to know it. Submitting, she let her half-smile rest on me until Riebenstahl drew her along and began the guided tour. "I'm an old fellow, not much use for much, but I have got my work."

Kenneth dropped down beside me with a little groan and an even-worse-than-I-expected look. I found a cup and poured him a jealous pittance of the wine, and from there we listened through once more to the list (it sounded rather more polished — is it possible he rehearsed it?) of Riebenstahl's activities.

Prytania, without effusiveness, made a better audience than Riebenstahl was likely to have again. She asked after the source of his machine parts and the prices of his books, and encouraged him to read a selection from his poetry (called *Manufacts* by now), which he did, and which was mysteriously bad, rhyming dextrous and dextrose; tensile, prehensile, and sensible. Then she demanded that he translate this into Chinese, which he also did, or pretended to do (for did he really know the Chinese equivalents of dextrose and prehensile?), folding his hands before his chest like a judge in *The Mikado*.

"Why, he's a sage," Prytania said delightedly to Kenneth.

Riebenstahl was so excited by her compliment that he almost straightened his back, and his chest puffed out to the size of a normal chest. He fairly danced, in sidewise heel-and-toe skips, to the Eiffel Tower — his thirtieth, by now — and signaled at it with a flick of his hands.

"Now, here. I like things to be perfect," and he extolled its flawlessness while Prytania circled around it, viewing it from various angles. The old man danced before her anxiously, elucidating every separate joint with figures of stress, dimension, and proportion. Prytania bit her bottom lip, and Riebenstahl stumbled backward, redoubling the speed of his spiel, peering to her face for affirmation.

"No, look," she said at last, with the solemnity his own anxiety indicated. "It won't do, it's all backward."

"Ha!" Riebenstahl ejaculated, this time in protest instead of triumph. He rummaged for the tower plans and spread them out before her. "No, no, no, *you* look. I copied these exactly, from a book up at the library. Exact, you see? Yes, yes, from the original."

But Prytania shook her head. "I see that," she said, "but the plans are backward then. When you come out of the elevator on the second level, you turn left to the coffee bar, not right. Otherwise you'd be looking at the Place de l'Alma from this corner, see? And you don't, you see it over here."

"She's right!" I said, and Kenneth added, "I say, she is, you know."

Riebenstahl grabbed his plans and held them backward to the window. "By God," he cried, "it was a blue-line print, a fool, a fool! A blue-line print," he shouted to Prytania, shaking the plans at her, "like a negative, I knew it, I even had to transpose the numbers and I didn't think of it! A stupid thing to do!" — and before we saw it raised his noduled fist came down upon the spire and shattered it to bits. The splintered matchsticks scattered on the rug at Prytania's feet, and he caught and kissed her elbow in an ecstasy of penitence.

"I have another, something special, something else to show you," his voice cracked in her ear, and trembling so violently that I caught my breath in alarm, he wheeled around and flung the sheet from one of the pedestals.

Beneath it was a new machine, contrived with wires and pulleys of the skeletal hand we had seen, and the bones of a very much smaller arm. He poked a button, and with a creak and whirr the hand extended, reaching to another switch at the farther side. A chalky finger fell upon that switch, and the motor stopped. The arm collapsed to its former position, but in doing so its elbow brushed the original button and snapped it on again.

Riebenstahl snatched up his glass and emptied it, busying himself with meaningless remarks and motions, fearfully awaiting our reaction. "The lady has no wine," he accused loudly into our fascinated silence, and lurched to the corner cupboard, drawing out another of the sheer crystal glasses. The bottle lip and the rim of the glass rang and clanked in short staccato notes. "Hey, hey, eh?" he barked nervously at Prytania, who turned and said, "But it's magnificent!" reaching to accept the wine.

At her words and the touch of her fingers on his own, Riebenstahl's hand flew open as if the muscles had been jerked from behind. With a little, "Oh!" Prytania caught at the glass, grabbed it mid-air in her fist, and . . . simply crushed it, as one crushes a brittle leaf. Splinters of glass fell among the matchsticks. Slur, snap, collapse, groan, the machine worked out its cycle behind her back.

Kenneth was beside her in one angular bound and gripped her wrist hard in the circle of his thumb and fingers. Riebenstahl stood with his arm still extended in an offering, and Prytania, in surprise but in no visible pain, stared at her clenched fist, where the blood was diffusing into the wine like a deeper red touched into a watercolor wash.

"Open it!" Kenneth commanded harshly, but she did not, so he drew her scarf off forward over her face and, pressing it to the back of her hand, prised at her fingers with his thumb. She opened it then, regarding the thin jagged splinters on her palm with attentive calm.

"Come into the light," Kenneth ordered, and rudely shoved her, still holding the wrist, down on to the couch beside me. "Hold it like that, *hard*," he said to me in so authoritative a voice that had he been offering me a bird's throat instead of Prytania's wrist, I should have obeyed. Firmly steadying her hand against the scarf on her knee, he slipped his thumbnail under one blood-drowned fragment just below her index finger. The piece of glass looked very small, and how Kenneth knew that it was buried glacier-like, I cannot fathom. But he knew; he pulled it sharply at just the angle it extended and at the same time clamped the cut so hard that Prytania's face, and the index finger, paled.

"Have you got some disinfectant? Anything," to Riebenstahl, who stammered, "I . . . I . . . iodine."

"Get it." And Riebenstahl stumbled off to get it.

Kenneth raised Prytania's chin with his free hand, leaving a smudge of blood along her jaw, and turned on her a look in which all the affection was obliterated by the strength.

"I have to see if there's any more glass in it," he said. "It's going to spurt. Don't be alarmed. I have to see."

She nodded, and he let the skin-fold go. A perfect little geyser of Prytania's blood sprang forth, leaped to a height of about an inch and tumbled down the length of its own thrust. The column throbbed slightly, thrust, and thrust, and thrust; and I became aware at once of Prytania's pulse beat and my own. The blood pumped in my fingers just off rhythm with her wrist, mine heavier, racing after hers but never quite catching up. An uncanny sensation that my blood was pumping through her palm to feed that little fountain made my arm and fingers tingle. I was certain that if I let her go the source of the flow would stop, and I even relaxed my grip a little, but the column shot still higher and brought me to my senses.

Kenneth worked in a rhythm of his own, deliberately kneading the gash and the smaller cuts around it. When Riebenstahl came with the iodine and kneeled on the floor before us, Kenneth without looking up said, "Pour it on her hand."

"All of it?" The old man's voice was no higher than a whisper.

"Half of it."

So the darker color still went into the scarlet wash. The scarf was heavy with three colors, wine and blood and iodine, which settled into still different hues where they had begun to dry. The odors would waft and mingle and overcome each other by pungent turns.

Riebenstahl had brought a towel, and clumsily tried to press it to her knees. Kenneth lifted her hand. The old man removed the scarf and settled the towel, then continued compulsively to smooth it over her thighs, rocking forward and backward, whimpering.

Suddenly I wanted passionately to laugh. We were like a set of imperfectly synchronized percussion instruments, my pulse off-beat with Prytania's little miracle of spouting blood, Kenneth's hands deliberately off-beat with both; Riebenstahl's steady rocking and that absurd, indecent stroking of her thighs; and most of all that damn wired arm just turning itself on and turning itself off, oblivious in the background. I was certain, *certain* it was the kind of joke that Prytania would enjoy, but her face when I stole a glance at it was tight and drained, no longer "olive," but emptied of its light. I bit my tongue and strained so hard to choke the laugh that I made my forearm tremble, and Kenneth snapped, "Steady! Change hands if you're tired."

"Sorry. I'm not tired," I said.

Riebenstahl came to himself as well at the dry command. He withdrew his hands and started to rise, then his face blanched with a look like pain, the temple veins protruding to the limit of his skin's endurance. Half-risen, he kneeled again and crawled about until his back was to us, then picked up the nearest object, which was Prytania's dripping scarf; and awkwardly, guiltily shielding his groin with this, he hunched himself to a rocking chair, where he sat miserably huddled with his arms folded over his lap.

My God I hated him! All my choked laughter came up again in the will to call his ugliness to account.

Harshly, I said, "Can't you turn that damn thing off?"

"Huh? Huh?" he started up. "Well, no, well, no," he said forlornly, "no, that's the thing, I can't, you see. That's why I hadn't turned it on before."

"Hold still," said Kenneth imperiously.

I held, for what must have been a whole half hour. It began to seem to me that Kenneth was unnecessarily grim, was uselessly hurting and alarming her. But I didn't say so because I didn't know, and I knew that he would deny it with all the more authority if it were true. Once Prytania raised her face from her palm just long enough to turn a frightened look on him. He didn't acknowledge it, but when she looked down again, his eyes flashed toward me in a brief, deliberate smile.

At last he took her wrist away from me, and clamped the geyser closed. My whole arm ached and prickled to the shoulder, and my hand was weightless, so that I had to hold it down and rub the feeling back.

"It's an artery," Kenneth said. "We might as well go up to the Etrangers. I'll call you when they've stitched her up."

"I can come along," I protested, but his face went hard, and he threw a look in Riebenstahl's direction, boldly assigning me my bounden duty. I didn't want to stay, or to speak to Riebenstahl again, but I gave way instantly, paradoxically proud that I wasn't sure whether I could argue Kenneth down.

They went, Prytania's wrist and gash clamped in his two thumbs, two fingers. I turned on all the lights and found a cloth and dustpan in the kitchen. Brushing glass and matchsticks from the floor, I said, "She made a bigger mess than you," but it didn't seem to cheer him. I tried to turn the arm off, but this time Riebenstahl's plans were flawless: no matter from which direction I braked the elbow, it brushed the button as it settled into place. I didn't think he wanted it ruined, so I gave up. I said dutifully, "She'll be all right."

"Ah, yes, yes-yes," said Riebenstahl.

He didn't seem to want to talk, and I had nothing else to say, so after a few feeble attempts I said good-bye.

It was twilight, nearly dark, and though it had been stuffy inside the air was so sharp here that it was hard to breathe. The cold stung in my nostrils and made a little knot of pain above my eyes. I had not yet cleared the house when a wave of nausea swept over me; it rolled up churning from the sockets of my knees to my throat and down again. I steadied myself with the heel of my hand on the sill and forced myself to take deep draughts of the biting air. Riebenstahl was still sitting in the rocker, motionless. As I watched he drew Prytania's scarf, dried hard now, most of it, and now dark brown, up to his slightly parted mouth. He breathed at it through his mouth and set one rigid crease against his lower lip, making the lip flap as he rubbed it downward again and again. The gesture struck so strong a chord that my nausea quelled in the effort to recall it. It did not take long: it was Jean-Claude Bastien in his shabby mime, with his mouth on the flower that was not a rose. But Jean-Claude, I thought, had been rather more effective, rather more sincere about it.

I have regular habits, but they regularly include going to bed about two o'clock. I have discovered that if I settle myself with a book, and keep at it till my eyelids weigh, I will sleep more easily and wake more refreshed than if I try to get in a full eight hours. I do not know what time it was when Kenneth called, but I know that I had read longer than usual, and that I had not slept immediately, and that I was asleep when he called.

His voice was high and breathy, full of catches and nervous laughs. Prytania would be all right, she was all patched up, but she couldn't type for six weeks or so. She was afraid she'd lose her job: could I fix that? I said I could. I asked if there would be any permanent damage, and Kenneth said, well, no, well, no, well, actually he wasn't sure. A few scars, of course; she might not get all the feeling back in her finger, but that was all right. It didn't mean she couldn't use it, that is, she could type all right, just she had to let it heal for six weeks or so.

"I wasn't worried about her efficiency, Kenneth."

"Oh, no, good God, I'm sorry. I didn't mean that."

"I'm glad it's all right. You get some sleep."

"Well, yes." He cleared his throat. I waited for him to say good-bye, but he hung on, clearing his throat for so long that I finally asked, "Is there something else?"

"I just wanted to thank you, sir. It's uncanny to me how you understand these things."

I sat down on the arm of a chair and set my feet in a cushion. "What things?"

"Well . . ." he laughed. "Here's the fact, Prytania's going to marry me."

I said something that seemed appropriate and waited a little until I thought of asking, "When?"

"As soon as her hand is healed. I guess in a couple of months."

"Did she say that?"

"You know Prytania." Kenneth audibly smiled. "She doesn't come right out and say a thing."

It struck me that that was exactly what Prytania did, but I didn't say so. I congratulated him again and said good-bye, but he held me on for a while with I-can't-thank-you-enoughs, as if he wanted to make sure that I took the credit for the match.

"I want to tell you something really weird. Do you mind? Am I keeping you up?"

The answer to this was so clearly yes that I said automatically, "Of course not."

"Well, this afternoon when I was working on Prytania's hand . . . you know, early on I'd got the glass out. I just kept working at it I-don't-know-why. I was thinking about what you said to me, you know, about showing her what I can do. And I thought, dear God, I'm pretty good at this. Here's the fact, I knew right then she was going to marry me, I *knew* it. Do you know I didn't feel the least bit nervous when I asked her? Do you believe in that sort of thing?"

"What sort of thing?"

"Well, intuition. Things coming right all of a sudden. Like working on a formula that doesn't come out right, until it does, like that! and you can't figure out how you couldn't figure it out before."

"Yes, I believe in that sort of thing."

"Well, you turned the trick. I wanted to thank you."

"You've done that, Kenneth. I'm very happy for you. Go and get some sleep."

Really, it was amazing how tender my feet were. I suppose I don't go barefooted very often. The cushion was a velvet one with floss daisies worked on it, that Laura's mother made for us years ago. I could feel each flower separately in my arches, which have gone a little flat recently. I picked up a splinter from the hall parquet and had to take it out in the dark, sitting on the edge of the bed.

I could understand it; I could even picture it. Somewhere among those straggly trees that line the walk from the Etrangers, Prytania shaky and a little cold, Kenneth protective, but unawed, perhaps even bold enough *not* to offer her his coat. I could imagine Prytania turning up that timid face again, made more submissive still by gratitude.

What I couldn't do was decide how I felt about it. In Kenneth's eyes I clearly was committed to approve, which seemed unfair; he had asked me what to do, not whether I wished him well. She surely didn't love him, but then she rated him too low. He'd always be good in a crisis; perhaps she'd get in the habit of inventing them. A happy marriage, after all, is only the preservation of a certain point of view, and if I had helped, by accident . . .

I did something: stretched, or rubbed my foot or scratched my jaw; and a gratifying feeling of myself, that I displaced a certain volume of air, flooded me like drowsiness. I lay back feeling the weight of my body in all its separate parts.

Laura turned, mumbling, "What was it at this hour?"

"Kenneth. He called to say he's marrying Prytania. She cut her hand or something, and he got the courage to ask her."

"Poor Kenneth," was all that Laura said, and fell asleep again.

PART THREE

A King of Kings

Astonishing the way everything is like love. I myself
am a man of limited experience — much more limited
than my experience of letters — and yet I have never run
across a metaphor so unlikely that I could not in all
sincerity nod my head, saying, "Yes, yes. That too is
true." Statesmanship, cyclists, the cycle of the stars, tree
rings, correspondence, candy wrappers: cite me an entity
and I shall cite you a simile. They have not yet begun to
be all thought up and put down. And this further, from
my limited experience: that nothing is so like loving as
not quite loving.

Prytania returned after six weeks to UNICEF — with a
scar that her friends could not find without assistance,
and only a pinpoint of deadened nerve at the knuckle
— thanked me ineffusively for having kept her job, and
took it up again. Much was made of her engagement,
and the goodwill and the teasing she endured with the
same fixed smile, wider than her features were meant to
bear. On the least pretext she delivered herself of
speeches extolling Kenneth's virtues, and on any topic
she could cite some relevant view he held, which was

likely to be more thoughtful and less thought-provoking than her own. She excused her lack of a ring with intense assurances that they had not yet found one good enough, and she spoke incessantly of china patterns and linen brands, which, however, she made no move to buy. The wedding date receded in a perpetual "few months off."

She was more voluble with me than she had ever been; would choose my table in the cafeteria expressly to chatter of her plans for life; of English ghettos in Calcutta and gardening in Middlesex. It was as if, like Kenneth, she had some gratitude to spend, and found me the most likely creditor. Yet this new garrulity had an unwelcome air of prevarication. She would pass on, with unfeigned passion, Kenneth's lecture on skeletal composition or the structure of a cell. But when she concluded, "Kenneth is wonderful, isn't he?" I always found the transition a bit abrupt. I should have thought the point was that skeletons were wonderful, or cells were. I would reply, "He is," in a weighty way, to suggest that I didn't accept the question as rhetorical; Prytania would reward me with the extravagant smile that didn't suit her.

Meanwhile she and Kenneth settled into a public image of comfortable affection. Madame said of Kenneth that he had "the kind of youth that comes to terms without destroying itself," and of Prytania, "She brought me jonquils from the Bois!" — and could not be led into delivering an opinion of their betrothal.

Laura and I spent a week with the Bastiens at Jean-Claude's family home in L'Isle Automne, and another at Cannes, where we lay in the sand and discussed with sunburned strangers how beautiful this beach had been before *they* had spoiled it.

Yves Adam went abroad for a time, returned, and two weeks later opened his new season to general acclaim; the reviewers averring that Yves Adam was living proof of the profundity of whimsy, and that Jean-Claude Bastien had brought more skill to bear on his portrayal of a man with his right foot in his left shoe than was to be believed possible by those who had the misfortune to miss it. Only a few Left Bank journals of little influence observed that the mime was an art without a future, which Yves dismissed with so little din that it could be seen to distress him greatly.

When the parks flowered I went again to Riebenstahl, telling myself that he was after all an object of pity rather than contempt, and that I could easily steer the conversation from Prytania, of whom he was bound to want news; only to find that he avoided the mention of her even more studiously than I. To such an extent that when, toward fall, he mumbled something about, "P'tania and her young man," he hastily amended, "No, no, it was someone else," although it was hardly credible that, in his limited acquaintance, he should have confused Kenneth and Prytania with any other couple.

So that by September I should have said that the summer "passed without incident," although in fact I knew of and had even witnessed several incidents, which I would only in retrospect see to have been strange and improbable; as a boy from whom some extraordinary secret has been kept will only afterwards discover that people had not been behaving rationally, that the hall cupboard had never been locked before, that he had never been allowed to go to the park on Tuesday afternoons. And as such a boy will incessantly rehearse, not so much for his own pleasure as for that of his listeners, the articles of his hindsight — "That's why you sent me to the park!" — so later I would repeat in astonishment, not because I was still astonished, but because by doing so I was stirring a breathless delight, "Think of it! I never gave a thought to what old Riebenstahl could mean!"

Elena Bastien had been the most beautiful girl in the richest tier of a feudal fishing village near Alicante. Those riches would have been poverty in Paris, and that beauty might have been unremarkable had she not so well learned to carry herself with the poise that only being the most beautiful engenders. In Madrid she had been taken for a beauty because she behaved like one. Having taken Madrid, she took Paris, because neither silence nor trivia intimidated her, nor did she ever find herself in fear of being clumsy or inane. No conversation lagged when she sat by: she filled it from the top of her head, supremely, and so rightly, confident that a rehearsal of her day's routine would interest her audience. When she dined with us, Laura, like most women, listened to her. I, like most men, watched her.

She dined with us fairly frequently, whenever she could know in advance that Jean-Claude's rehearsal would run into his performance. She would call Laura and say, "Jean-Claude won't be home Thursday. "I'll come to you, unless you're having squid." Laura, who had never invited herself to dinner, and only accepted an invitation after an imaginative reckoning of the probable inconveniences entailed, was disarmed beyond expression.

"Maybe Jean-Claude will be late to pick her up," she would say hopefully. And Jean-Claude, who spent his entire stock of punctuality on the Poche, often was.

Certain seafoods with which she had been too intimate in her early life were the only lapse in Elena's palate. Otherwise she ate superbly, like someone with a gift for it, who has known hunger as well. One evening in June we served *poulet en papillote,* and Elena, behaving her appreciation of it, spent the evening on the couch, arms flung back, talking slowly and inconsequentially in a sated comfort wonderful to see.

Jean-Claude came shortly before eleven, to Laura's poorly concealed regret. "You won't take her away yet; she hasn't even properly digested. A liqueur?"

Jean-Claude refused and accepted in succession, kissed his wife and said they must get home, unbuttoned his jacket and eased himself down beside her. His legs were long, even for his body, and he seemed to sit more deeply than anyone else in a given cushion.

"How did it go?" Elena asked.

"Tonight? Not brilliant. I wore myself out this afternoon. I'm getting closer to it, though." Jumpy, for Jean-Claude, but in high spirits, he ran his hands down to his ankles and stared at the space between them.

"The trouble is," he said, "that we're stuck with the body. I hadn't looked that far back for it before."

"Yves would love *that,*" Laura observed. "Cognac, or a sweet one?"

"So I just have to make the body something else. For instance, supposing I deny its point of balance?"

Bent over, he raised his head expectantly to us. Laura was crossing to the tray of liqueurs. Elena yawned luxuriously. I hadn't understood him. With an impatient gesture, Jean-Claude rolled forward on to his head and one forearm, hung his legs asymetrically in the air, and wound his free arm in a crooked oval.

"Now," he demanded, "if I were to stay like this for

thirty-six hours, do you think you might begin to think of me as something else than a person wrong end up?"

As he spoke his tie, a bright, deep red affair in silk shantung, slunk down his shirt front and draped itself languidly over his face. Elena sat up for the first time since dessert.

"Jean-Claude," she said, "your taste is beyond salvation."

Unable, anyway, to get the tie out of his eyes without altering the pattern of his arm, Jean-Claude put his legs down and sat up on the floor.

"It's the principle of motion sculpture," he said listlessly. "I think it is, I'll have to ask a motion sculptor. You're freed to see the pattern of a thing precisely because it's doing something that it isn't meant to do."

"Did you *buy* that?" Elena insisted.

Jean-Claude tucked the tie possessively back into his jacket and gave his wife a look mock-wounded and mock-resentful. "I did," he said, "but it was a sentimental purchase."

Elena pressed her toes against the rung of the coffee table, making her foot arch hard.

"All right," she said, "you may wear it as much as you like at home, but I won't be seen in company with it." She smiled oddly. Jean-Claude took her foot and traced a ring around her ankle with his finger.

I must have remarked this, because I now remember it. But I was looking at Jean-Claude's tie and thinking of that red, remembering the radishes again from so long ago that it seemed someone else's memory. The rectangular garden plot in the Evanston grammar school, the broad for-your-own-good face of the teacher — whatever was her name? — and the furtive bite of radish freshly pulled: sweet, warm, a little gritty with clean earth, and then the unexpected sting.

It was complicated: the odd secondhand guilt of that stolen radish in my memory, and then the fact that I had got there only indirectly by way of Jean-Claude's tie, and Jean-Claude and Elena sharing a look that was palpably pre-coital enough to make me feel I was eavesdropping; so that when, minutes later, Elena began to talk of Prytania's dress, it seemed not only a logical subject, but positively a discreet one.

"Except for Jean-Claude I can't recall so much wanting to take anyone in hand. I'd like to put her in a Givenchy. I bought one yesterday for Mme Denille, Jean-Claude — all bunchy *bouclé* pleats on a high-rise waist. Mme Denille will look a boxcar in it."

"Would you like to have it?"

"Oh, you do make me impatient. I'd look like a boxcar too. Don't you see, there's a certain kind of dress that a woman with a bosom can't wear . . ."

Laura, at last, had engaged Jean-Claude's attention to the liqueurs, which she hawked in whispers, all but reading the labels off to him. Jean-Claude affected indecision, and I listened to Elena's lecture on the certain kind of dress. Somewhere in the last few sentences she had shifted mood, up out of sleepiness into vivacity. She was developing the philosophy of something called The Empire Line, which was also the name of a shipping firm we dealt with at UNICEF, and conjured up a few arresting images for me, of one-stack steamers with over-abundant bosoms.

"Her shoulder bones are good, you see, which is rare on that kind of frame. Jean-Claude, are you listening to me?"

"No, my love," he said, and for no very apparent

reason kissed her soundly. He had settled at last on Cherry Heering, and now sat down beside Elena skeptically comparing its color with his tie.

"Jean-Claude," Elena concluded suddenly, "you ought to ask her to dinner." This time I did remark, even at the moment, that she seemed absurdly pleased with her suggestion; but I had no reason for noticing that it was ambiguous, that having avoided the phrase "over to dinner," she might, if one chose, have meant "out."

Jean-Claude replied with a "Damn, left my cigarettes at the Poche. All right," so indifferent, so clearly indicative of his having no intention of it, that I seriously doubt he could have mimed it better.

The Poche Adam was a squat white box almost concealed in a cul-de-sac off Raspail. It had been designed, with considerable thought, and at no insignificant expense, to be entirely devoid of ornament. There were no moldings, cornices, sills or knobs. The lobby walls, and the endless tiers of stage drape, were of a flat black cloth that bore more resemblance to burlap than to the velvets of the Right Bank theaters, so that no one ever guessed it was hand-woven, hand-dyed raw silk. The shallow-cushioned seats, likewise, looked so severe, without in the least looking modern, that people rarely remarked their comfort, nor would they have believed it had they been told that the frames were specially designed in Denmark and were made of solid teak. "Our only ornament is *Art,*" Yves said, of course, which made very good newspaper copy and, since he happened to believe it, did not offend even those who knew he had put the company in bottomless debt to avoid any curve or color or superfluous frill.

Tuesdays at the Poche, every initiate to this monastic ruse received in his program an insert inviting suggestions for improvisation. This was another example of Yves' *Art;* for while the improvisations provided a unique study for devotees of the mime, they also generated the excitement of a lottery. Housewives, matinée lovers, critics who had space to fill in the lean weekdays — all flocked around the box, and unlike any other repertory group in all of Paris, the Poche could count on a full house on the worst night of the six.

Laura and I occasionally made a part of it, and on a Tuesday in late July we decided, in spite of an angry, unexpected rain, to take in the last improvisations of the season. We had seen the bulk of the program several times, so we came in only in the second intermission and pushed through the steaming lobby to find our seats. The auditorium was over half full of those who, barred by the weather from the cul-de-sac outdoors, had chosen to keep their seats or mull in the aisle exchanging ideas for the mime. A smaller group stood before the stage-right apron, gravely depositing their papers in Yves Adam's suggestion box: a dilapidated and odiferous garbage can.

We sat, and I scanned the napes in front of me to see how many Tuesday habitués I could recognize. Laura took the suggestion card from her program and worried the edges of it with her pencil.

"Stanford, help me think. What shall I put?"

I had an improbable notion that the black chignon on the aisle six rows ahead belonged to Prytania. Prytania didn't wear chignons, but this one was unskillful enough, pleasantly awry enough, to have been her attempt. The improbable thing was that she would have been with the bulbous towhead, certainly not Kenneth, on her left, or that if she had come alone (also unlikely, I should have thought), she would have taken an orchestra seat one range more expensive than our own.

"Stanford, I've an idea. What did Jean-Claude call the sketch he did at our party? You remember, the one . . ."

"The American."

"Yes, that's it!" She wrote it, exuding by some non-sensual means I have never been able to understand, the self-importance of her excitement; and hurried down to join other latecomers at the garbage can.

I counted couples from the left of the row up ahead, but the seating was ambiguous. There were three men together at one point, and at another a woman and a girl. Probably it was someone with the towhead after all. If not I could find it out after the performance.

Laura was back, and the house was quickly filling. It was hot, and whatever stray rain had found its way inside diffused with body heat. My own raincoat was damp and heavy on my knees.

Dramatic dimming was a speciality of the Poche. The lights played as they died, teasing over heads and curtains, one bright spot chasing through them until it directed our attention to the smelly pail containing our ideas. Now at the other side of the apron the darkness thinned a little, and a mime set up the easel of a sidewalk artist, doodling at his poster as the stage faded back up to watery dawn.

Into this Jean-Claude the scavenger shuffled from the back. I do not know — I never knew, I never noticed — whether or not the spotlight picked him out. He didn't need it. He had the sort of face that, had it been a voice, one would have said it carried. Without insisting on itself — expressing nothing now, in fact, but poverty and

dullness — it drew the eye as if our whole damp darkness
had been arranged to set it off.

With the most stupid conceivable slowness Jean-
Claude approached the garbage can, languidly eyed the
sidewalk artist, and thrust his arm deep under the lid.
The piece of paper he withdrew was rolling and crackling in his hand: we strained to recognize it, and fell
into startled laughter when it turned out to be an insect,
which hopped away into the wings as he shied from it.

One by one Jean-Claude drew out suggestions for his
mime, and as he found them uninspired, he turned
them into toys to charm us with. One scrap became a
handkerchief he honked noiselessly into and stuffed
deep in his pocket. The next he licked and rolled into
the treasure of a butt. For an uncertain instant as he
opened up the next, I thought I saw him lose composure, but then his start expanded into moronic astonishment, so that it was more likely to have been
planned. I suggested, "The American?" to Laura, to see
if she had noticed it too, but she was staring ahead with
a concentration almost sour.

Jean-Claude flipped the paper upside down, peering
incredulously until we recognized it as a piece of abstract art. He studied it over his shoulder and between
his legs. The audience began to titter.

Holding the page obsequiously before him, Jean-
Claude approached the artist with a blink and bow. The
painter in his turn stood on his stool, sighted over his
thumb, squinted, scratched himself, gave up, and
shrugging heavily tore the page in tiny pieces. Jean-
Claude wandered back into the wings; the sidewalk
artist wrote, "Les Parapluies" on his poster card.

A murmur, liquid and inexplicable, rose at this, and
poured into a joyful sigh, as if "Les Parapluies" fulfilled

one excruciating expectation and raised another. This always happened, no matter what the choice.

"Ah, too bad," I said to Laura.

Silence instantly fell again when Jean-Claude reappeared, shivering beneath an imaginary umbrella that he forced before him against the wind. He entered a heroic competition with the storm, to decide whether his umbrella was to be convex or concave. He was just on the point of proving champion when he stumbled — over ankles that turned out to be ankles of a most absorbing aspect.

Jean-Claude's improvisation concerned an accidental meeting in the rain between two people whose umbrellas betrayed their mutual attraction, tapping on one another, bouncing from contact, catching to prevent their parting yet holding them apart. It suffered, as *L'Express* observed next day, from the fact that Jean-Claude must mime the existence, not only of the girl, but of her umbrella and his own as well. It was not his best, and I had seen enough of Jean-Claude's work to know it. Yet I played the sycophant as eagerly as those around me. His tautness held us and commanded us. An altering of his balance and we gasped like fools, believing he would fall. A muscle of his mouth announced that he was going to be funny, and before the joke was out we lay in slack collective laughter. We obeyed like an elephant stupid but highly trained, whom Jean-Claude bade rear up, back off, lie down. With a stunning suddenness I saw how a man like Jean-Claude might want to be an actor, who had no personal vanity and was irritated by specific praise. What would be the value of the housecat's admiration for having mastered the behemoth?

Finally, Jean-Claude and his invisible partner yielded

to their umbrellas, and they left the stage together, spokes and handles inextricably intertwined. Applause stampeded up behind him.

As the lights went up again, Laura surprised me with a curt, "Let's go."

"Go? You don't want to see Yves?"

She charged up the aisle and I followed, puzzled by her disgruntledness. We were halfway down the cul-de-sac before I remembered that I hadn't looked again at the girl with the inexpert chignon.

"What's the matter, Laura?"

"Well, I'm just a little surprised at Yves. That thing was rigged! Didn't you see the paper he picked to do?"

"Yes; not particularly. Was it marked?"

"Marked! It wasn't even the same color. It was green."

I wasn't sure I liked missing half of what I'd come to see for the sake of Laura's easily outraged honor. But I was preoccupied with the new light in which I had just seen Jean-Claude. I wanted to think about it. And then, the rain had temporarily abated, so we got a cab more easily than we would have if we'd stayed the performance out.

I meant, the next day, to ask Prytania whether I hadn't seen her at the Poche, but she was called to the telephone just as our morning's dictation started, and Miss Recheuse took her place. Later in the day it slipped my mind.

Then it happened that I saw her again in the late afternoon. I had stopped in to call on Riebenstahl, on purpose, it almost seemed, to be irritated by him. He was sorting a box of cycle parts with mystic fussiness, stopping only to propound a few universal principles

for me. The little house was steaming in the brilliance
after last night's storm, and at the end of a half hour I
found my own warmth, and the sight of Riebenstahl's
sweat spreading in deep patches under his arms, beyond
endurance. I said aloud that I had to go, wondered once
more why I had come, and escaped into the more open
heat of the Parc Fasseville.

Paris was rich as a hothouse that whole July. The
dahlias were big as chrysanthemums, and in the park
they thrust their faces as high as the children's hands, so
demanding attention with their insolent golds and reds
that the children broke them off and spread them ankle-
deep in the paths; but more shot up and burst their
borders and crushed against the grass.

At the center of the park, Prytania was sitting, bare-
armed and bronze, at the feet of a bare bronze Dio-
nysius. Although the sun was high and hot, she sat in
one of the few spots of sharp light, for the chestnut
branches lunged toward every corner of the square and
shaded every dusty clearing. She played her fingertips
over great bronze fruits that tumbled from a cornucopia
and trembled in the sun as if they, too, had more force
and weight this season than they could contain. She was
waiting for someone, her mouth half-open in expectation. She divided her attention among the paths, fixing
briefly on every face that passed her, her hurt hand
lightly caressing the curves of fruit.

I waited my turn to reach her line of vision, ready
with that smile of mild triumph that, God knows why,
we always turn on people who see us later than we see
them. Finally her glance fell on me, her eyes as milky
with sunlight as the eyes of the blind. They rested for an
instant on my foolish smile and without the least sign of
recognition passed beyond.

I didn't call to her as I might have, and barely broke
my stride to watch her stare slide over two or three
others wandering up the path. I realized that she was
fitting the image of a face on all the faces that did not
match it, discarding them like imperfect negatives. It
was not flattering to me, but there was some recompense
in it.

"Well, Kenneth," I said, "perhaps it happens. Perhaps we're going to pull it off after all."

Jean-Claude insists that I met him moments later
turning off Wagram, and that I neither saw him nor
heard his greeting. But I don't know, of course, whether
this is true, or whether he says it to tease me, to defend
Prytania.

All late summer and early fall Prytania drew away from
me in a manner that wounded my affection and my
pride. She ceased to look for me in the cafeteria, and
apparently more often than not she lunched away. Her
preoccupation in the office was so invulnerable, her
conversation so banal, that two or three times I could
have slapped her gladly, and I was in perpetual danger,
which luckily for once I recognized, of divulging my
part in her projected marriage. I had solemnly adjured
Kenneth to forget it, but in the end I grew to consider it
small thanks that the two of them should drop me so
completely. Mme de Verbois had once said, in reference
to my daughter and her husband, "The reason that
people cry at weddings is that weddings are the public
affirmation of a private shutting out." Yves had once
snarled, as if I had denied it, that, "Art is a holy
holocaust of rejections." Astonishing, I thought, the way
everything is like love.

One evening in October, a year since Harold had

predicted the arrival of Prytania, Laura appeared in my study with the evening paper in her hands.

"Stanford! You didn't tell me your friend is exhibiting at the Poche Adam."

"My who? Is what?"

"Your Riebenstahl is opening a show, and Jean-Claude's choreographed a mime for it."

"A show of what?" I asked incredulously.

Laura spread the page out on my lap. Three columns wide and a full ten inches high, eyeless from the way the flashbulb had caught his glasses, Riebenstahl was bending over one of his machines. His mouth was open in triumphant ejaculation — one could clearly see that he was saying "ha!" — and below him in piquant italics a caption demanded, *"Ephraim Riebenstahl — the Grandma Moses of Motion Sculpture?"*

"Why didn't you ever mention it to me? How in the world did he get to know Jean-Claude?"

"I haven't the faintest idea," I said, although a faint idea threatened even then. Laura began an animated summary of the facts, but I said so sharply, "Let me read it," that she left in the rigid haste of martyrdom.

The article was written in an exuberant condescension, so self-congratulatory that one might have supposed the discovery deserved less credit than the discoverer. The critic found the grandfather of eight "as *sui-generis* as his machines." He was charmed that Riebenstahl had never heard of Jean Tinguely, in ecstasy that he had never heard of motion sculpture, *bouleversé* that his knowledge of art was naïve as "a precocious chimpanzee's." What he brought to his work (the word *oeuvre* appeared in every sentence) was a knowledge of his tools acquired "in the murky workshop of real life" and a passion never yet encountered in those who had set about to dehumanize the arts. The exhibit in the lobby of the Poche would open tomorrow night, when it would be accompanied by a new production, *Mimes Mécaniques*, inspired by and dedicated to the new sculptor, conceived and choreographed by Jean-Claude Bastien.

I let my cigar ash burn down to my fingers, and then with the skill of long practice I carried it, four inches high, unbreaking, to the ashtray at my desk. I got my coat and left the house without saying where I was going. I caught a taxi on the boulevard de Port Royal and directed the driver to Parc Fasseville. At the rotunda I paid him off and walked, crushing chestnut leaves in the deserted paths, to the little house.

The house was dark and locked; but to make sure I called at the porch, knocked on the doors, and finally, feeling irritated and ridiculous, climbed on a garbage can to rap at the second-floor bedroom window. It was nearly eight o'clock.

I retraced my steps to the gate. The same cab still sat there in the lamplight, and its driver cocked an eye at me, inquisitive and hopeful.

I hesitated. I had been to see Riebenstahl only the day before. He had struck me as unwell, as nervous, even for a man whose nerves were normally taut as catgut. He had skittered about in meaningless preparations for my comfort and made observations on the universe even more than ordinarily disconnected. I had remarked the absence of several of his sheet-draped pedestals, and he had barked, "Housecleaning, yes! You've got to face it sometimes." I knew of only three people besides myself who had met both Jean-Claude Bastien and Riebenstahl, and although there was no proof that Madame or Kenneth had not found occasion to introduce them, I could see no feasible reason, were that the case, that he should have concealed it.

"We could count it as one ride; I know how to set the meter at zero," the cabbie confided.

I climbed in, and he snapped his cigarette in the gutter.

"I want to be let out at the Poche Adam on Raspail near Vaugirard."

The more I thought about it the more preposterous the whole thing became: that a half-mad gaffer who made his living on matchstick models and grew tomatoes illegally in a public park should be hailed as an artistic hero; and that even Riebenstahl should be dense enough to suppose he could keep secret from me an acquaintanceship which, even if he himself proved hardly worth the mention, was certain to be reported in every newspaper in the town.

The driver stopped at the inconspicuous slash between buildings that led to the little theater, and taking him at his literal word, I paid the meter reading without a second tip.

"*Merci!*" he shouted venomously after me.

In the cul-de-sac a poster the colors of mourning warned: NO PERFORMANCE TONIGHT. I tried the doors, and the third one yielded.

Inside, the lobby of the Poche had undergone a metamorphosis mobile, audible, shocking, and complete. A labyrinth of wire and twisted metal wound around the flat black walls, which made so sharp a background that they might have been intended all along as the Devil's gallery. Freed of their Victorian clutter, the machines were so sinister and so sinewy that even I, in spite of my annoyance — indeed, it made me angrier than ever — stood a moment as if I had lost my way. The skeleton arm was there, mechanically killing itself and bringing itself to life; though the only other "sculpture" I had seen, the original, rather domestic one, was not. There were other bones — the critic had been struck by a preponderence of bone — that snarled themselves in mazes of machine: a jaw that chewed motorcycle spokes into furious revolution, a pelvis rocking the pendulum of a rusted, gutted clock. In one corner a tangle of chalky fingers perpetually regrouped themselves into hands, which joined each other in mocking clasps of greeting until the joints and the metal joinings snapped, and the finger pieces fell away to become the parts of other hands. The central wall just opposite the doors was taken up by a sooty hulk as tall as I. A six-inch jet of butane flame at its base burned up toward a cradle of molten lead, and from this an ivory Chinese back-scratcher dipped up dripping handfuls. These disappeared in the bowels of a refrigerator motor, from whence they were spewed as little gears with teeth the shape of human teeth, which in turn attached themselves to the grinding frame about the whole. The frame whirled up in jerking arcs toward the summit of the thing, and each wheel as it reached the top plunged off the track, plopping into the bowl of lead to be melted down again.

I started as I sensed some movement incongruously fluid, and looked up to see Yves Adam coming toward me from the auditorium arch. He grasped my hand in both his tiny ones, evidently too excited to be surprised that I was there.

"I think he's done it, I think he may have done it, my blessed boy!"

He drew me toward the inside door, my arm clasped

in his wrists, speaking under the clamor in an urgent whisper.

"It's about to start. Come on! I haven't dared to say it to him, I've been exploding with the news. Jesus bless Apollo you showed up!"

"Apollo didn't send me," I said. "Have you seen the evening paper?"

"Of course, yes! Stupid critic, they must get born in taffy factories."

"Then you think Riebenstahl's an imposter too?"

Yves stopped on the threshold.

"Imposter!"

"Well, not that, perhaps. A senile, morbid fool."

"Carrion crow! Would I give my lobby to an imposter or a fool?" He bit his lip as deep as his beard and tapped on my shoulders as if he would bring me down to size.

"Oh, look, we aren't tuned up to these things; I grant you it's gory weird. But you've got to stretch your mind for it like I do. It isn't part of our coronary generation."

"Riebenstahl is fifty-seven!" I gasped.

"Yes, yes, it's nothing. Wait till you see Jean-Claude. I think he's done it."

He pulled me on, then stopped again as the lights began to dim. "Look, Powers, I was wrong. I thought I'd goad him into it. But the fact is — not that I care! — it isn't me that did it. It's the girl."

The lights went out.

"The girl, of course," I said.

"Shhh! Wait, it's starting. Wait till you see what he's done to me! Be quiet now."

He shoved me into an aisle seat and dropped himself several rows ahead.

The curtain opened and a spotlight cautiously began to fade up on a figure in the center.

"Too fast!" shrieked Yves. "On a count of twelve!" and the light, which had been barely perceptible to me, went out and began to dim still more slowly up again.

Jean-Claude's new show began with a short vignette, which occupied *in toto* less than a minute, of which time nearly half was taken up by the crescendo of the light. But before it was over I understood what he had been trying to explain to us long ago, and ill-disposed as I was to be impressed, I had no doubt that in his own terms he had succeeded.

He sat — or, it seems more accurate to say, he had been set — on a steel gray pedestal more than four feet high. Except for his bare right arm and the narrowed oval of his face, Jean-Claude was gray himself, from his crossed knees to the tips of his left fingers, clothed in some substance defining and metallic. The covered arm was extended, rigid, with the thumb pointing stiffly up, and the bare one dangled elbow-out, not moving so much that one could say it moved, but just perceptibly animate, and ill at ease. Only that arm and a stiff goatee bespoke something human — and the beard left doubt; it jutted forward like a cone of iron shavings.

When the light had reached its zenith the living arm began to move. Gauche and painful, the elbow never quite where it belonged, it strained across the metal chest and reached for the other hand. With grinding effort it attained it, flexed, and depressed the thumb. Then the whole machine collapsed and shivered, the bare arm rocking back to its place, but striking sharply when it had almost settled, the metal beard. It froze with shock, and by now the robot was so inhuman that this hint of realization seemed more grotesque than its insensible progression. The elbow shivered, the arm reached up and began all over again.

Of course it was Riebenstahl's machine, but it was also Yves Adam — the famous Zitzio, with the elbow and beard and the perpetual thwarted scheme. I saw at once what Jean-Claude had meant, what Yves had hypocritically denied. The mime evoked not Zitzio but the idea of Zitzio. It was not, like Yves in his rôle, affecting, although it was a little awe-inspiring: it was satisfying, like just deserts, or a theory's proving true.

The lights blacked out, and Yves screamed some instruction at the booth. I peered about me in the dark and tried to tell who, and how many, might be there. I could make out little groups of shapes and some scattered single ones, not more than twenty people in all, and none of them Riebenstahl for certain.

I groped for my hat in the seat beside me, almost on the point of leaving, but the curtain flung aside and I still sat, thinking that I had nowhere to go but home.

I saw the whole rehearsal. I had seen it in the lobby. Each of the fantastic, phantasmagoric machines was there; and each, by being made of bodies, was more terrible than before. A rasping echo from the outer room ran under the whole performance, something gnawing at the mind. A human wheel of spoke-like limbs whirled at the prodding of a corpse-sized bone whose knees and feet were teeth. A golden-headed woman swung upside down from a clockwork mat of men, and others urged her back and forth with obscenely insensate hips. A pyramid of steely figures, so balanced that the arms were legs and the legs were iron rods, ground forth a string of human gears, which joined the whole, and plunged by turns to a hot metallic death.

The curtain fell on "A Show of Hands," in which whole bodies joined in clasps and slowly broke each other's bones. The little audience clapped and cheered, but its scant acclamation fell as thin in that afflicted silence as spilt pins.

"The girl, of course," I mumbled.

I waited for light enough to leave, but it didn't come, and stagehands began racing back and forth in the aisles to Yves.

"*No, no!*" he shouted petulantly. "We'll have to run the cues again," his voice surcharged with triumph he dared not show.

I stepped uncertainly into the aisle and, peering for a footing, saw a woman coming toward me. She was too tall to be Prytania, but the visibility was so bad that she was upon me before I recognized Elena Bastien.

"You're here!" I involuntarily exclaimed.

"I always come to final dress. So I can badger him next day and keep him from getting overconfident." She led the way toward the feeble exit lamp. "What do you think?"

"I think Yves is right. I think he's done it."

"Yes, I think so too. Funny how well we thought he talked, and how little he explained."

"Are you very sorry?"

"Sorry! Why?"

"You told me once you hoped he wouldn't — that he needed an illusion, don't you remember?"

"Oh, that." She shrugged it off. "That was frivolous of me. I thought it *was* an illusion all along. Maybe there's nothing Jean-Claude can't have if he wants it after all. No, I'm delighted. More than that. It's a great thing for him to have accomplished something of his — own." I thought I detected a hesitation before the final word. "Would you like to take me out for a drink?" she asked.

"You aren't going backstage then."

"Good heavens, no. They haven't time for us. They'll be screaming at each other till half-past two about what went wrong."

"Did anything go wrong?"

"I didn't see it, but I won't say so tomorrow. Well?" she insisted. "Will you come?"

It seemed urgent, but I couldn't quite comply. "Give me a raincheck, Elena? I'd like to talk to Riebenstahl."

"All right. If you change your mind I'll be at the Chèvre Aveugle for half an hour. Good night."

Others were coming past me to go out, substantial business-looking men and heavy-lidded women in furs, arguing in low excited tones like members of the trade. I turned and felt my way back down the aisle toward the backstage door.

"Who put that amber gel in?" Yves was shrieking toward the stage, where the lights, of which I had seldom been aware, were going through their parts without the mimes.

The dressing-room hall was white enamel and conveyed — I hadn't the least doubt it was Yves' intention — a hospital corridor. Even the shouting behind closed doors and a faint odor of sweat could not destroy the sharp illusion.

Blinded after the two-hour darkness, I groped along the walls, making out Adam's modest name-card on the first door I came to, and going on. I reached the second, which was ajar, and was about to knock when a shock of color stopped me. The crack gave on to a mirror, which threw back a slender vertical column of radish red. As I got my bearings a voice detached itself from the rumble of the halls.

". . . as if I don't want it as badly as you do, Prytania. My God, what must you think of me if you can think that of me?"

"I didn't mean it that way. Oh, Jean-Claude, forgive me, please."

I set my back against the wall where the mirror was out of sight. His voice rose slightly, though it whispered, with a hint of rectitude.

"No doubt it seems absurd to you that two people on two salaries have as little to spare as we do. I suppose it is shocking. I suppose it's bourgeois of Elena to want to save for a house."

"Jean-Claude, it's unfair to say that to me. I know she's more generous in this than either of us."

"But for God's sake, then, what can I do? Every franc I spend on you I take from her."

"I know, I know. I'm sorry. I didn't mean to bring it up *tonight*. I don't complain, you know that, Jean-Claude. It's only that we have nowhere to be alone."

"I've told you I'll come to your place any time you'll let me come."

"I *can't*, Jean-Claude. She's Kenneth's aunt!"

"Whenever she isn't home."

"She's always home. Oh, it isn't that. I couldn't do it to her. It wouldn't matter if she knew or not, not in her house."

"Then don't you think I feel the same about Elena?"

Prytania's voice slipped on her words like feet on icy ground.

"Listen, Jean-Claude. I have enough. I even have some saved. I can take a little apartment near Montparnasse. No one needs to know I have it."

"*I'll* know. Good Christ, Prytania, do you think I can let *two* women pay my rent? Why don't you send me flowers backstage, too?"

Sharp silence fell. I strained against the wall and held my breath until my heart rapped out in protest I could hear. Then Jean-Claude's breath broke, and I heard Prytania's muffled sobs.

"I didn't mean it, I didn't mean it, oh lord I'm sorry, my love. Sweet Prytania, please, I didn't mean it."

I flung myself from the wall and made for the auditorium door, not well enough aware to know that hurrying footsteps would not be noticed, but not caring, only wanting to get away before they found me. The door swung open in my face and knocked me off my balance. Riebenstahl stood on the threshold blinking at the searing light. His temple veins were pounding and his eyes behind the staring glasses were as red as those of someone drunk or dying.

"It's you, eh, is it? Ha! I knew you were bound to find me out." But he said this as if he had rehearsed it, and had no interest in it.

I gripped his elbow, wheeled him round and propelled him up the aisle. I didn't even stumble in the darkness. He went as weightlessly as fallen leaves, and his bones in the hollow of my palm were just as brittle. I could have crushed him in my fist and not even hurt my hand.

"I'm glad to know you realize that," I spat against his ear.

"Oh, yes, dear yes, I realize, eh? That's the matter with me, no doubt."

I wouldn't give him the satisfaction of a reply to this anxious boast. I shoved him on. He held back in the lobby, but I took him, coatless, through the outside door.

"Look here, hey? Where are we going? Don't you want to look at my machines?"

"I've seen them. I think they're hideous, deformed."

"Yes, yes. I knew I could count on you, Your Excellency. Where are we going?"

I stopped at the entrance to the cul-de-sac and faced him squarely, furiously.

"We're going for a walk," I said, "and you're going to tell me exactly what in hell you think you're doing."

He moaned, a sound like a wounded cat, and followed after me whimpering, anxious to keep up now, and out of breath.

"Well I don't know now. That's the thing. No! Everything was clear as day before. I just don't know, I couldn't tell you. What would you say to suicide?"

I gritted my teeth to keep from making the noise this absurdity deserved and resolved that I would say nothing until he ran himself out of chatter. I held to my pace, and he panted after, away from the Chèvre Aveugle and up the rue de Rennes toward the Seine.

"I had no idea, Your Excellency, I really had no idea. The young one, Jean-Claude, he's a fine lad really, you don't know. He said to me, 'You make machines behave like people. I'd like to make people behave like machines,' he said. He asked me, 'Would you mind?' He really meant it. Well, now, that's a thing I can understand, now, wanting to do that. 'No,' I told him, 'go ahead.' I even said I'd help him at it."

Riebenstahl tried to look at me. He plucked my arm, but I drew it away and squinted out across the street, where couples sat at tables on the sidewalk with red beer and cloudy glasses of Pernod.

"I don't mind admitting to you I was proud when he said he wanted to show my things. You wouldn't blame me for that, now, would you?" There's not many people had seen them, and they all seemed to get something from 'em. This fellow from the paper started talking about my 'work.' Well, it is work, I didn't see any harm in that at first. Do you know what they want to do with me? They want me on television! Ha! Oh, yes, they do, they want me to do a debate with this John Tingly. Your Excellency, when you first came to me, did you know about motion sculpture?"

I said nothing. He stopped to catch his breath, but sprinted up to me when I didn't do the same.

"My God!" he cried. "It's got a name! They've got museums for it! Yes, yes, it's the trinkets all over again. They won't leave me alone. They talked about my de-*vel*-opment, and they said I'd got per-*cep*-tion and a sense of the ab-*surd!* I'd chuck it and be damned to them, but no one's going to let me now. No, no, no, no! Your Excellency?"

"You *are* talking about your machines, aren't you?" I said.

"Well, yes. Well, yes, I am. What else?"

"I just wanted to be absolutely certain."

"But I've been figuring it out, I still can figure a thing or two. There was a big one in a fur collar talked a lot about survival. He said I started late — d'you hear? — started late! At what, I wonder? Yes, he said, it was out of the run of things, but I'd got a chance at this rate of making something to survive me. Outlast my lifetime, that's what he said. He said that's all that matters."

He took my forearm in a grip from which this time I couldn't shake him, and dragged his footsteps on the pavement to hold me back.

"Matters!" he shouted. "What matters, eh?" And, his energy returning, he fell into phrases more like the epigrammatist I had known.

"Ever had that put to the test, have you? Listen, I'm an old fool, but I know what I'm saying now. Nothing matters, that's the secret, there's no such thing as necessity. I could tell them where their arguments take 'em, I can tell you just as well. Art is necessary to civilization, one of 'em said to me. Good. What's the value of proving that? Taken as given, yes, but is civilization necessary? That's what I'd ask. It's necessary to man, you say. So. Ha! And is man necessary?"

I jerked my arm away in anger and rounded on rue Dauphine.

"Don't wave me away, Your Excellency, I mean something different. Beavers, you see, are necessary. Biologically, if you'll allow me. Given two beavers, you can't get away from it, no, they'll reproduce and build a dam. You see? That's necessary, that's what I call necessary. But once you've got reason into it, once you're dealing with people, it's no longer any such thing, you see. Does man have to eat? Does he have to copulate? Does he have to build a house? Well, no, now, ha! Sometimes he doesn't! It's necessary if he's going to live, I grant you that. But man, Your Excellency, man is the only animal that knows he hasn't got to live. That's all that reason amounts to, yes. Man isn't the only rational animal, I've never said he is. No sir, ha ha! Man is the only rationally su-i-*ci*-dal animal. That's how I've got round to suicide, eh? Well? What do you think of that?"

We had come so fast that we were crossing the Quai Conti toward the river bank. A clutch of students, mostly Negro, were dancing with guitars on the bright Pont Neuf. I waited until their noise was far away

enough in the background that I could answer Riebenstahl in a normal voice. Then I stopped and leaned my
back against the parapet.

I said, controlled, "I think that those who talk about
committing suicide don't do it."

He took his glasses off and rubbed them on the front
of his shirt. His eyes were almost hidden in their
swollen, reddened sockets.

"Well, yes, no doubt there's something in that," he
sagely, generously conceded.

"And I think what you have committed is an immoral
ugly act."

"What's that?" He blinked. "Eh?" What d'you say?"

"And I further think that you know it, and that all
this jabber about having your idiot toys misunderstood
is a play for my sympathy. But I don't think, Riebenstahl, you're going to get it."

He gaped at me. From his open mouth a broken
wheeze came forth.

"Now tell me just exactly what's your part in this
affair between Prytania and Bastien."

"Oh, them. . . ." The wheeze became a sigh, and, to
my infinite repulsion, Riebenstahl, quite oblivious,
cupped a hand against his groin. The tears came out of
his eyes the whole length of his lower lids, and ran in
every direction over his wrinkled cheeks, like a deluge
finding troughs and furrows.

"Oh, there's a thing, you can't imagine the beauty of
it, Powers."

It had always irritated me that he bestowed a title on
me, but now his so suddenly using my name drove me
half to fury. I became aware of a splitting head. I urged
him on again, along the walk.

"What have you had to do with it?" I demanded.

"Nothing I could really claim, but they don't leave me out, you see. Oh, if you knew. They come to see me. They say it's the only place they've got to come. If you could see how he looks at her, it makes me want to cry."

He *was* crying. I bit my anger back and said, "What have you done?"

"I don't know, only what they've said. There's only M. Adam and me that knows. At least till you. I try to help them how I can, listen to them, that's all I can do. And I gave them my machines. But they say I help. They say . . . they said they loved me, Powers, can you believe it?"

I could have knocked him down and left him senseless in the gutter.

"No," I said, "to tell you the truth, I find it hard to believe. Now if you'll do me the kindness to take your hand out of your crotch" — he started and flung the hand away — "I'll tell you exactly what I think you've done, and why you've done it."

"Your Excellency . . ." he whimpered and hobbled after me.

"You don't know Elena Bastien, do you?"

"No, no . . . I never had the pleasure. . . ."

"But you do know Kenneth Stoddard, and you know he's to marry Prytania."

"Oh, yes, there's that. . . ."

"And if you're so per-*cep*-tive as your critics seem to think, you know that Prytania hasn't a chance in China of holding Bastien."

"But they're in love, Your Excellency. . . ."

"Do you dare to mention love? Do you really mean to turn around at this late date and tell me they're in *love?*"

"I was wrong, I didn't understand. . . ."

"And you still don't understand. Jean-Claude would fall apart without his wife; he couldn't tie his tie. Kenneth would never recover, and Madame would simply cease to live. Is that what you want? Is that how you intend to thank her?"

"Nonono, no, no."

"You killed you wife, and now you're going to kill two other marriages."

"But it isn't me. How can it be?"

"No? Isn't it?" I hissed. "You give them a place to come, you say. You give them your machines. That's wonderful! And is there anything else keeping them together?"

"They love . . ."

"Shut up! You accused me once of wanting to manipulate."

"What, I? I said that? No, Your Excellency, I never said that."

"And I say now you've manipulated an acquaintance into an affair. And I say you've insinuated yourself into it because it's the only way to keep her by you. You're lusting after that child yourself, you demon, and you know it."

"No! No!" he wailed. A woman passing us clutched herself against her partner and hurried on.

"Do you think I didn't see it the first time I saw her in your house? Do you think I don't know what you want, and what you're settling for? My God, I wish they'd locked you up the first time they called you mad!"

"They call me mad . . . ?" he sniveled, and suddenly I had to get away. I turned and ran the way we had come, down the *quai* through the strolling couples, who detoured round me and melted on without so much as a frown.

I went home to bed. Riebenstahl went to throw himself in the Seine.

In Heaven, the existence of which I do not for an instant credit, I hope it may be written in the black that I awoke the next morning before dawn. It was about five, and for more than an hour I lay twisting in the gray half-light. I dressed without rousing my wife and let myself out into the morning.

I breakfasted on bread and coffee at a small sidewalk café, under the eye of a sleepy waiter, whom I gave the cabbie's tip. I walked all the way, two hours of it, to the office in Neuilly, and I got there early, hoping that by some miracle both Prytania and Papadeneau would be ill.

But the day started even worse than I could have feared. Disaster in India, totally unforeseen, and no one's fault. In May, our sluggish spring just lagging into sight, it had been high summer in the coastal plains of southern India. I suppose someone must before have discovered, someone we hadn't thought of asking, that in such heat modern miracles lose their power. In such heat, seventy thousand tubes of contraceptive foam, recently distributed to village schools, had ceased to do their part in the alleviation of world poverty. The villages would produce this year their usual progeny. The schools would have to retrain and reconvince their skeptical students. We would have to negotiate for the insurance, and a new product. To make matters worse, one of the useless tubes had been found in the possession of an unmarried girl in purdah, and the doctor had been hounded out of town.

I was no more responsible for this expensive failure than I was responsible for Riebenstahl's senile lechery. I had done nothing but ship the stuff, and it had *arrived* intact. But the report lay on my desk as insistent as a mote in my eye. Progress without Westernization, I thought, and to show for it, one initiated innocent in the whole of the southern plains. The remnants of last night's turmoil, encouraged by a lack of sleep, plucked at my joints and sent them shivering like catgut. Papadeneau, solicitous to the point of insolence, assured me that I had aged ten years. He went so far as to ask if I wanted to talk about it, but I was not up to the reprimand this deserved, so to appease and get rid of him I sent him for bicarbonate. And, ruefully, I recognized he was right. I wanted a confidant, but in that field I knew no one but myself who met my standards.

I read the report over blindly for more than an hour, jumping whenever the door cracked with the apprehension that it would be Prytania, which it never was. Secretary Haverill, on the way to his office, stopped in and asked if I wasn't feeling well. I indicated the report, and he admonished me, smiling in his mild-mannered way, "I expected the youngsters to be upset, but not you, Powers. Setbacks are our business."

I made a gesture, but he took the report and buried it in my file. "No, it's true, they justify our existence. We're the great clean-up of the aftermath of war, and if things could be set right without a struggle, we'd be out of a job and a purpose. Besides, old man, you had nothing to do with it. Take the day off, why don't you."

It was a welcome suggestion, and I took it. I walked in the direction of the Parc Fasseville, and though I kept mentally plotting routes that would swing me west and south of it, I knew all the time that I was on my way to Riebenstahl.

The house was as tight as the evening before, which should not have alarmed me, for I had no way of knowing whether he always locked up when he went out. But it struck me as out of character, as slightly sinister. One can always tell a bed that has been made from a bed that hasn't been slept in. In a mechanical repetition of last night's round, I knocked and called and climbed on the garbage can to rap on the window.

Then I went back to the rotunda and asked the patrolman if he had seen my friend.

"No, Monsieur. I don't see him often. He keeps pretty much to himself."

I said I knew that, but he was unwell and I couldn't seem to rouse him. I had a notion he hadn't come in at all. Would he make a routine check?

I waited on the steps among the fallen leaves. After what seemed an inordinately long time, he reappeared with a notebook in his hand and said apologetically, "They have somebody at the morgue in the *douzième*. A hobo, they said. Fished out of the river. That wouldn't be him, would it?"

"I hope not, but I'm afraid it's worth a check."

I had a vague notion of a morgue as some place made of corpse-sized filing cabinets and naked light bulbs, so the knobbly, comfortable old building took me somewhat by surprise. The black-clad guard who came to greet me had a soft, funereal demeanor more like a genuine undertaker than a cop, so that I should have liked to tell him he had missed his calling.

"You mustn't assume it's Mr. . . . ?"

"Riebenstahl."

"Riebenstahl, sir. We get quite a lot of these fellows who sleep under the bridges, and one day they just roll off. It's rare they turn out to be anybody someone wants to claim."

I asked, "Is he very . . ."

"Damaged?" the guard anticipated. "No, he wasn't in the water long. Some students on the Pont Neuf heard the splash. They were just too late."

"What time was that?"

"About three A.M."

"Had they noticed him before?"

"The students? No, sir, no one had. As I say, they aren't a very noticeable sort."

I was relieved. "May I see him?"

"Yes, sir. Please, sir, come this way."

Even in the morgue itself, he was laid on something more like a camp bed than a slab. There was a tactful suggestion of formaldehyde in the air, and this, together with the cared-for whiteness of the sheet that covered him, made me think of Riebenstahl's underwear drying in his kitchen. It suits him better than the Poche Adam, I thought, and the guard turned back the sheet with concerned efficiency, like a nurse, just to the depth of his chin.

I don't know what I had expected, but not repose. The temple veins, which had always been the most striking part of his face, had paled and receded beneath the skin as deep as the guard's, or mine. He had always seemed lean and crinkled in the cheeks, but the flesh sloughed toward his ears now, making it smoother, fuller. His puffy eyes were closed, but they hadn't been able to make his chin stay up, and his mouth was open as it had always been. I could hear him saying a gentle, final, "Ha."

I turned away, and the guard rather anxiously replaced the sheet.

"Is it he, sir?"

"Yes, it's he," I said.

"Oh, sir, I'm very sorry. I'm sorry for what we

thought, but you see, he hadn't even a coat. No money, and not a speck of identification, just a pocketful of junk."

"I'll make the arrangements," I said, "and sign for his things if you want me to."

"Well, are you kin, now?" he apologized, leading me back to the outer room. "We have to have some sort of proof, you see, that he's who you say he is."

I produced my United Nations card, which had all the effect I could have hoped, and more, for he startled me by beginning, "Your Excellency . . ."

"Just Mr. Powers."

"Yes, Mr. Powers. I'll get his things for you."

Workshirt and trousers, dried and unironed, the way he always wore them. Shorts and a sleeveless undershirt, darned socks, much-mended shoes. A cotter wedge, four bolts, six nails, an onion, some copper wire. Filed and welded from a scrap of bicycle chain, a shiny ring with the key to the little house. The official list said, "Handkerchief," but he hadn't carried one. It was Prytania's once-white scarf, gone limp with river water, and the colors faded into one pale stain.

"There's blood on there," the guard said anxiously, "but it isn't new. He hadn't any cuts on him, Mr. Powers, no sign of violence at all."

"No, no. He probably had a bloody nose sometime."

"That's what we figured."

I signed for the bundle and took it. The guard tiptoed after me to the door.

"I wouldn't want you to think we wouldn't have tried to identify him, Mr. Powers. But you see, we get so many of these fellows. . . ."

"On the contrary," I said, "you've been more thoughtful and thorough than I could have hoped. I appreciate your concern."

"Why, thank you, sir." He sighed with satisfaction, and stood bowing after me in the door; impressed, raised in his own esteem by my compliment and my call.

I was old enough to have seen a few friends die. I had waded through the thick, excreted perfume of a dozen rites, wanting to feel myself the most affected, sparring for greatest grief with others of the former friends. I had seen death, but I had never been its harbinger.

There were a dozen sons and daughters who must be notified by nightfall; a patrolman, my wife, a newspaper and four others to be told. Yet I carried my bundle and walked along the Seine toward the Pont Neuf, not ready to become the messenger, not willing yet to share the death of Riebenstahl.

I felt I had been walking for a hundred thousand years. My shoes were meant for walking. They were bought for it. My feet weren't sore. But the pavement pounded upward through my body like my blood itself. It thrust its rhythm on me, I could no more stop than if my heart had fed on the mere force of my pushing on where I was headed, and when I reached the bridge that I had thought my sentimental goal, I didn't pause for it. I walked up-river.

Scum in little eddies sucked the dry leaves down by fistfuls at the piles. His glasses would have gone like that; they would be interred by now in the riverbed. Anonymous refuse tumbled down the muddy current, will-lessly, end over end. I walked against it, as if I too were in the tide, yet strangely unaffected by it, thwarting its strength with steady energy from a source as deep, as distant as the river's source itself.

I was stopped at last by the peal of the hour from

Notre-Dame-de-Consolation on Jean-Goujon. It was three o'clock. I wasn't ready to portion my knowledge with Madame, but the UNICEF staff went home at five and Madame must be told first. I turned from the river as from something certain into the unknown.

She was addressing envelopes in her kitchen. A stack of them leaned against the wall, and others drying in the feeble light lay spread before her like a game of solitaire.

"You here at this hour?" She drew me in, her pleasure betraying the tedium of her task, and then glanced sharply into my face and told me to sit down.

"You wish something to drink. Kummel?"

I accepted with a nod, and she poured two glasses, not pressing me to begin. In her window a vase of hothouse peonies burgeoned, pink and white and red, their great heads searching stiffly toward the corners. I chose a chair with my back to them and the light. She handed me the glass and sat herself; the stuff was sweet and burning. I had left my package in the stairwell, but now I wished I had some way without the words. I had set my back to the flowers, but Prytania was everywhere: a stack of brilliantly jacketed records, an English novel open face-down on the couch. Three dining chairs were ranged around the radiator with their backs to it. Each was covered with newsprint and a wet cardigan, their dead arms dangling.

"You wash her sweaters," I observed. I wasn't stalling; it seemed relevant.

"She washes them herself. Tell me, my friend."

I rolled the stem between my fingers.

"Riebenstahl is dead. He killed himself, Madame."

She made a gesture half to her face, which trailed then rising into the air. Those gestures had made everything right, made everything possible in my youth, and they had not lost their multitude of meanings. This one said, "I am sorry," and, "It's not a shock, I half expected it, don't think of me," and, "What of you?"

"He told me he was going to, and I didn't think he meant it. I thought if he meant it he wouldn't say so, and I told him as much. He agreed with me. I suppose I didn't know him very well."

"You are not," she said slowly, "young enough or foolish enough to think that places the blame for it on you."

"No," I said, and smiled to reassure her, "I'm not that young or foolish."

"Good."

We sat in silence, letting the sticky liquid slide beyond our tongues, as if it were necessary we should taste every drop.

"Do you realize why he did it, Madame?"

"No, I do not know the reason, but I always knew it was in him, underneath. Do you wish me to know?"

I nodded. "He said it was his machines. You've seen the papers?"

"Yes. But you do not think that was the reason."

I roused myself and took a breath of sugared fire. "He did it because he loved Prytania, and she . . . is in love with someone else."

Madame took this in — she took it all in, for she presently replied, "Someone not Kenneth."

"Jean-Claude Bastien."

"Oh. I see."

"I was harsh with him, I said some things I wish I hadn't. I don't blame myself for his death, but it takes an effort of the will not to blame myself for that. Of course, my first thought was for Kenneth and Elena."

She looked at me in a way that made it clear that for

the first time she was uncertain where I was going. She put her head on the side and smoothed a thumb against her fichu.

"I haven't any idea of — reparation," I said, "but I've been thinking all day of what he said of them, Prytania and Jean-Claude. I think perhaps he was right, and I was wrong. We dislike change; infidelity disrupts our sense of order."

"What is it that you want, my friend?"

I set my glass down, fingered it and picked it up again.

"They haven't any place to go. They must meet in bars, I suppose, and in the dressing room of the Poche, where there's no privacy for them. The nearest they had to it was the little house, and Riebenstahl was always there."

"Yes?"

"Prytania won't have Jean-Claude here because she won't risk hurting you. I don't know what Kenneth knows, but evidently you're her first concern. Of course they can't go home to the Bastiens'. You can see where that leaves them — sneaking and sordid. It doesn't suit them, does it?"

"What do you want to do?"

I drained my glass before replying, and swallowed the answers I might have made like so much fermented cumin.

"The little house is empty, Madame," I said, "and the morgue gave me the key."

She lay back in her chair and shut her eyes, for so long that she might have fallen asleep. A little spasm of fierce hope contracted her lids.

"She will refuse," she said, and then amended, "She could refuse if she wanted to."

"You'll do it for her, then?" I pressed.

She rose and set her face to rights, automatically smoothing the sweater on the nearest chair. "No," she said, obscurely distant, and when my heart had skipped its beat, "for you."

I went to her and clasped her hands, but she impelled me backward toward the door, first with the pressure of her arms, and when she pulled them free, in little waves of wanting to be rid of me.

"Kenneth is yours in a way that Prytania is not, Madame," I said, resisting the force, not physical, with which she urged me back. "May I be certain that you won't think better of it, and interfere?"

She listened hard, like someone deaf or hearing through a tumult, and only stopped before me when I was safely in the hall.

"Kenneth is his own. I hope you will never find it necessary to say that I interfere."

"My apologies, Madame," I said, trying to take her hand again. "I know you better."

But the fingers fled from me.

"It is easy to know others," she replied, and closed the door.

This time I took a cab. In the UNICEF lobby Secretary Haverill was sorting papers with the receptionist. He greeted me with an approving laugh in which, after a moment, I joined him.

"Can't we get rid of you for a day?"

"If we've got to pick up the pieces, we'd better get on with it," I said, and he clapped me lightly, fondly, on the back, as if I had been a much younger man.

In the office I spread my bundle on the desk and extracted the key. I took Prytania's scarf and folded it in my lowest drawer. Then I wrapped the rest again, more carelessly, and threw it in the basket to be taken down and burned. I went to the outer office and called Prytania.

I had not been ready for Madame, but in my studies of the care of children, Prytania had been my special field. I believe I was eloquent in my simplicity. I gave her only information, and not all of that. I didn't tell her it was suicide, although I didn't say it wasn't. Nothing required me to offer my opinion — not even the morgue had specified with greater certainty than "either . . . or" — and I knew Prytania well enough to know that she would just as soon not have it. I told her, briefly, the story of his wife's death, and how by his own account it had affected him. I described by what signs I had known that he wasn't well, and the shock with which, as a man who believed in nothing but tasks and the tangible, he had heard himself described as an artist of "promise" and "caustic vision." I said that he was bewildered, tired, and not himself. I described my visit to the morgue, and indicated that I had told Madame.

She sat with the notebook still open in her lap for the dictation she had expected. Her hands lay motionless on the page, crossed palms set up and open. She might have been offering the little scar. Her sweater was clean and brushed, her skirt in no evident disrepair, and on her insignificant breast a piece of metal hung by a slender chain, the bold suggestion of a broken hand cut out of steel. I recognized the work of Riebenstahl.

She took it almost as calmly as Madame. She only occasionally swallowed and nodded, to show that she was following. Nor did she challenge me to reveal why I thought she should be told, and when I did not offer any explanation, she accepted this, as always, with the flat and literal grace of giving up.

"We worked him too hard," she said at last. "We kept forgetting he was old."

Madame's words came back to me, and, covering and tracing the rough round of the bicycle ring, I said, "You are neither of you so young or foolish as to blame yourselves."

She replied with mistrusting hope, "It was an accident, wasn't it?"

I had to choose then. A great swelling of wanting to tell her why he had died rose up in me like nausea or flatus. I choked it, willfully, and said, "It was an accident. There were students on the bridge who saw him stumble."

She accepted this. She accepted everything. I paced to the window and watched the leaves detach themselves from the blighted branches and glide away to the ground.

I told her that Riebenstahl had had no opportunity for last requests, and that if he had, they should not have been sentimental ones. But he was a man, I said, who put great faith — whatever faith he could be said to have — in making use of the objects at one's disposal.

"He was fond of you both, Prytania, although I doubt he would have said so. And the only thing he couldn't bear was waste."

I laid the key in her open hand, across the severed artery. She studied it for a long while, not asking what it was or what I meant by it, but waiting until she herself should understand. When she did so she turned her eyes to me, brown and violet with the colors of the autumn window.

"Oh, really, I don't want it. Marraine . . ." she explained, and when I only nodded and smoothed her hair, lightly, as if her decision were of no personal moment to me, she elaborated, "I couldn't take it. Thank you, but it wouldn't be right."

Her words unsettled her as mine had failed to do. She closed her fist around the key, searching vaguely for some place to set it down. Her left hand wandered clumsily on her thigh.

"I don't want it," she insisted more determinedly, "it wouldn't be right," chagrined and shocked that neither of us believed her.

Riebenstahl had never got round to donating himself to science, and a daughter came from England to claim his body and debris. She was pregnant enough that I wondered with some resentment whether there had been no one of the seven less so to do the job. She found nothing to apologize for in the fact that, having had no use for the man, she wanted possession of his meager leavings. The uselessness in her eyes of most of the objects in the little house inspired her with listless pique, colored only by flashes of accusation which I was handy to absorb; and she assured me with a vehemence that expected disbelief, that her father had arrived only five years ago with as many hundred pounds!

She left the books and took the imitation jade spittoon. She tossed the bones into a cardboard box with impatience and repulsion, but, grudgingly satisfied, she lined her tin trunk with the unmatched cups, wrapped in his underwear. She stripped the windows of their floral curtains, which had not been his, but I didn't interfere, and only when she eyed his wooden bedstead covetously did I explain that the furnishings were the property of the city. At my suggestion, she gathered the books and equipment she didn't want and redelivered them to the Left Bank *boutiques* he had frequented. They didn't bring enough to pay her fare.

Dutifully just, I showed her the reviews of the double *succès fou* at the Poche Adam, and gave her a taxi ride, the one thing she enjoyed, for a look at his machines. Like Kenneth, she asked what they *did,* and when I replied with their inventor's, "Nothing!" she set her hands on the boll of her belly with incredulous revulsion.

"Cor! They an't wath anything, now, are they?"

I said, "There are those who think someday they will be."

"Someday! There'd be no use catting 'em back, now, and that, would there?"

"The freight would be expensive," I agreed.

"What'd you say they'd bring in, now?"

"Do you mean *now?*" I wanted to be sure, for the word seemed to have no temporal connotation in her vocabulary.

"If I was to try and sell 'em."

"Well . . ." I hung my thumbs in the armholes of my vest, in the only attitude I could be sure would convey contemplation. "You couldn't call him famous. I'm not sure you'd get a buyer, but I liked the old codger" — she snorted appreciatively — "and I might be willing to pay you for the lot."

"How much?" she asked me, eager and suspicious.

"Oh . . ." I thought it expedient to count the money in my wallet, not wanting to suggest it was worth a check. "I might go twenty pounds."

She squinted to cover an instant's startled greed, and looked at me so narrowly that I feared I had gone too high. In the end, however, she only upped me ten.

"Make it twenty-five," I shrugged with irritation just short of impoliteness, "but I'll want a receipt."

"All right then." Her indifference was as feigned, but not as skillfully feigned, as mine.

When she had gone I presented them to Jean-Claude.

I had seen him with Prytania only once. I had let them treat me to champagne in their Alsatian bistro, after the fourth performance of *Mimes Mécaniques*, when both the gloom and the triumph had lost their first full strength. We toasted Riebenstahl, and Prytania began to cry a little, but this Jean-Claude would not allow. He lifted her hair to show me a break in her symmetry, that the hairline at the nape of her neck was lopsided, and he said, "You have to be slightly fuddled to overlook a flaw like that!" When he had her laughing, he adjured her, "He would have hated all the fuss." He thanked me for the key, simply, attempting to convey his gratitude with no emotion more cumbersome than delight. To match his tact, I excused myself when the bottle was yet half full.

But Prytania had insisted that I was to come as I liked to the little house, which she called The *Little* House, as if it were a name; and so the day after she moved from Madame's I followed an hour behind her from the office.

The trees were nearly bare, but Riebenstahl's tomatoes still stood half the height of the porch, and the red fruit rotted on the ground, while the green continued to tug at the bowing branches. In the vestibule I stumbled over a washtub of more of them, and the living room, with the furniture piled in the center, was dotted with bowls and baskets of still more. Jean-Claude was balanced on a heap of covered chairs, and Prytania, in a tattered shirt that reached beyond her knees, her hair tied out of reach of her spattering, was mixing buckets of yellow paint with a broomstick.

"Glory lord!" I greeted them.

"I'm going to make green tomato pickles," she explained proudly, "but you can't make green tomato pickles in an aqua kitchen!"

I recognized the arbitrary dictum as Jean-Claude's brand of whimsy. Both of us laughed, and he threw me a tomato.

"The whole house has got to be yellow," he said with tolerance. "For Elena it's always white."

Prytania made a face at him. "Luckily, Jean-Claude has no opinions of his own, so it's not a competition." She glanced quickly sideways at me, I think to see whether her levity had shocked me. I sniffed the tomato and dropped it into a bowl.

"Don't you want some help with that?" Jean-Claude asked her.

"Not in those clothes!" she exclaimed, complacent, horrified. "You'd make a mess of yourself!" At which we once more, because her sneakers were entirely yellow and her shirt was stiff with enamel patches, laughed at her together.

"But if you want to be useful, the two of you, you could pile the upstairs furniture."

We mounted to do so, and when we were alone I said, "Jean-Claude, I have a present for you. Although, in fact, it's already in your possession."

"Prytania?" he inquired with an unsure laugh.

"No, no. It's really mine to give away." I handed him the receipt, which I had endorsed to him. He sat on the bed and stared at it, shaking his head in wonder.

"Good Lord, sir, you go too far! These things are worth a fortune."

"They may be, but if you'll notice, his girl had a limited idea of fortune. I cheated her, of course, but as far as I'm concerned I did it justly. She'd seen the reviews, she thought they were junk herself, and she jumped at it. None of his children did anything for him in his lifetime. I see no reasons he should support them now. He'd rather they were yours, I'm sure of that."

He was willing to follow this argument. He folded the paper carefully in half.

"I won't offer to buy them from you, because the money doesn't represent their worth. But I'm indebted."

"Don't declare any obligations yet," I said. "I want something in exchange."

"I'm not easily frightened. Ask and it shall be given."

I said, "Don't tell Elena."

He looked up flinching, and the receipt, which was almost in his pocket, came down again to rest on his knees.

I laughed to reassure him. "Put it away. I don't seriously mean it as a condition."

"I'm sure you don't, but I'm not sure you know exactly what you're asking. I appreciate what you've done, believe me, but I can't expect you to concur in Elena's and my way of looking at things. Elena doesn't feel she has to hate Prytania just because I love her, you see, and I don't feel I have to hide where I've gone or what I'm doing. I've never deliberately lied to her, and if I did so now I'd have violated our marriage as another man would have violated it by being here."

"I have nothing against modern marriages, Jean-Claude," I said gently. He caught at the word.

"Modern!"

He flattened the receipt out on his knee and folded it crosswise to the crease he had already made.

"You'd say our apartment was modern, wouldn't you? And yet there's nothing of interest in the décor that didn't belong to one of Elena's peasant aunts." He threw a gesture at the wall, where fantastic blossoms quarreled with extinct red birds. It would take three coats to cover those birds with yellow.

"She offers me feudal freedom, that's closer to it; and I return the compliment. If it falls in with the current fashion, so much the better. But Elena comes by it honestly, like the terra-cotta jugs."

I wanted to ask how often the philosophy had served them, but I knew that I wanted to ask this only because I was pretty sure that it had not. So I didn't; it would serve no purpose to win an argument with him.

"Jean-Claude," I cajoled him instead, and sat beside him on the faded ticking. "On the contrary, it's you who don't accept enough. Such as that, for instance, I respect the tenor of your understanding with your wife. I think the world would be better off if it took you for an example. But you must understand that the 'civilized' world does not, and that, belonging to that world, I've taken a certain risk in it. My wife shares your regard for Elena, but not for Prytania, you see. And she wouldn't understand any of our parts in it, especially mine, as well as the four of us."

"You're right, of course," he answered quietly, trying for the sake of my generosity to concede a point which was in fact beyond his willingness to grant. "Prytania would agree with you entirely. Kenneth Stoddard still thinks she's been a sort of unpaid amanuensis at the Poche, and that there's some kind of 'career' in store for her there if she handles it well. Things seem so much simpler to me than people make them, but evidently somewhere I miss the point."

"But I disagree. It's we who miss the point. We do make things more difficult. All I ask you to understand is that we do. Elena would never willfully hurt me, but neither would she realize that she was doing so."

"I could ask her . . ."

". . . to lie for me? And lay the burden of it on her when, really, she has nothing to thank me for? Would that be making it simpler, Jean-Claude?"

He frowned and traced the floorboard with his toe.

I asked, "Have you told Elena yet that I've given you the key?"

The question made him uneasy, and he continued to fold the receipt until he had made a slender bar of it.

"You mustn't think we haven't any topics of conversation except my mistress. I told her Riebenstahl had died, and that we had access to his house. That's all she wanted to know for the moment. She doesn't pump me for details."

"Exactly," I said. "You see, it isn't a question of deliberate lies. And if she ever asks, it's true as well that the dispensation of the house is in Mme de Verbois' hands, and that Prytania has her consent to use it. It's a matter of minor importance that I came between. It's also true that Riebenstahl's daughter offered the machines at a ridiculously low figure, and that the Poche has acquired them. It isn't very much I ask. And you will have given me the security of knowing that my wife will not find out. I'd prefer your kind of security, but it isn't in my grasp."

He unwillingly surrendered by slipping the paper in his pocket.

"You win," he said, and performed a grimace that purported to be a yawn.

"Now let's move this thing, or the mattress will be as yellow as the walls."

Under those stubby and maladroit hands, The Little House changed its nature, became sparse and tropic, alien both to the woods behind and to the traffic at its doorstep.

Riebenstahl's daughter had done her a service, really. She had usurped, dismantled, stripped, discarded, until she had peeled Riebenstahl off like a layer of lichens from a rock, leaving nothing disquieting or even familiar; leaving Prytania nothing to contend with but the original deficiencies of the house and furniture.

She set out against these by further negatives, challenging them calmly and entirely, as she had challenged the Roman numerals on the Arabic school. The difference was that she had proved an indifferent secretary. She was brilliant as the mistress of The Little House.

She exiled further furniture to one unused room upstairs, leaving in the living room nothing to sit on but her stool, my chair, and the couch where Jean-Claude liked to lie oblique. She stripped the walls of frames and fixtures, blotted out their patterns with her bright mat paint, chopped off the legs of the workbench, even unhinged whole oak doors.

Then she made her additions: all alive, or newly dead. Pale fish stared from a tinted bowl, dried leaves sprang up at every sill. Knife-petaled flowers succeeded each other with such frequency on the mantelpiece that they seemed rather to transform themselves than fade. She did not, like Riebenstahl, try to diminish the room's queer length, but emphasized it by setting the stunted workbench down the center from one wall. From this there sprouted the fronds and spines of torrid vegetation, and though they narrowed the room, they narrowed it as a banquet hall is narrow, as if at any moment a tribe of pygmies might arrive for the floral feast. At the other end the whole wall was commanded, giant to the pygmies, by a rubber plant as high as the cornice, which shied from the opening of the door and snapped its leaves.

I didn't force myself upon them. I never came unannounced, and I let some invitations pass unheeded. I was careful to come equally often when they were together and when Prytania was alone, when she was likely to be lonely. They rewarded me with a welcome that could not be false, with informal lunches for three, an abundance of green tomato pickles, and a perpetual eagerness to display their love, to recount their small adventures. Nor do I think this was particularly strange. Secrecy was alien to both their natures, and they acknowledged with high scorn the fact that, everyone most concerned being perfectly in accord with their arrangements, they yet must pretend in public to be mere friends. Their greatest game was flaunting their affair in the faces of those they fooled. No aspect of The Little House so drove them to delight as that it was set in the center of a public place, and that they were flanked on the one side by meticulously shielded innocence, on the other by a swarming thoroughfare.

Weekends at the Poche were given up to *Mimes Mécaniques*, but the weekday productions proceeded as before, and scarcely a Tuesday night went by that Jean-Claude did not choose for improvisation a suggestion written on green paper, reenacting for four hundred strangers, and the pen of Wednesday's critics, whatever scene of their week's rendezvous Prytania had found most interesting. When they quarreled, they resolved their quarrels in this way, by setting them on view, and they had no disagreement harsh enough that it could survive the pompous, respectful retelling in the arts pages of *L'Express*. Beyond these sketches, Jean-Claude

had no new projects immediately in mind, but reviewers who had before found him only consummately
skillful, now, since the stunning reception of his mime,
were ready to find new depths of feeling and perception
in him — and I am not prepared to say that Prytania and
Jean-Claude disbelieved them.

Perhaps because of this disdained secrecy, perhaps
because there was about The Little House, as well as the
Poche Adam, something in the nature of a charade, they
imbued their every moment with a significance beyond
itself. If when I arrived I found Jean-Claude's scarf on
the living room floor, Prytania would tell me, "He's
incorrigibly untidy!" as if this intelligence might explain the source of the universe to me. If Prytania
pronounced the cheese too strong or the burgundy too
sharp, Jean-Claude would confide. "She has no palate,"
in a tone so heavy with meaning that I might have
thought I should take notes, except that the next moment, whatever the quality of the cheese, they could eat
no more of it for laughing.

I laughed as well, and accepted their declarations
with whatever awe or gravity seemed due — and which,
in fact, I felt, because their intensity was catching. They
had that before which a man of sixty must stand in
helpless wonder; a continuing purity of ecstatic love.
They lived the present as if it were the past. They
recognized in every moment that preciousness the discovery of which is usually confined to love remembered.
They savored each other's voices, foibles, bodies, with a
sweet self-consciousness that could only be improved by
their having one spectator.

"Well, do you like it?" Prythania would demand of
me, including Jean-Claude in the sweep of her eyes
around her new décor, kneeling on the raffia rug and

rising from the shelf of plants like some dark landlocked Venus. "Do you really like it?" Adding once, absolutely without emphasis, "It's the only thing I've ever done."

I have said they quarreled. They quarreled in front of me, and not at first, I think, because they had no pride with me, but because their quarrels always began as something else, as banter or simple chatter, and none of us knew they had begun until too late.

Jean-Claude asked of Prytania a curious thing for a lover; only that she not invent obstacles to their happiness; that she not pretend their emotion owed a fraction of its strength to the existence of his wife. This was the law he laid down for her. He was quick to think she questioned it, or doubted his own or Elena's perfect ease.

She would say merely, "Don't get too comfortable, or you'll get home late again." He would answer with something or other vaguely teasing, and before a half-dozen sentences had been exchanged, we would find — all of us, for I think they were as uncertain as I how they had got there — that they were arguing about Kenneth Stoddard.

"Have you seen him yet or haven't you, Prytania?"

"I talked to him. He's busy himself, you know."

"You spoil everything with your silly cowardice," Jean-Claude would flare. "Please do me the honor not to think I'm jealous. If you want to marry him, that's fine. But what good you're doing him this way is beyond me. And I'll be damned if I can see what good you're doing us!"

Prytania went stiff when she was angry, and spoke in a parody of her own style, outrageously and enragingly calm. "You think everyone in the world is taking lessons from your wife. Have you any idea what Kenneth would think of me? I can't imagine anything I'd rather *not* do than sit in a bistro and share us out with Kenneth."

"You don't love him then."

"Who said I did?" She would weep in that startling way she had that he had forced this confession from her; her face unclenched, her eyes wide open, her mouth set just ajar.

"I don't. I never did, and I don't see how it's got to the point that I have to apologize for it to you."

Tears totally unnerved him; Elena was never known to cry. "Prytania, don't. Please don't. I'm sorry. But you'd have to tell him all the same, my love."

He was right, of course, and, pressed for my opinion, I agreed. So Prytania promised, and the quarrel was over until perhaps she said, "I was to meet your mother, but you never take me. When do I inspect the family mansions?" Then, a reply relevant by any standard but the logical, Jean-Claude would ask her whether she had told Kenneth.

She couldn't do it. I saw that, days before she asked me to do it for her. She waited so long, called him so infrequently with the excuses she half-believed, that at last she had to fear he would come to check up on her at Madame's.

"I've always been a coward," she admitted shyly, as if by speaking of it she had already begun to impose on me. "Jean-Claude knew how to make me understand what Elena feels, so he doesn't understand why I can't do the same. But I'm *not* Jean-Claude, and Kenneth isn't me: what can I say? 'I'm in love with a married man, but his wife doesn't mind, so you shouldn't either.' 'I'm in love with somebody else, but it turns out that I never loved you anyway, so it's not his fault.' Do you see

how difficult it is? I'd *like* him to forgive Jean-Claude. I
keep forgetting to say that to Jean-Claude when he
jumps at me. The trouble is that I'm not . . . I'm not
eloquent enough."

This was the longest (and incidentally the most eloquent) speech I had ever heard from her. She would
have made it longer had I required it, but she half-
smiled, Prytania-smiled at me, asking me not to make
her add, "eloquent like you."

I said, "I'll do it for you, if you like."

She gave up artfulness with a positive shiver of relief.
"Would you? Is it too weak of me? I was afraid to ask."

I laughed at her, which puzzled her, and she added, "I
don't want you to think I use you." I shook my head,
and she let me take her hand, still laughing, and kiss it
very lightly on the palm.

I asked him to meet me at a little bar on the corner of
boulevard Courcelles and rue Courcelles, where we
could sit in a high-backed booth and see The Little
House across the intersection. He came looking somewhat seedy, in a sour, disheveled sort of mood. I had
wanted to give him all the due I felt Prytania didn't,
and his seeming neither to want nor warrant it put me
out of sorts. I wasn't eloquent; I was careless. Identical
mirrors were mounted over the seats, like those in an
English train. Each threw back the image of the other,
making an endless telescope recede, mirror upon mirror, beyond our cubicle. As I talked I watched my cigar
smoke rise between them, its undulations redoubled
with each succeeding reflection. Kenneth listened to me
without interruption, only cracking his knuckles without making any noise and studying the crease in his no-
color cavalry twill.

Love and guilt had made Prytania callous to his

intelligence. She had taken his acquiescence for credulity, misconstruing him worse than he ever had her. So little of what I told him now was news — a name, a few details of circumstance — that indeed Jean-Claude might have felt he gained his point. He evinced no surprise and asked not one single question. Once, when I raised my hand between the mirrors and watched my infinite fingers curl in the reflections, he squinted up at me, his eyebrows darting toward each other like attacking insects. It was the only time he took his eyes off his knees.

"All right," he said bitterly when I had finished. "But what's the point of your breaking the news? I suppose Prytania asked *you* . . . to."

His sarcasm stumbled as he discovered mid-sentence that this might be so. I admitted it as kindly as I could.

"I just think I'll check on that," he said, abruptly quitting me, the booth, the bar.

I dropped a bill on the table and followed, but here his youth had the jump on me. He was running, and out of sight around the rotunda before I had crossed the street. By the time I reached The Little House he was in the living room, confronting Prytania across the bank of plants, not looking at them but aware of them, his arms pinned to his sides. I realized what it must be like to take in the charge at once; as if Riebenstahl's litter had started up and put forth spines. Kenneth's face wore a look incredulous, outraged, aghast, so that it took me some time to understand that he was offering himself to Prytania as a blind.

"In spite of Father Mentor here, the fact is that everybody doesn't share Mme Bastien's view," he said.

Prytania winced at this and glanced at me.

"The only way you can really be safe from the nuisance of public opinion is to keep a fiancé. It's a much better screen than a wife or a husband, in fact. We might even make a foursome now and again."

"Don't mock me," Prytania pleaded, turning again to appeal to me, but Kenneth put himself between us and assured her gravely that he meant it. She backed off from him and sat looking away from both of us.

"How could you want this extraordinary thing?"

"I'm unencumbered," he stiffly explained. "I can outlast him."

"Unencumbered!" she repeated with a wondering shake of her head. "Oh, Kenneth, beside Jean-Claude you have all the wives of St. Ives on your back. Look at you — you want to saddle yourself with us this time."

"I can outlast him."

She pressed her hands along her jaw. "Oh, God, I'm so surrounded by generosity I'll suffocate in it. Why am I the only one who knows that possession is nine points of love?"

"Your knowing that is something," he smiled pityingly at her.

She sank back into the chair in defeated assent. She might have been forced to some arrangement disadvantageous to her. "You may have a lot to outlast," she warned. "He doesn't know he has to choose, and he may never find it out. As long as he doesn't, I'm going to make him right."

"I'll take that chance," Kenneth said kindly.

"And if he does, there may not be much left of me worth your having."

"I'll take that one too," he said, and without touching her, or acknowledging my presence, he pushed through the vestibule and out into the park.

Prytania came to me. She cried often now.

"I didn't know, I had no idea he'd turn against you. It's so absurd of him. I am so sorry!"

"I wasn't eloquent enough, that's all," I said.

"Oh, God, I never meant to cost you Kenneth!"

I took her face in my hands, her jaw still red from the pressure of her own fingers. "It's no surprise to me, Prytania. It's a very old fact of life: the messenger gets beheaded if he brings bad news. Luckily Kenneth's friendship is worth less to me than my head."

"When I think how much I owe you . . ." Prytania began, but I silenced her with my hands across her mouth.

There were two things Elena could do, and the lesser of them was to take a confidant. I expected it, and did not blame her. My wife was the least unsatisfactory prospect, and I came into it incidentally, because I was there, and because it would never have occurred to Elena to ask a wife to keep a secret from her husband.

I found them together in our living room one night. Laura met me with a face of terrible significance, and Elena smiled at me dry-eyed, just a little apologetic. Laura caught me up on as much as she had heard, and Elena finished her story in simpler terms, with few superlatives and no accusations.

There are people who maintain balance and proportion by a skillful cancellation of their excesses. Elena was one of these. She never came sober from a feast or unheated from a slight; but when she forgave, she forgave absolutely; when she dieted she lived on water, and could continue to cook voluminously for Jean-Claude without temptation. She spent her monthly salary in seven days, and then she managed the house on less than a quarter of Jean-Claude's, because nothing would induce her to touch their savings. She had put her faith in the Virgin Mary until she was twenty years old; when she transferred her faith to herself, she had not kept her rosary.

Elena knew this of herself, and knew that it was she who had defined their marriage. Jean-Claude, as little inclined to soul-searching as to sin, would never of his own have asked for absolute freedom, or absolute openness.

"I said . . . I thought I said, to Jean-Claude: I want what is really you, not some figment of a 'husband' patched up out of other people's notions. I said: I will give you me, and if I find part of me in the body of another man, you may have that too. I don't know where we misplaced what I meant by honesty."

There was no question of her resenting Jean-Claude's reaction to the girl. She had shared it herself, had been touched by the innocent, determined invasion of his mime, and she had seen half a dozen models in the summer showings which had made her think that, there! Prytania Obée would make of that what the designer had in mind!

When he told her of his meeting with Prytania in the park, of how confused Elena's attitude seemed to make her, she had laughed with him in complicity and pride.

Even when it turned out that Prytania might offer him something she had never been able to, some kind of involvement in his work that had always been beyond her, this was so clearly to Jean-Claude's benefit and enhancement that she could hardly claim she had less of a husband than before. He was not thick or dull, Jean-Claude; he had anticipated her.

"We mustn't go so far as to pretend that jealousy doesn't exist. If you ever find out that you can't stand it, Elena, tell me so. You won't have to explain. I'll simply stop seeing her."

But she could stand it. All he had done was settle the responsibility on her. If at any given moment she asked, "Is this more than I can bear?" — the question had no certain meaning. What is the limit of endurance? She was eating, she was working five days a week, her mind seemed very much intact.

He had always been good about calling her if he was likely to be late, and now and again in the fall he had telephoned from the Poche to say, "I'm too keyed up. I'm going to take Prytania for a beer," or, "We feel like a walk on the river. Will you not wait up if we go ahead?" Even this was a tribute to their confidence, each in the other, and it had been easy enough to reply, "Of course, my love. Are you sure you've got your key?"

But The Little House had no phone, and the nearest public booth was three blocks away. If, toward December, dinner was cold when he got home, he would simply repeat this information in an easy apology, perfectly confident — hadn't she taken pains to make him so? — that she would understand.

The Monday before Christmas was the first time he failed her altogether. She was sentimental about Christmas, sentimental about Mondays too, which, in their irregular life, had been the longest space they had together. She was late herself tonight with shopping, and apprehensive of whether she had planned a dinner too elaborate for the hour. They were due at a party at the Chaumbrés' at half-past nine.

She had one ungainly package, a clotheshorse for Jean-Claude. Her great anxiety was how she should manage to get it across the hall and into her own closet without his seeing her. She lifted it up three stairs at a time, and set it down with a caution that made her forearm muscles ache. At the landing she sloughed her bag and her other parcels to the mat, removed her shoes, and, in a panic of haste and stealth, slipped off her coat and hung it on the form. The key made complaining little squeals and the door, however slowly she swung it, moaned a little at her ingress. She held her breath. He hadn't seemed to hear her. Quickly, she wheeled the clotheshorse around before her so that she might have been carrying her coat by the shoulders, and swiftly tiptoed across to the open bedroom door. Thank God he wasn't there! She dashed across the carpet, short of breath, and triumphantly buried her surprise behind her dresses. She put her coat back on and tiptoed to the door. Her shoes, her bag, her packages; she turned the key once more as loudly as possible and swung the door both in and out, then called, "Hello, love! Sorry I'm late," and tripped into the living room.

The clock ticked harshly, insisting that it was seven twenty-four. The paper was folded as she had left it on the ceramic coffee table. There were no shoes or sweaters strewn about, so it was hardly worth checking the other rooms. But she did so, calling and threading through the kitchen, his office, her sewing room, the spare.

"Wasted," she said aloud, and then this word seemed so immense that she needed to get rid of her little burdens. She stumbled back to the living room and spilled them on the floor; let her coat fall likewise, as if she had been Jean-Claude; sat down, got up, and threw her shoes one after the other at the fireplace.

This seemed silly. She was a sensible girl. "What have I got to worry about? He hasn't been run over," she said to herself. "He's with Prytania, and not ready to come home. Would I rather he were someplace I didn't know?" But she was shuddering all over with the effort not to answer, "It's Monday night! It's Christmas week! We have so little time!"

She hid her smaller secrets without looking at them again, hung her coat, and put on a pair of flats. She went to the kitchen, deliberately singing, deliberately following the words, and prepared as much as would wait without being ruined: Parmesan croquettes, ready to fry; the steak seasoned, lying in the grill; the *cresson* washed with the dressing standing by; the potatoes peeled and resting in cold water.

After that, she read the paper over again. At nine she put the croquettes in the refrigerator — they would have to do without an hors d'oeuvre tonight. By nine-fifteen it would be too late for potatoes, and they followed. At ten she rewrapped the steaks and ate a little of the sharp *cresson* herself, unseasoned. She lay down on the bed for a while and tried to believe she was tired. Her tear glands had never been very active, a physical matter, and now, though the muscles under her eyes were flexing and burning, she did not cry. "Is this more than I can stand?" she asked directly, but she didn't know the answer. All she knew she couldn't stand was lying in that bed, so she got up and walked, but she had no place in particular to go.

Like most women, dramatic and timid in a crisis, she sat down and wrote a note of temporary good-bye. It said, "Darling, please make my excuses to the Chaumbrés. Nothing drastic, but I need to be away from you for some time. Don't worry. Love, Elena." She laid it on the mantelpiece. Then she put on the black dress which was his favorite, with small jet buttons and a cowl of Spanish lace; skillfully made up her face, put her hair up with such care that each of the four thick locks twisted into their knot took ten minutes, tore up the note, and sat down to wait for him.

At a little after eleven he came home, noisy and

breathless, red and cold from having run in the night air after a shower. He slammed the door aside and into the hole in the plaster he had worn with a thousand similar slammings, calling, "Elena, where are you? Are you furious?"

He hugged her hard, but the damp cold of his cheek, and the smell of some soap she never would have chosen, made her involuntarily recoil.

"Elena? Hey?"

"God damn you, Jean-Claude," was all the inadequate reproach she could seem to muster. He peered into her face, trying with the energy of his remorse to elicit forgiveness. ("His face was very beautiful and funny," Elena said. "No one would have guessed he was thirty-one years old. I had to laugh. I always have to laugh. After five years of marriage my breath still catches when he looks at me directly.")

He panted a little with relief. "Prytania was varnishing the floor. You don't dare leave it half-done, and I'd promised to help."

She recoiled again, but this time didn't show it. It was in her mind to ask, "Is varnishing so strenuous a job that you have to bathe?" But it was a tactful lie, and she realized that her own smile was another. She wasn't sure that hers wasn't the more culpable deception.

She said, "I'm keeping something from you," because this notion had just forcefully occurred to her, but when he looked hurt and scared again, she batted him on the ear and explained, "It's Christmas, silly."

So they went to the party late, and Jean-Claude was brilliant, and when Elena found herself ravenously downing platters of toast *crevettes,* she admonished herself that, the fact was, she could stand it.

"Why, my dear child!" Laura broke in at this point in

her narrative. "You're a martyr! You're out of your mind! Jean-Claude has to be brought up short, it's as simple as that."

"Elena doesn't want to make her husband take the blame," I said. "She wants to keep him," and Elena turned on me a look of astounded gratitude.

Soon after she showed a sudden inclination to be gone, and on an impulse I offered to escort her. Laura declared she would hear of nothing else. Elena demurred, but feebly, and once outside she took my arm and held it hard.

"There's a little more. Do you have to hurry? I've got a raincheck from you, do you remember?"

I led her into the same *brasserie* where I had breakfasted the morning Riebenstahl had died. It was late; the same morning waiter had come on.

"I hope you won't think ill of me for not wanting to say this to Laura too. . . ."

I stopped that line of argument.

Elena said, "I knew her reaction would be just about what it was tonight, but she was the only person I could think of. I suppose there just didn't seem to be any particular reason that you should understand."

"There isn't any particular reason," I said. "But I have so far, and it doesn't feel as if I've reached my limit."

Elena ordered the first of many *absinthes-fausses* in that gaudily lit café, and she relaxed, not in genuine ease, but into a kind of torpor with the mere familiarity of her troubles.

"I've begun to dream that he's slipping away from me. In fog, in sand; the most obvious sort of thing. I told Jean-Claude about it. I said, 'Don't you think it's a bit insulting of my subconscious to be so obvious as that?' I must have meant for him to laugh, but when he laughed I was a little disappointed. He just said, 'It's not too bad, is it, Elena?' I can't measure 'too bad' any more than I can measure 'bearing' it. So all I could answer him was, 'not too bad.' ''

One weird change also was effected in her. As if she were still the small girl of her village, she began to be afraid of the dark. Their apartment was in an ancient building, haven beyond retrieving for cockroaches and mice. Elena had learned to live with these creatures (at least, she went about thwarting them in a very methodical manner, and tolerated such as survived). But one night when she came from her shower barefooted and gowned toward bed, a particularly large and ugly beetle darted from the corner and brushed her toe. She screamed. Jean-Claude sat up, saw the insect run into a corner, protested, "Oh, Elena, for heaven's sake!" and squashed it with the spiral of his paper.

She lay awake until dawn in nameless terror, afraid to wake him for fear of annoying him further, afraid to turn her back on the dark, afraid of cockroaches, shadows, burglars, death and the Devil. She fell asleep only when the light made the shadows innocent, and woke two hours later trembling and exhausted, on the verge of her rare, sparse tears. Jean-Claude was incredulous that she should not have waked him — much more so than at the fact that she should have been afraid — but he did not seem to notice any relevance in her terror to Prytania.

I think she must have been very beautiful that morning, a self-sufficient woman in need of unreasoning protection. Certainly she was beautiful when, ashamed and confused, she told me of it. She sat haggard over her empty glass, toying at the ice with a spoon.

"Well, do you still understand? Will you advise me?"

"Yes, I will," I said, "because my advice is that you've

chosen wisely, and that all you need is the courage to persevere. My advice is that you must continue exactly as you have done, so that when Jean-Claude comes back to you he'll be certain it was his own choice. Elena, Jean-Claude will tire of this little girl. We've nothing else to do but wait for that.''

"Thank you," she said, "and thank you for the 'we.' Does that mean that I can talk to you sometimes?''

She did that, and she took my advice as well, but she also built a second defense of her own, which for the time she kept secret even from me. I suppose she was not the first to try it, and I should not have been very surprised had I known of it. The wonder is not that she determined to have a baby, but that our century had provided her with the means. I, who act as a dozen Majesties' purveyor of contraceptives, never fail in awe that science has put this power in a woman's hands, to gamble on the hour of her pregnancy without her husband's knowledge, and to call it an accident if she so wishes.

They played the whole gamut of passion, or played at it. Jean-Claude, of course, could feign any emotion that had a name, and Prytania became so adept at the various poses of female submission and coquetry that she was something more than a straight man to him. He would put on the face of a pious Englishman or an American gangster, taunting her for her pleasure with the indifference of either. She would fling herself in passionate supplication at his feet, incidentally tickling his ankles, which were cruelly sensitive; or in another mood she would rub her thigh against his arm, arching her belly like a lean kitten, and like a kitten predatory, unabashedly sensual. Jean-Claude would raise the Englishman's eyebrow at me and observe, in a tone of sociological frigidity while she bit his ear, "It's the Negress in her," and all of us would laugh.

But what warmth there was was of their own making. In winter The Little House was all but unheatable, penetrated by the damp of the park behind, whipped by the wind where the boulevard forked before it. Prytania learned, and took great pride in it, how to maintain the level of her fuel supply, but the old pipes wheezed with unproductive effort, and the thermostat that Auguste de Verbois had installed was always at odds with Riebenstahl's thermometer. When the three of us were there, a coal fire in the grate, the air thick with the smell of my cigar, I sometimes even shed my jacket, and Prytania would lift her hair from her neck and let it tumble for a fan. But she admitted that when she was alone she felt the winter, and that her isolation made it deeper.

She said to me once, oiling the elephantine leaves of her rubber plant. "You've no idea what it takes to convince a tropical plant it can live in this atmosphere." Sometimes I was startled by her observations, at once intense and banal, so that it seemed some *double-entendre* must have been intended. But I had seen too many mistake her literalness for conscious subtlety, and knew that she was only speaking of the weather.

She talked incessantly of spring and summer, of restoring Riebenstahl's garden and opening the windows to the park. Jean-Claude had promised her an invitation to the Easter family festival at L'Isle Automne, and this date took on the authority of the calendar for her; so that, oddly, when she said, "Automne," she meant, "the spring."

Meanwhile the year had only just turned over. She struggled to keep her plants from drooping and, increasingly, to keep her spirits at the pitch Jean-Claude exacted. She sometimes failed at this. One night when it happened that we left together, Prytania reached vaguely out toward both of us and said, "I wish I didn't know I was living in a dead man's home."

Jean-Claude cheerfully, not unkindly, scoffed.

"So are ninety-nine per cent of the other Parisians," he assured her. "For that matter, you're probably living in a dozen dead men's home."

After that, he made it more than ever a point to speak with unsentimental admiration of the old man, whose accident was to be infinitely lamented, but certainly not the occasion for inventing ghosts.

As always, Prytania instantly adopted Jean-Claude's tone. But when he wasn't there, she spoke of Riebenstahl — and of Kenneth and Madame — in a different way. She made the comment on their friend's death, that it had come at the moment of his life's only triumph, and without that triumph's having caused him anything but confusion and pain. She wondered how much Madame blamed her, and whether the stairs were becoming more difficult for her. She tried to justify, what she could scarcely articulate, that now that Kenneth was proven to have accepted them without reproach, she felt more guilty toward him than before. She came back, like someone tonguing a toothache, to these three. I listened, neither agreeing nor reassuring her, which seemed to afford her some relief, for when Jean-Claude came she could tacitly, enthusiastically deny — by jumping to dish his *julienne*, by averring chagrin at the mud on his shoes — that she had any concerns that were not he.

When, as more and more frequently happened, Jean-Claude spent Monday evening with Prytania, we performed a ritual of my invention at which the others became even more original and adept. At about a quarter to ten I said that I'd have to go or be locked in the park all night. Prytania affected dismay, and Jean-Claude assured me I could easily scale the fence. I protested age. The two of them threw up a screen of laughter, Jean-Claude demonstrated in mime how an octogenarian could do it with a hand-up, and Prytania calculated my probable age in centuries. In such hilarity, I could escape, they could get rid of me, without our having suggested that I was leaving them to bed.

But I didn't leave the park before the gates closed. I stuck to the fence-side of the trees, where the patrolman wouldn't see me, remarking from the clearings when the living room was dark, when the lights went on upstairs, and when they too went out.

Prytania hadn't invited me up to the bedroom since her décor was done. She ought to have done so, for as I wandered in the dark deserted park I had an awful image of that room, that the red birds on the wallpaper had pecked through the paint like shells, and that it too was filled with armored plants. I pictured these sprouting from the sill (which, however, gave forth a perfectly regular rectangle of light), and from stunted banks about the bed. I could see — could not *not* see — Prytania dark and taut among them, and Jean-Claude oddly out of place in the person of his scavenger, too exuberant, too pale, loping foolishly in search of his clothes and saying (her mouth flashed down at the outer corners, a second's stung pain that he didn't see), "Dress now, lazybones. I won't play ladies' maid."

When the police went off the beat I sat for a moment on the monument, rubbing my hands over Dionysus' rough cold peaches, that had been so smooth and trembling in July. Then I took another turn, made inventory of the chestnut trees, and when I supposed Jean-

Claude had gone, I sought a spot I had discovered in the fence. The pedestal of a concrete urn stood half the height of the picket railing here, and on the other side a tree trunk forked conveniently. I could get up, across and down in three clean thrusts, without any of those gutturals that old men make.

Jean-Claude was the last of them to confide in me. And with good reason: Jean-Claude had Prytania. When he had worked back and forth between Riebenstahl and the troupe, he had used Prytania much as one uses a dictaphone, storing ideas there to recall verbatim and at will, not discarding them but setting them aside, so that for once his mind was stripped down free to the work at hand.

He was an incessant and enthusiastic talker, as if he had to use up his stock of words in order to keep silent on the stage. In The Little House he lectured on his work to both of us, stretched on the couch and, later, in a changing mood, pacing the length of the room and pricking his hands against the plants. At first, as with Elena, I was but an auxiliary listener. Then later he would leave with me and we would walk together up Wagram, Jean-Claude gesticulating, cogitating, unaware that he sparked interest in every passing woman because, whatever it was in Jean-Claude that needed an audience, it was not egotism.

Things were changing around him, he said, for he had not changed. This was untrue, of course, and Jean-Claude saw that it was as soon as the words were out. His very manner of moving had been changing, as if he'd bought spare energy from a questionable source. He admitted to muddle and (once for every leaf in The Little House, once for every lamppost on Wagram) tried to explain again.

It had, muddle had, caught him first at the Poche, the least appropriate possible place, for it was here that he had learned, under Yves' irascible tutelage, that most things are not as difficult as they seem if clarity and health and industry are brought to bear upon them. It came in the form of expectation for his future, which, as the months went by and he had no sequel outlined for *Mimes Mécaniques*, took on a skeptical, even a taunting, air. He was conscious himself of a void in his mind where a project ought to be. He made no symbol of Riebenstahl's demise; they had worked together to some purpose, but he had never supposed that the partnership was a permanent one. He had on the contrary simply assumed that when he had squeezed this one idea dry, what he wanted to do would be as much clearer to himself as he had made it to his colleagues and the press, and that other incarnations would spring like mushrooms in the dark.

It didn't happen. All his images were of human machines, or else they slipped back into the anecdotal mode of mime that he had by now committed himself to defy. It didn't help when he discovered that Etienne D'Arno, who had never exhibited the least resentment of his prominence among the protégés, was making dire predictions behind his back. Or when Toto, with a laughter vaguely unpleasant, warned, "You'd better come up with something soon, old man, or they'll call you a one-shot and give all the credit to your sculptor friend."

He did the thing he had always done, which had always worked before, and which had prevented his having to feel the isolation of the favorite: he confessed that he made no progress, and that it worried him. Individually the troupe was sympathetic, but that did not impede his noticing that some conversations stopped when he arrived, or his suddenly realizing that his closest friends were waiting, and would not be broken-hearted, to see him fail.

Yves was more patient, but he was not used to seeing Yves be patient; and the open affection, sullied with respectfulness, that marked the master's behavior toward him now, was as ungratifying as the cant of *politesse*. Yves, when Jean-Claude admitted, or rather insisted, that his mind was blank, said only, "Work and wait and wait and work," which was no conceivable use, and was so unlike the goading anger he had come to lean on, that he was almost angry for the first time himself.

"You're getting old, Yves," he chided in return, and was dismayed to hear the indulgent, sad reply, "Yes, yes. I was thinking it was time you noticed that."

Not that Adam stopped giving him advice. Only that he indulged insinuations now instead of dictums, and that Jean-Claude felt this as betrayal. One afternoon when Jean-Claude was called upon to demonstrate improvisational technique to a class of tyros, Yves found his performance lacking in variety, and made the occasion an excuse for a lecture bearing only indifferently on the mime.

"Never to get trapped," he bombastically announced, and some of the little idiots took notes, "by a theme or an idea or a woman, is the first tenet of a productive life. Every fiddler has to be a Nero, remember that, and if he burns his fingers that's the hazards of the game. Never put a girl to bed for anything but fun," — a titter ran around the room, signifying that the master had gained in popularity — "and never follow your fancy once you see it's turned a dud. Crutches only make a sound man clumsy."

Jean-Claude left the classroom with high color in his cheeks, first because he had been reprimanded in the sight of his inferiors (this was the wrong his reason fastened on) ; second, because the meaning was so bald; third (we were well into February before this last came out) , because the message had hit home.

The odd thing for him to discover was that adultery had never much attracted him. Thanks to Elena, he'd never had to give it any thought, because she'd freed him to follow the impulse of the given moment. He should have used the freedom, certainly, but it shocked him now to feel it as a duty. The arguments against their establishing a routine of assignation had been so practical and so conclusive that he had been totally unprepared for the advent of The Little House.

"It's one thing to have two women waiting in bed for you," he said. "It's another to find two women hanging curtains."

But worst of all for Jean-Claude was the drain on his time, and the sense that, without a single word of reproach from either of them, he was giving insufficiently of himself to both. Elena had never since they married, directly or by insinuation, complained that they spent too little time together — not even in the weeks before an opening, when he got home only to sleep, not even when he left her for whole months on a foreign tour. Now she watched clocks, set sauces cold and congealed before him, outlined the schedule of her week in such a way as to make it clear that, very likely, they should not see each other until Monday. Prytania had, all the time he was embroiled in *Mimes Mécaniques,* been simply there, whenever he wanted her, making no demands on either his attention or his time. Now she incorporated into their love a fantasy that every hour they had was stolen, and stunning as she was in this little melodrama, he could not but see occasionally that she believed it. It was spoiled for him when he found himself reacting: dammit, that's absurd!

Yet he couldn't really say that they were wrong. He would be late to the Poche from having lunch at The Little House, late home to dinner from having detoured for a cocktail with Prytania, late to Prytania from a long rehearsal. He was fundamentally unpunctual; no one had ever blamed him for it. Now everywhere he felt the same reproach: I have to be up at eight, you know. When are you going to give us your new mime? The waiting was agony, Jean-Claude!

An American tour for *Mimes Mécaniques* was proposed, and when in March the papers were officially signed, Jean-Claude was excited to a spurt of new ambition. He found himself with a few tentative ideas for choreography. Was it possible to base a mime on a series of sports and games? He talked it, walked it out in the living room of The Little House, plotting a chessboard on the raffia rug, conjuring a company of ebony and ivory figures that insensibly maneuvered each other off the board.

One Saturday I ran into him as we were both headed for the park, and for my sake he walked the long way around. He was discouraged.

"I haven't been out of the Poche since breakfast, and I've got to be back for costume call in half an hour. It hit me all at once what a cut-and-dried race war it's going to seem, and if I dress them in other colors the critics will only be confused. It's a goal of mine to do intricate things and never to get called obscure . . ."

He was still talking when we entered the house, and stopped just over the threshold, more bewildered than anything, to see Prytania on his sofa prostrate and dumb

with grief. We stood for a dazed moment; then she rose
and stumbled to him.

"You . . . promised to arrive at four."

He stroked her hair and questioned her with desperate patience, trying to find out what calamity had be-
fallen her, unable to comprehend that it was only his
being late.

"Oh, Jean-Claude, don't you see I have so precious
little of you. I try, forgive me, but every day revolves
around whether you may be here or not. When I expect
you and you don't come, I can't see beyond the night I
have to face."

I thought I should have been the more conspicuous
by going, so I stood rooted in the doorway while he
stroked her hair and she wept.

"Oh, Jean-Claude, if we only had some whole unbroken time together. Sunrise to sunrise, or — think of
it! — a week."

"Yes, yes, my love, of course I want it too." His eyes
were pacing out the room, not rid of the chessboard
yet.

"You've no idea how good I'd be, what a help to you,
and how happy."

"You've always been a help to me, Prytania."

"Oh, no. Not now. I ask too much of you. Jean-
Claude . . ." she raised her eyes with a fearful flicker to
his face and buried them damply again in the side of his
neck, ". . . if I could go along to America, you'd see
how good I'd be."

"Shhh, hush, Prytania. We haven't got the money."

She lifted her head once more, for a long while
watching him to see if this were the only objection he
would raise. Then finally, with fresh tears falling from
under her giant lids, she pleaded, "But we do, I do. I've
enough to pay my fare."

Her fragile skeleton shuddered with the effort of her sobs. She wrapped herself around him with a weight that dragged him down.

"All right, my love," he said. "Don't cry. All right, we'll go together."

Elena said, "I was just out of the shower when he rang the bell, winding my hair up in a turkish towel. There's so much of it — my hair — that I have to use a bath-sized one, and then it looks like one of those medieval cone headdresses; it looks absurd."

She wasn't expecting anyone at this hour, and she thought Jean-Claude had forgotten his key again. She put on a robe, likewise of toweling, which caught most of the water, though she still left footprints on the parquet and the rug.

"I'm coming!" She slipped the latch and opened the door, ready with a reproof. It was a tall blond boy she'd seen somewhere before, though she didn't place him.

("There were puffy creases around his eyes that didn't suit the smoothness of his skin, the way a baby's flesh will crease where there are no joints.")

"May I come in?"

She would have said no, but he had already done so, passed her and crossed to the window, with too much effort, too many movements to accomplish such a small distance, and no apparent reason for doing so, for when he got there he looked not out of the window but at the wall beside it. She followed him, looping the belt of her robe tighter and sliding one collar under the other up to her chin.

"You don't remember me," he said, turning, his hands in his overcoat pockets and his legs splayed for balance. There was no hurt in it, but enough surprise that Elena answered, "I'm sorry . . ."

He shrugged.

"Kenneth Stoddard. I'm engaged to your husband's mistress." ("Like an eight-year-old who says son-of-a bitch," Elena told me, "not the least interested in the meaning of the words, but its being important to him, necessary, that he shock you.")

"My husband isn't home," she said.

"Your husband is at the Parc Fasseville," Kenneth told her, again harshly, wanting an effect, so that Elena, who knew perfectly well where her husband was, was a little piqued.

"That's right. And I was taking a bath, so if you'll excuse me . . ."

"There's a bar called Aux Deux Courcelles where the boulevard meets the rue. It's got a plate-glass window, and if you pick the right spot you can get drunk in full view of the house."

But he wasn't drunk. She doubted if he'd had a full glass of beer. He plopped himself down on her sofa, trying to be impudent about it, but spending too much energy to succeed at that. He took out a pack of cigarettes and lit one, the first match breaking as it struck, so that he had to stamp the flame out on the rug. He glared at her for it, and when she saw how his clumsiness mortified him, she was no longer angry. She'd have liked to offer to light his cigarette, but he managed the second match all right and sagged back, puffing hard. It was more to be generous than anything, to fool him into thinking that he'd achieved his effect, that she said sarcastically, "Thanks. If I ever want to get drunk in that particular view, I'll remember it."

"There's also the Bateau Blanc down by the entrance, but he doesn't use the entrance. He takes the fence right there at the flatiron, without even looking around. You'd think somebody'd stop him sometime, but nobody ever does. That's what I mean, you see. You'd think somebody'd stop him. It only takes him a second. He's better coordinated than he looks. That fancy-man type usually turn out to be corseted jelly when it comes to it."

Elena left him and went back into the bathroom. She put on her slippers, unwound her hair, and let it fall, picking up a comb. Then she went back.

"If you like," she said, "I'll insult Prytania, and we can spend the evening that way. I don't see much point in it, but if it would relieve you, I don't mind."

She went to the mirror over the mantelpiece and began to comb her hair. There was just enough curl in it to make it tangle, and there was no use hurrying the process. It had to be done a lock at a time, starting at the bottom and working back up toward her scalp by inches. She didn't really need the mirror for it, and the sight of her face afforded her no pleasure, for she thought herself unhandsome without make-up, not the sort that looks best in strong sunlight, straight from the sea. But she didn't know what else to look at. Not at the boy, whom she ought to have sent away and didn't send away because . . . because he was company, perhaps, or perhaps because it was sweet to have someone trying so hard to make her angry.

He said abruptly, petulant, "I came here because I find that I don't know exactly what I'm doing, and I thought maybe you could tell me."

At that, she stole a glance at him in the mirror. He was hunched into his overcoat as into a small cave, his eyes vacant but for fatigue. A spark dropped on his collar, hung glowing for a moment and went out.

"What is it that you're doing?"

"I'm being generous, and sane. It seems to be the

local pastime. The English don't like to be outdone at sanity, certainly not by the French and Spaniards."

He laughed joylessly. That anyone should have to handle anything so badly, emotion like a double handful of balanced eggs, touched her, endeared him to her inexpressibly. It would have seemed natural to fold his blond head on her bosom and stroke it, saying, "There-there, there-there."

"My aunt must have given them the house, but she's getting no returns, as far as I can see. As far as I can see she's losing a hundred and twenty francs and about a kilo a month for it. And she can't talk about it, or she won't. I offered to be useful to them, but I couldn't tell you why. It seemed the only alternative, but now I could think of several, like wiring the fence or catching him hard in the stomach with my fist."

"Or coming here to take it out on me," Elena said.

"Because they don't even do that — make use of me. Every couple of weeks I take Prytania out for a walk or a drink, and I let her fidget till it's time to go home. Oh, I let her. I thought perhaps you could tell me why."

"No, I don't think so." She tugged at a snarl. Jean-Claude outrageous, mouthing the flesh below her thumb and smelling of Prytania's soap. Because whoever loves most owes most, she could have said, because the debt lies with the one more loving. But she said again, "I don't think I could."

"The whole thing seems to have been your idea, you see."

"My idea?" Elena said, and turned to face him. "*My* idea?"

"I thought it might turn out to be as simple as that you don't give a damn. If it's that simple I might know where to start from, to start over again."

The sullenness trembled along his boy's jaw as he glared at her, ready at any instant to collapse into some other trembling. ("All at once — no, not all at once but in two distinct and separate parts, I was aware of how bare my skin was underneath the robe, and how easily I could take that boy to bed. Right now, in that robe that makes me bulky, and my hair clammy, clinging to my neck. One kind word, one hand on his shoulder and he'd have tumbled into me like a pile of leaves. I couldn't remember the last time I'd felt that certainty. It would do him good, I thought, and that pleased me, made me faintly proud. I thought it might have done me no harm.")

"I guess," she said, "that you had better go now."

"I'm sorry. I didn't really think it was that simple."

"I'm not angry. I just think you'd better go."

He stood and thrashed the air aside with a slender, impotent hand.

"Total acquiescence, is that it? We've got no weapon but patience, and we aren't even going to look for another, is that it?"

"It's a question of alternatives," she said.

"I've heard that before. I even listened to it. All I want to hear from you is that we aren't going to do anything. Is that it?"

She replied, careful not to be too gentle, "Nothing we can help each other with."

("I left the room before he did and went back into the bathroom and waited till I heard the latch click. Then I slipped off the robe — I don't do this sort of thing — and looked at me. Oh, don't bother to look yourself, I won't show for months yet. But if I relax my muscles and throw my weight forward I can see how it will be."

(She instinctively did so as she rose to leave the *brasserie,* braiding her fingers across the false mound and ever so slightly rocking, smiling at me, holding on to her belly as if it were a point of balance.

("Not total acquiescence all the same," she said.)

Prytania was in a high fury of little plans. She bought some clothes. She was thinking of flying for a weekend to New Orleans. If only Jean-Claude could make it too! She'd had to have new luggage.

She modeled for us a crackling dress the blue of gas flame — not the sort that Elena would have chosen for her, but suiting her youth and, above all, her mood, perhaps better than high fashion could have.

"Is this too bare for Easter? It'll be stifling in Louisiana in May." She chattered around us, pirouetting so that the brilliant cotton flew and exposed the polish of her thighs.

"Hotter than Paris was last summer. You can't imagine it unless you've been there. Wait. I have another one for evening."

She skipped away to change. We watched the legs flash up the stairs and out of view.

"And Elena?" I asked. "What does she say to it?"

Jean-Claude stretched back on the couch and slid his feet between two potted cacti.

"Oh, well . . . I've been making a study of the sins of omission. I find they're distinguishable from the deadly ones. It was you who gave me my first lesson in it, remember?"

"I remember," I said.

"And you think this is all right too?"

"It seems to me," I replied, "that the essence of honesty is being essential about it. After all, one doesn't tell one's mother, 'I find you utterly ridiculous, but I love you anyway.' One's mother would only hear the first part of the sentence. One must find what's true for oneself, and then translate mere facts into terms that will make it comprehensible to another."

"The mime — or any art — is a lifetime's effort to do exactly that," he assured me gratefully, and took his legs off the table again.

Prytania returned in silk, and then in a suit the color of wheat chaff, and then carrying two black valises of finest pigskin. When Jean-Claude left she was nervous, and held him almost bodily back, then walked with him to the fence. When she returned her high spirits had spilled over into skittishness. She opened the larger of the cases and hurriedly began tossing scarves and sandals into it.

"You must have been very frugal with your salary," I said.

She hastily denied it. "I remember being poor, but I never learned how to be frugal." She closed the lid on the evidence of this and slipped the cases out of sight in the stairwell.

"I had quite a lot of money suddenly in England. It was meant to keep me in vac, but I always got asked to someone's summer place. I got to taking those summers as my due, and not realizing I hadn't spent my allowance on them. You know that got me in trouble once before."

She was, I saw, consummately oblivious that she had betrayed herself with this "before."

The days were lengthening now, and it was not yet dark, but the house had kept its chill, and a light rain splintered against the panes. Prytania made a fire. I watched her rolling newspapers into rods, coiling these about her fist and tucking the edges in, laying a bed of them to support the coals. Her hands performed the actions deftly, with a vanity that stabbed the heart. So might a palsy victim master a thimble or a pen, announcing with his expression, "I'm getting on — I can do for myself."

She struck a match and turned a little from the mounting flame, her features caught golden in the first brief flare. I had never altogether lost the sense that her flesh was wax. In certain lights, like this one, the impression struck with double force. She expelled a little breath that served for a laugh, and I could predict before it came the expression, defiant and self-deprecating, that would mold her features as she explained herself. Familiarity ought to be a little wearisome; but this foreknowledge, fulfilled on her face the instant it came to mind, gave me a sense of sway, delicious and disquieting. It was as if my thought had been translated by her skin; as if, made malleable in the sudden heat, that substance could be rearranged at a signal from my brain.

"I used to be the darling of everybody's parents. When I didn't know how to use their salad forks and butter knives, they'd pat me on the head and tell me, never mind, I had the makings of a perfect lady."

The bridge of her nose produced its one high wrinkle of distaste, and she laughed. She moved her stool back from the fire and set it against my chair, cupping her knees in her hands and swinging them lightly from side to side. The hem of her skirt swished on my shins.

"I just bought clothes and clothes, and then things to keep them in, and then I'd give them all away. When I finally passed the sixth form I just took off for the Continent. It didn't occur to me that I wouldn't be able to live the whole year as well as I did on a holiday . . ."

Her voice trailed off and her knees stopped swinging at the angle nearest me. They were trembling.

"Imagine . . . imagine never having any money to manage at all, and then having more than you know what to buy with. It's demoralizing, really."

The thought of helping her go away, even for a short time, chilled me. But I saw there was no help for it, and in a wild flash of humor I remembered telling Harold, "I don't expect she'll write for a million francs, and if she does she won't get it."

"How much do you need, Prytania?" I asked gently.

She sprang from her chair and gestured vaguely to where her luxurious litter had been strewn, murmuring, "I didn't dare to tell him I'd overspent. He'd be angry, he can't get any, *she'd* never have been so foolish . . ."

"Five thousand francs?"

"Oh no!" The exclamation was more for relief than shock. I stood up, and she came toward me. "A thousand is all I need. The fare one way. I'm awfully stupid. I'm awfully sorry . . ."

"Well, well, we can't have you stranded in America, can we?" I said archly. "I'll get it for you in cash tomorrow; that will be easiest."

She leaned and kissed me clumsily on the lower cheek.

"Jean-Claude is right. Everyone conspires to make us happy," she said, smiled broadly and dissolved immediately in tears.

"Jean-Claude mustn't know." I pulled her to me, and she let herself be folded against the roughness of my jacket, resting with the sudden stillness of a broken bird that surrenders itself at last to a human palm.

PART FOUR

*The Dancer
from the Dance*

*L*UCE AND HAROLD came home for the holiday. We met their plane at Orly on Easter morning and went directly on to Seine-et-Oise; exchanging, after a year and a half apart, such vital information as that vegetables were high and that from above the Channel had looked calm.

We were lucky in the weather, which was sharp but windless, of a stunning clarity, and had brought the maximum holiday mass out toward the suburbs and the country. Our train clacked lazily past the deserted factories and the still-brown dahlia farms, which gradually gave way to myriad hills of pregnant sheep; finally (not an island at all, but a steep little plateau caught in a hook of the Oise) the walls and red tile chimneys of L'Isle Automne.

We climbed to the Bastien home and entered by the cobbled carriageway of the oldest building. We wandered in the court until we located our hostess, Jean-Claude's mother — a woman like a benevolent Medusa, with an immense, impressively ugly face, awesome masses of springing hair and a manner so mild that one suspected fraud. The women began to speak of domestic outrage in the fields of delivery and part-time help.

The family houses of the Bastiens and the Charles-De Vries, one ancient and three modern, formed three sides of a flagstone terrace, which opened on the other to a garden-orchard leading into woods. Flagstone, again, in the form of a knee-high wall, set off the garden and, leaning into it with igneous determination, seemed to have scooped it up like a bulldozer and made a stage of it. Thus elevated, fifty of the clan, and as many more who might be supposed to wish Jean-Claude success in America, drank and sidestepped chocolate poultry, marzipan rodents and small children, the latter desperately employed in an egg-hunt among the shrubs.

I was struck with an uncanny force that each familiar member of the cast — surrounded by the multitude of extras, juveniles in the main — was overacting a role intended for someone older and of opposite demeanor. Jean-Claude, for one, was fidgety, a little shrill and haggard, compulsively downing quantities of dry white wine and edging back and forth along the wall. Yves was melted into a clutch of elders at the back, his beard drooping over the bosom of a matron in conspicuous mourning. Elena's softness had gone thick and taut, her pallor harsh, so that I thought, "Take care, my girl; you're on your way to being well preserved." Prytania, like one of those limp marionettes whose sagging joints deny the inflexibility of the parts between, stood in no particular place with her attention somewhere else, on one foot and another, vaguely chattering without a pause into a group that listened with intense uninterest. Kenneth had lost the energy of his angles; no extraneous gesture, no gratuitous flexing of the knees or ankles marred his deliberate glide of middle age as he carried a brimful glass across the lawn. He paused, exchanged with Elena a greeting wordless on both sides, and continued toward some old lady gaunt with the gauntness of formerly full flesh, who sat consuming a green pear with a fork. She had been placed, this lady, in a wooden chair with a child's hoop set against the side, so that for a space of half a dozen glances while I watched the sober Kenneth, I believed that she was seated in a wheelchair. Gradually it invaded my consciousness that wheelchair tires are unlikely to be yellow, and only then did I focus on the ancient, and recognize Madame.

I excused myself and picked my way among the children, two of whom chased each other around Prytania's legs without her being in the least aware of them. When I called her name she focused sharply and left her listeners in the middle of a phrase.

"He hasn't spoken to me. I don't even know which *is* his mother."

"Come," I said. "My son-in-law is here. We're going to spring you on him and see if we can make that Teutonic jaw fall open." I grinned to encourage her, and she followed obediently after me to where Harold was terrifying two Charles-DeVries children with his amicable advances. I noted once again that my son-in-law was large, simply and entirely; even the small of his back was large, and his voice was the size of a tank when he turned and discharged, "How d'you do?"

Prytania returned the phrase and waited, with a profound lack of expression, to be recognized. It was the same look she had first turned on Kenneth, but now, I knew, she had brought it forth at will.

"Do you live in Paris?" Harold asked too forcefully, like someone who resents having to begin the conversation. Not the remotest glimmer crossed his face.

"Miss Obée, has spent some time in Frankfurt," I replied. "An afternoon." I thought my manner as broad as a dig in the ribs, but Harold observed with the severest gravity, "That's not enough."

Medusa Bastien, with a benignity that was generally interpreted as a threat, intimated here and there that luncheon had been laid, and a collection of grass baskets by the children, of children by their parents, and of parents by aproned female Bastiens ensued. A pair of lunging adolescents separated me from Harold and Prytania, and they moved off ahead. Elena was at my side.

"Well? You see that he's asked her here. Do I have to take that too?"

"You don't have to take anything, Elena. You never have had to. I thought it was something you'd decided on."

"Sorry." She touched my arm and walked on very erect beside me.

We herded each other into a hall that was severally used for dinners, family musicals and bookbinding. The imperfect setting of the ceiling beams and a certain disuniformity of the plaster betrayed that the room was the work of amateurs. Not so the profusion on the trestle tables. It was hard to believe that even the Bastien fields had provided running room for so many legs of lamb. Sauces pungent with their wines, wines with the vitality of spice, and minor masterpieces of a vegetable nature crowded as they might among the cutlery and crystal. Buttery vapors mushroomed forth from a quantity of mashed potato that staggered the imagination. One would not have dared compute the number of teeth required for the mastication of such a feast.

No doubt at every table in the room some form of sparring and maneuvering took place. At ours, Mrs. Bastien conscripted Jean-Claude and Elena and installed them at her flanks. I was already next to Elena, so I stayed there. Laura slipped in beside Jean-Claude, too quickly for Prytania, who rounded the table and sat on the other side of me. Luce and Harold, Kenneth and Madame came hard upon us, Madame panting a little at Kenneth's urging. Yves passed by us and lodged himself with Jean-Claude's father at a farther table.

The scraping of chairs continued for considerable time, under cover of which everyone either did or did not acknowledge his neighbor. Prytania looked steadily toward Jean-Claude, but he ignored her altogether and uncorked three bottles in quick succession.

"Mme Bastien," I said, "I don't think you've met Prytania Obée, and Kenneth Stoddard."

Mme Bastien nodded her bristling hair to Prytania and beamed on Kenneth.

"Aren't you the doctor? Really, I think everybody should be a doctor."

Prytania, her voice thick with disappointment, said that she was enchanted.

Elena, who was unaccountably attired in the kind of dress that a woman with a bosom can't wear — a bulk of pleats hung from her highest rib — sighed lightly, and Jean-Claude filled all his mother's glasses.

"And from England, too!" Mme Bastien amplified Kenneth's virtues, "like the Powers' children." She widened her horrendous smile to Luce, who ameliorated things a little with some observations on Channel crossing.

Jean-Claude declared, apropos of nothing, "Alley

oop!" and spilled some wine in the vicinity of Elena's glass.

Mme de Verbois was saying something about children, which got Laura successfully launched on the subject of her own. Harold involved Kenneth in an immediate assessment of the cricket season. Prytania stared at her soup plate, with bewildered glances at Jean-Claude.

"Some salt," I suggested, and she jumped a little and reached for it, just as Elena half-rose to do the same. Their hands lit on the cellar in the same electric instant; the stubby ones not altogether innocent of ink, and the long ones, lustrous with the care of lacquer and expensive cream. Their eyes met over the bridge of my nose — I think I drew in my chin — and of course in the derangement of the day, Prytania broadly smiled and Elena stared with blank indifference.

I leaned between them to my soup, wondering if the glance would break or bend around me, and concentrated on whether the turtle was mock or not. It must have broken. It was Prytania who finally withdrew her hand; and Elena, with a purposeful fist, took possession of the salt.

"I do say," Mme Bastien pleasantly remarked to her daughter-in-law, "That these new fashions make a woman look four months pregnant."

"Surely not so much as that," Elena answered, shaking the cellar with a vengeance. "That's a cliché quite unworthy of you, Maman."

"Unworthy, unworthy," Jean-Claude pronounced, and waved a bottle in the air. I felt Prytania's shoulder stiffen into my upper arm, and realized with her that Jean-Claude was roundly drunk.

"For the love of Christ, Jean-Claude," Elena said.

But Jean-Claude exchanged the bottle for his glass. "To the love of Christ," he proposed, and drained it down.

A silence. Medusa Bastien picked up her glass and smiled in general appeal.

"To the love of Christ," she repeated with such reverence that there was nothing for it but to take our goblets up. Prytania sat rigid with dismay, but I clinked Laura's unsteady rim across the table, and the rest made uncertain gestures and furtive sips. At the table next us someone repeated the toast in religious tones, and the love of Christ went on being proposed to the frontiers of the room.

"Purest love that ever was," Jean-Claude insisted, beaming on his triumph, and although Laura took up a rapid catalogue of Luce's accomplishments, her breathlessness could not hope to cover Kenneth's steely, "Tell us all about it, Bastien."

"I will, I will," Jean-Claude promised, but he did not just then, for three serving girls descended, whisked away the soup plates and took the steam lids from the platters of lamb.

"You must let me know whether you marinate in vinegar or lemon," Laura demanded of Mme Bastien.

"Kenneth," Madame pleaded in a murmur.

Luce said, "The English think a lamb is an undersized mutton."

"Shocking," I put in.

"Tell us all about pure love, Bastien," Kenneth repeated, glowering.

"Oh, but surely," said Jean-Claude's mother, in what would have been a fluttery tone if it had issued from any but that awesome visage, "it was Christ, wasn't it? Sir," to Kenneth, "you must have an Easter egg."

Kenneth snatched one from the basket and began shedding its painted shell on his cavalry twill.

"Someone care to share it?" He challenged Prytania with his eyes.

"I will," Elena said.

Prytania watched him slice the egg and deliver half across the table. Her fingers sought my own beneath the table. I clenched them hard. Kenneth deliberately took the whole half hard-boiled egg in his mouth.

"Tell us, Bastien."

Jean-Claude looked up and gave Kenneth one of his handsome, open smiles.

"Now I've been giving considerable thought to that, and have come to the conclusion that our definitions are inadequate. We seem to lose the last vestiges of objectivity." He was either altogether addled, or else he was parodying his own style of argument. He held his fork like a pencil and described a few miniscule arcs, evidently representing definitions. Then he tried to hang the fork on his ear, but it was too heavy to lodge there, so he slipped it tines-foremost into his pocket instead.

Harold laughed loudly. Elena turned to me with a gesture of frank appeal, but, pressing Prytania's fingers, I only shrugged with my eyes. Laura signaled a desperate series of dry swallows. Everyone, apparently, looked to me to set things right. I gently disengaged my hand and helped myself to lamb.

"I agree with you," I said. "Even the most detached of minds become hopelessly muddled when they get to love. Whereas, essentially, there is no reason we shouldn't bring the same methods of analysis to bear on that subject as on any other."

"This man understands me," Jean-Claude generously announced. He looked at his cutlery and, finding no fork, picked up his spoon and began very correctly eating small mounds of potato purée.

Kenneth spat out a contemptuous noise that would have done credit to Yves.

"I see what you're getting at," I corrected, composedly, "but I can hardly understand you without having heard you out. What definitions would you like to see embraced?"

Laura gaped at me.

"Definitions of love embraced," Mme Bastien explained at large, and giggled a little, but it was not a contagious sort of giggle.

Jean-Claude pushed back his chair and rose to a professorial stance. He propped his plate against the bread basket to make a lectern of it, and a dribble of mint sauce ran onto the tablecloth. He cleared his throat, patted his pocket and, discovering the fork, clinked it loudly against an empty bottle. The sound reached only the nearest tables, but their obedient hush spread raggedly to the edges of the hall. When the stillness was complete Jean-Claude held his two filled glasses aloft.

"Ladies and gentlemen," he expansively proclaimed, "we are fortunate in having among us two superlative sorts of wine. The white a Puligny-Montrachet — a little young, be it observed — but nonetheless on that account as exciting as it is dry. One might say thin, but one does not ask rose leaves to be thick. The red a heady, heavy Chambertin; fruity and vital, rich and ripe, with the authority of a vintage year. Ladies and gentlemen, I propose a toast to: wine."

Cheering and laughter as Jean-Claude drank off one glass and then a second, and others all around us did the same.

"The Bastien cellars!" someone augmented the salute, and Jean-Claude's dapper father took a bow among the shouts. Jean-Claude let the fork ring out again, and waited for silence.

"We praise our women as our wine," he orated, almost sang, "with this subtle difference: that we fully appreciate the one only when it's empty, the other only when it's full."

A raucous roar broke instantly, only afterwards subsiding into hesitant titters as some began to wonder which of the possible paradoxes Jean-Claude meant. He rapped the bottle again; the noise died quickly, trained by now.

"Great love and true love are distinct from separate entities," Jean-Claude went on. His tone announced so patently that he was "going on" that except in our immediate vicinity the hush was calm; patient for his revelation of how this was relevant.

"Great love and true love," he repeated. "Nor is endurance a sufficient test for either. For ether will wither a living thing, but what endures indefinitely in a vacuum may decay in a matter of hours in air."

He paused an instant to let this sink in, but I am not at all sure that it did so, for not an expression altered in the room. At our table, a single-minded concentration on the cutlery, around us a pleasant air of expectation and goodwill.

"Great love involves impossibility," he explained. "Great love is great because it inspires toward the sense of all that cannot be." He inclined himself toward Prytania, but he looked at no one. He cupped his hand and stared into it as if he were reading notes. His tone announced precisely a speech prepared in advance.

"In every historical or fictional great love is an in-

226

herent contradiction; we pay tribute to these loves because they cannot be. For this reason we weep for Antony, Phèdre, Narcissus, Nicolette. For this reason we weep for Troy and not for Helen, because there is no reason her marriage or her affair should not continue. Therefore: since what can be accomplished is never vast, the vast, the great love is based on all that cannot be accomplished, which is always vast. And the great crisis of any love affair is the realization that it could continue."

He briefly paused and passed a hand over his brow, as if confused, but almost immediately straightened, laid down his "notes" and spread his arms pontifically.

"Which brings us to true love, another thing altogether than great love. True love always contains some lesser hint of the unknowable, the inexperienceable, the inexpressible, the unshareable. True love is in this sense to great love what art is to experience. It is a compromise; a making-do, with sufficient vitality of its own to accept the fact that it is precisely this: not impossible."

He stopped again, took a deep breath, then hesitated once more and simply said, "Ladies and gentlemen, I propose a toast to: love."

But Jean-Claude's own glasses were empty, and the bottles were dry as well. He turned them all successively upside down, with a shrug for each, and the laughter as the toast was drunk was scarcely less cheerful than before. Here and there a few glances conferred and acknowledged — indulgently, however — that Jean-Claude had had a bit more than he could handle.

Harold drank. I liberally partook of sautéed mushrooms. Jean-Claude sat down, and the hubbub gradually rose again around us. Among us, a kind of movement and conversation started up that suggested its innovators had lost coordination of their limbs and tongues.

"Then," Kenneth said in a deliberately reasonable tone, "anyone whose love is not returned is a greater lover than any coddled husband or coquette."

"That kind of impossibility, of course," Jean-Claude said coldly, "doesn't count."

For the rest of the meal, no one found any topic but his food.

After the final course, in which a great quantity of *crème au beurre* — not mine — was left to waste, Prytania lifted a blanched, bland face across to Harold.

"Perhaps you'd like to see the grounds," she said. The invitation was palpably absurd, as Prytania had not seen the grounds herself, and Harold, as he immediately indicated, had; but the company apparently heard nothing in it save a signal to disperse. Elena bore some plates away. Laura herded the children toward the sunlight. Jean-Claude stood and stalked out of sight without a word to anyone.

"I'm glad to see," Mme Bastien murmured to me with a twinkle of her awful eyes, "that others have the same difficulty managing my boy as I always had."

"Not at all," it pleased me to answer, and pleased me even more to see that she accepted this as a cant demur to the apology implied.

"He'd had a bit to drink, I'm sorry to say," and she moved away, her visage announcing that the mystery was now solved.

I stepped to where Kenneth was levering Mme de Verbois from her chair.

"Your tactics are wrong," I said. "You'd do well to give them a review."

"Sir?" He jerked his head above Madame, and the old

lady, too, was yanked almost upright with the force of
his start. She grunted a little and remained as she was,
slightly bowed in the support of his hands, gathering
forces to complete the rise.

"Your tactics," I repeated.

"I'm sure I don't know what you mean."

Without looking at Madame I gave her my hand,
which, after a brief hesitation, she elected to grasp. Hard
fingers hung on my wrist like hooks, and with a low
noise like the sound of rust she managed to stand. The
hands recoiled.

"I mean that you've chosen the rôle of Penelope —
make it Job. If you show your temper, and you did just
now, your stock goes down."

His face, rather squarer, I thought, than heretofore,
twitched slightly with dislike.

"If you're talking about Prytania, I'm only following
your advice. You pointed out that all I wanted was a
contract and consent. It's all I'm asking, and I'm going
about it reasonably enough."

"Reasonably," I pursued, "but not quite reasonably
enough. You haven't learned that creditors are apt to be
disliked. Therefore, they have to keep close counsel.
They can't afford mistakes."

"Quick with the metaphor these days, aren't you?" he
replied. The blood mounted to his face in such a fury
that I suddenly thought he was going to strike me. I
offered my arm to Madame, but she made no move to
take or touch it, so I nodded to her and followed after
the others to the woods.

I chose a little knoll above the houses, not quite halfway
to the playground from whence came the splat and

twang of tennis balls, the squeal of swing chains, and children's voices calling, *"Plus haut! Plus haut!"*

I sat on my overcoat on a mattress of pine needles, my heels wedged, because the incline was steep, against a corner of blue rock. The rock rose gently at my left in a low ledge, expressly formed, it seemed, to support my arm. Behind me a little crowd of pines bristled against each other and fought for the sky, but equally failed because they grew too dense. Some sort of berry bush with curling thorns and clusters of inedible, unripe fruit stood at my right, concealing the crooked path by which I had climbed. It gave off an acrid sweetness almost animal. The hill below me fell away, irregularly open through the trees on rivulets not yet rushing, patches of brilliantly pallid sky, the red roofs of the village of L'Isle Automne. I could see nothing of the Bastien houses but one plaster chimney stack, where the refuse of our feast was being fed into the air.

All of us have moments of unmixed and unsullied joy, when the light falls right and the very air seems of one temperature and one substance with our bodies. I think it was cold, but I had no desire to put on my overcoat, to walk with the others, or to move at all. A torpor took me, less like sleep than like a vegetable stillness running sap. A profound silence lay at the source of everything, and over it were picked out, clear and separate, distant sounds. The balls above spat back and forth. Somewhere in the valley a dog barked once. From the town a church bell clanged as if the brass had been long cracked, and now and again a bird shrieked, scolded, repented, and was still. My watch, which I did not hear on my pillow in Paris at night, ticked off the seconds uniform and dry.

A shaft of light fell over my right shoulder, and illuminated in the berry bush the tiniest cobweb I had

ever seen. It was the size and shape and brilliance of a
silver dollar; its symmetry might have been planned by
a machine. It must have been fragile, I thought; anything so slight must be fragile. But the light made metal
of it; it was invulnerably whole; the seven strings that
splayed from it were welded on seven thorns, as invisibly
as the cables of a far-off bridge, and no less sure. I
counted the interstices of one radius and another, super-
imposed each wedge of air on the one at its left to check
its shape, compared the spaces of its perimeter between
the anchor threads, assuring myself that its perfection
was absolute.

I don't know how long I entertained myself with the
appreciation of this triumph, but my absorption must
have been worthy of it. Even the sounds went beyond
my consciousness, and when I became aware of them
again, the bell had stopped and the birds had either
gone or gone to sleep.

I thought at first it was these that broke my day-
dream, as a stop will wake a man who has dozed on a
moving train. Yet as I tried to remember how long it
had been since I heard the bell, some slight noise came
from the path. I recognized it, and realized that I had
been hearing it for some time, yet I don't know what it
was; it could have been the crushing of damp pine, or
the brush of a woman's stockings against each other.

I tried to catch the light on the cobweb at the same
angle as before, turning and following the shaft from
where it broke through the trees. It fell without warning on Madame's head and torso. The light hung
harshly on the downward creases of her face, and she
studied me in a cold, tired way.

I suppose she had not really lost a great deal of flesh;
it might have become her as a girl. But now she had
borne the flesh too long, and it had lost its resilience. All

the lines of her body sloughed toward earth, all the excess in her face converged toward two deep lines along her mouth. We remained facing each other in frank appraisal.

"We will all lose her," Madame said abruptly.

I let a smile break, rose, and offered her my arm.

"May I take you back to your chair below?"

"All of us, and you as well."

"Madame," I remonstrated gently, "you take things very much too hard. I shouldn't have suspected you of giving up so easily. Why don't you simply ask Prytania to visit you sometimes?"

"Because," she said, "she might come, and she might not really wish it."

"As you will. Will you take my arm?"

She continued to stare at me and, very slowly, turned her body in the direction of the descent.

"When you need someone to talk to, and somewhere to go, I shall . . . receive you," Madame said.

Her hauteur was so queenly that I bowed, the mocking gesture of a sycophant. Madame began laboriously down.

Her skirt clung to the bush and carried it bending with her a little way. Then the branches shot back violently, and I saw the cobweb shudder. She had broken it. Regret swept over me, and for the first time I felt the chill. I raised my hand and thrashed it through the torn strands with much greater force than I need have to destroy so small a thing. It added no resistance to the air. It simply collapsed and clotted into the dampness of my palm.

For the ten days left Prytania bought, pressed, packed, unpacked, repacked. I saw her home each day to The

Little House, recklessly, I suppose, but I never stayed long, and I hardly think she noticed I was there. Her industry was slightly grim, and occupied her wholly. She never mentioned Jean-Claude's conduct at L'Isle Automne, at any rate not to me, and I should be very much surprised if she mentioned it to him. She only once, when I ventured to chide her for a labor clearly useless, stopped and fixed me with a wistful look, and pushed a handful of her hair aside.

"Once we get off, you see," she said, by way of vindication.

Jean-Claude behaved peculiarly, but she either didn't see it or else, I should think more likely, she chose to treat it as the norm. If he was due to arrive, she could be sure he wouldn't do so. But at unlikely hours — once in the middle of rehearsal, more than once at midnight — he would appear, lie on the couch, pretend to supervise her packing, and then leave suddenly with a minimal good-bye. Like her he seemed to be restlessly enduring the trivia of the interval before a change.

On the night before their departure I dined alone in a sandwich bar, and then I went to The Little House, deliberately intending to stay until I was asked to go. I had told my wife that I wouldn't be home till late, but I don't think I made much effort at excuse. Laura didn't care where I went or when I returned these days. It had occurred to me that she believed I was drinking. At least I thought I caught her once surreptitiously sniffing my breath when I got in bed. Sometimes, to oblige her, I stopped at the little bar below our apartment and held one whole neat whisky in my mouth as I climbed the stairs.

April, all of it, had been mild, with only intermittent showers of the kind poetically assigned to April. Now in

the first week of May all the residue of winter was being
emptied on us, as a woman might overturn a pot of
souring soup. It was a heavy, stupid, blundering kind of
storm, with thunder enough to serve a dozen times the
lightning. There was nothing liquid in the rain; it
might have been lard or mash or half-cooked peas. The
whole park hurried mud that sucked at my heels and
slapped my ankles. The Little House grunted and trembled under a force that threatened, not to wash it away,
but to hammer it headlong into the soughing ground.

Prytania called for me to come in. I left what water I
could behind me and eased into my chair. She was
kneeling before an open suitcase, over which hung a
new trenchcoat stiff as parchment, and with the flat of
her hands she was trying to coax the wrinkles from her
fake Scotch coat. She was dressed in a wrapper faintly
Eastern, threadbare, negligent, but under it she
glistened of scrubbing and special care. On her eyelids
were two streaks of uneven green, foolish and touching,
lost altogether against the brilliance of her eyes. She
rolled a cuff between her fingers, considering the wear,
and I noticed that she had painted her nails some heavy
melon color. It didn't suit her, of course; the fingers
were wider than before, and as blunt as if she had
chopped them straight across. She drew a blundering
breath, and frowned beyond my ear.

"Change frightens everyone," I said.

Her eyes slid up to locate mine, then fell away again.

"I was only wondering if I'd need the plaid."

Jean-Claude had, needlessly grave, as if he were
wheedling a child, warned Prytania that he would spend
the last evening with Elena. Prytania had said she
understood, with the solemnity of farce. And so, as I
think we both expected, about nine o'clock he came. He

said there were just a few brief points he wanted to double-check, but when it came to producing them, he was at a loss. He told her not to forget her passport, which, as he well knew, had been zipped in her bag for a dozen days. He repeated the name of the station and the hour she must arrive, which were both of them things Prytania was much less likely to forget than he. Then he said he must be going, and he installed himself on the couch. At intervals he got up and wandered to the window or the door. He would say, "I'll give it ten minutes more," or, "It's bound to let up soon" — when clearly it was not that kind of rain.

Prytania laid the coats aside and filled her two new bags, which I think she had newly emptied when she came from work. When there was no item left she could reconsider or rearrange, she stood up from them and stared into her shuddering rubber plant, as if wondering whether she might not get that in too.

"I'll need help strapping them," she said to the rubber plant. But it didn't respond, and Jean-Claude only peered through the banging pane.

"It's a hell of a nasty night," he said profoundly.

I went to her and closed the lid on the larger case. Then, while she straddled it, I slipped a strap through one brass buckle. The case was black and waxen, almost slippery to the touch. It was pungent with departure, as only new leather is. I pulled the strap as far as it needed to go, then I forced it to a farther closure.

"Your hands are shaking," Prytania announced.

I smiled up at her, where she sat astride her precious luggage, grasping two corners of it as if she expected it to fly, her smeared eyelids stretched upward with surprise. I wondered whether there were something I could say to make her laugh, but I couldn't think of anything,

and I didn't dare to fail. The planes of her cheeks were
waxen, but they seemed to me now not so malleable as
slippery, like the surface of the suitcase.

"I suppose I'm a little nervous," I admitted with a
shrug.

"We all are," Jean-Claude decided without turning
from the window. "It's the rain," he said. Neither of us
saw fit to challenge him. I buckled the second case.

"That's it, then," Prytania said loudly, and trying to
be light, but she sounded rather as if the thought
distressed her. She cast about for something to do and
amplified, "I'm ready."

Jean-Claude turned and looked at her at that, or
looked at the space that would have been there if she
had not. Prytania ended by laughing and putting a hand
up to her hair.

"Do I need combing or something?" she protested.

"What? Oh. No, no." He focused and started to turn
away, then swung back, suddenly frowning at her face.
He went to her and pulled the blunt hand from her
brow. She plucked it back but he tightened his grip and
stared at her fingernails. She helplessly hid the other
hand behind her back.

"It's nothing," she said. "I can take it off. I thought
. . . I thought you liked it."

He stayed for a moment looking at her hand, his
nostrils slightly distended in distaste, and under the
grimace of scrutiny the hand became grotesque to me. I
should like to have hidden it, and I raged against him
inwardly for exposing her.

"I like it on Elena," he said distinctly.

Prytania looked as if he had struck her, and my own
face froze with the same sensation. I said, "Good Christ,
Jean-Claude, what does it matter?"

His grip relaxed, and Prytania took all her fingers to her lap.

"It doesn't," he said. He added, "I'm sorry," but his voice bespoke nothing but fatigue.

"I've got to go," he said, but once more he turned and stared at the rain. Prytania's eyes flailed through her plants and she bounded up. She swung both suitcases across the room and aligned them beneath the rubber plant.

"We should have a little drink," she called above the storm. "I think there's half a bottle of wine. Listen!" she babbled to me with a bogus brightness that verged on hysteria. "I found the weirdest thing this afternoon. I turned the mattress. I thought I should let it air or something — I don't know, isn't that what you do?"

I laughed in her own volume to encourage her, and assured her that I was certain you did something of the kind.

"Well, and there's a little ledge underneath, in the corner of the frame. A kind of support that runs across the corner, do you see?"

"Yes, well?" I prompted.

"Well, guess what I found there, you'll never guess!"

"Four million francs," I said.

Jean-Claude asked, "Shall I guess?" and Prytania threw him a glance of fierce revenge.

"No, you don't count. It wouldn't mean anything to you." She laughed, but the laugh was nasty, only pretending to pretend. "Guess!" she insisted.

"Something of Riebenstahl's, then."

"You're getting warmer."

"Tomato seedlings. A box of bones."

"No!" she said. "The glasses!"

She tossed her head, set her hands on her hips and

surveyed me for the effect. I tried to look as mystified as she would have me.

"Of course!" I exclaimed. "I should have thought. His daughter never found them."

"Well, isn't that the strangest thing you ever heard? Why do you suppose he would have hid them?"

Then, evidently not expecting me to have any reply to this, she darted from the room and to the kitchen.

"What glasses?" Jean-Claude asked, but Prytania was immediately back, with a half-filled bottle of Beaujolais and a little cardboard box.

"The ones I cut my hand on. Wait till you see how fine they are. There are four of them. Do you suppose they're very precious if he hid them?"

"I'm sure they are," I said, "or else he decided they were dangerous."

She unwrapped the glasses with trembling care and set them on the mantel. Then she chose one and took it toward the window, senselessly, for no light came from there, only belching wind and rain. Perhaps she did it for the pleasure of having Jean-Claude follow after, who seemed bewildered and dubious, at the excitement we displayed.

She lifted the glass at the window, defying him with the full exposure of her hand.

"Don't touch it," she said. "It's fragile, and you're too clumsy."

Jean-Claude's confusion broke into an exasperated sigh at this. He flipped a hand at the glass as if to say it was nothing special, and would have retorted to her taunt had the silence not been broken for him by a scraping at the door. All of us heard it, but all of us strained to it, not quite sure that we had. It was so unlikely that anyone should be calling in the rain, when no one had ever called at all before, that our glances concurred in a vision of prowlers or thieves.

Wet wind tumbled on us from the vestibule. The rubber plant reared and whipped. Something fell against the wall. We were frozen, all of us, and when a little stillness succeeded we couldn't seem to thaw. Prytania drew a breath as if she needed it to cry out, and then Jean-Claude and I found our voices in the same instant to call, "Who's there?"

Slowly, measuring her progress like a little child, Elena came in and steadied herself with a hand against the wall. She didn't look at us at first, but studied the hand and the deltas of yellow wall between her fingers. Her hair was plastered down her cheeks, which ran rain and tears together. Her dark slacks clung and twisted at the knee; her wool coat, like a giant sponge, slipped water in pools around her.

Her focus wandered slightly without lighting on anything, then the suitcases fell within her line of vision, struck sleek and pimply in the bursts of lightning. She looked at them for a moment, and a low sound from deep within her throat, like someone shouting at a great distance, came, "Aieee, aieee."

She weaved a little. She drew her eyes with an effort from the cases and cast them aimlessly until they happened on Jean-Claude. She smiled. Her cheeks stood out, blanched with strain. She said, separating the words like someone who has memorized a foreign phrase, "I came to say that I would like you to choose now, but I . . . see that you . . . have already done so."

"No," burst from Jean-Claude, but it seemed that he could neither move toward her nor go on.

Elena continued to smile, a hideous grin of agony. She put her free hand to her forehead and turned herself by the pressure of the other on the wall. Her glance wavered again, over the bank of plants where the leaves were scrabbling at each other noisily; took in Prytania without seeming to register her, wandered again and came to rest on me.

I had thought her fully spent, but now her face recoiled in a swift fang-baring disbelief. She wiped at the space in front of her eyes and squinted. Her mouth convulsed and she began to scream. Her shrieks struck one by one, short, sharp and undiminishing. They seemed to give thrust and purpose to the wind itself, which hit out in cold brief blasts. Staring toward me, drawing no breath but taking force from the wind she forced around us, she screamed until Jean-Claude finally stepped forward and slapped her, hard.

She stopped. She backed from him, and as her shadow receded from the lake her dripping coat had made on the rug, we could see long strings of blood lazily uncurling in the water, settling more heavily into the spaces between the raffia strands. Elena, backing, averted her eyes and pulled her coat in fists about her thighs.

"I tried to wait for you at home," she pleaded. Her shoulder brushed into the rubber plant and she wheeled, shrinking from it. She receded jerkily, then missed her balance and grabbed at it for support. She continued to back, at once recoiling and hanging on to it, so that the top bent toward her, poised, and slowly inverted its arc. It bent in toward her, rolled on top of a suitcase and crashed to the floor. She let go of it, jumped, and a cry broke from her into the ceiling beams.

"Oh, God, I'm bleeding," she screamed. "Don't you understand? Jean-Claude, it's going."

She didn't fall, but Jean-Claude caught her up as if she had. He forced his shoulder under her arm and pulled her whole weight to him. The water from her coat and hair fled staining into his suit. Without a word he swung her around and half-carried her to the door, but Prytania, with a spring and bound, snatched at his arm and hung there.

"Choose!" she said savagely, digging her fingers into the flesh at his wrist. "Choose now, choose now, choose me!" she whispered wildly.

He batted against her grip as against a gnat and pulled Elena forward, then finding the resistance too great, he squandered one full-face glare at Prytania and flung her with all his force from the arm. She fell back whimpering and let him take Elena on into the rain.

She stood a moment longer moaning, the wet wind buffeting her hair. I started for the door to close it, but as I moved Prytania sprang before me, raced to it and slammed it. She recoiled and wheeled as if it had shut in her face, sped to the window, where we could dimly see Jean-Claude swing Elena up to carry her like a child, leaped back from this and turned again. She ran. I should not have thought it possible in so small a room. She made for the stairs, bounded once upon them, bounced back to the floor and spun. She leaped, pounced on her rubber plant and swung it upright in both hands. She shook it, pounded, rocked it, like a woman furiously churning butter, until the roots broke free and the pot went tottering, clattering by itself to the wall.

"Prytania!"

She cast the plant down, whirling in the direction of my voice, spied the glasses on the mantelpiece and made for them, her arms stretched out before her, blindly running.

I stepped in her path. Her full weight, which was not very great, struck into my chest and shattered. Her body went limp against me; she lay against my shoulder sagging into my arms and knees. Her arms were trapped between us, her hands crumpled just beneath my chin; they were full of the odor of twisted leaves and the flat, stale smell of bark. Her hair had flown before her across my shoulder. I buried my face in it. It bristled against my cheek and smelled of rain.

I held her there, stroking her bent spine gently, rubbing her back in long slow sweeps from her neck. She had gone so limp that her back formed one shallow arch to the top of her thighs. I set my hand against her buttocks and drew her carefully to me. She began to shudder, and the shudder sent itself to me. I felt that I was stroking liquid life into a part of my body that had gone numb.

I clasped her to me and carried her before me to the couch; she was so light that I scarcely needed shift her weight as I lay us down. She had made no sound, had moved no muscle; only trembled. Now she moaned and let her face fall into my neck. She gave off the heady scents of fur and leaf and tempest; at once the storm, the animal that hid from it, and the thicket where it hid. The essences swept and sickened me, and no part of me seemed alive except for my right hand, to which all my senses gathered. I kneaded her thigh and felt that it molded to any shape I willed; I pressed her hip and the very bone bent and yielded beneath my palm. A heavy rasp broke from me — I had forgotten I had a voice — and then as I forced all my weight into the little handful of her breast, I seemed to break myself; the veins of my temple split and I thought the blood ran in my throat.

There was a great blackness in my head which shifted and rolled itself into the vision of a forest. I stood at an elevation from a multitude that neither cheered nor bowed, but stood in dumb submission while a storm raged that touched neither them nor me. They were the color of Prytania, and they had her hooded eyes. They were fantastically dressed in skins the color of summer flowers, and wore hats like small pagodas weighted with clamoring, jangling bells. Their mute, mouth-open worship built a buoyance under me, on which I weightlessly ascended into the overhang of trees.

I think I was briefly unconscious. At least I was not aware of the vision's going, or of Prytania's stiffening under me. I only gradually learned a sharpness struggling at my weight. Small arms like steel struck at me and I fell heavily away.

"Stay with me," I found from somewhere sufficient strength to say. "It can be the same as always. Stay with me."

"The same!" Prytania spat, and sprang. Her limbs and fingers struck into my flesh like nails as she scrambled to the floor. "The same!"

I forced myself to open my eyes, to see the face that must accompany such a voice. But Prytania's face had no expression; not disgust, not even anger. Her eyes were vacuous as black water, a void where a man might wander and stumble and never reach an edge. She raised one hand and lowered it, took a breath and turned away.

"You . . . had . . . better go now," she said in a voice without a tone; and then, drawn up with dignity, she mounted her stairs, sliding both feet one after the other on each step till they reached the rise, taking a new grasp on the railing for every step she gained.

She came to say good-bye to me, which she might not have done. I think of that sometimes, I sometimes speak of it to Madame.

She let herself into my office in midafternoon, by the

back stairs from Supply. No one but Papadeneau ordinarily uses that door, so that when I heard it open I said without turning, "Not now. I'm busy."

She came around to stand by the chair before my desk, from whence for more than a year she had recorded my dictation in that slant scrivening that served for shorthand.

"Now, please," she said, and gave me the shallowest of her smiles.

"I'm going away," she said, "but not to America, of course. I think I'll go to Spain. I'd like to see where Elena lived. Is that strange of me?"

I shook my head. I had been making strokes with my pen in the margin of a letter. I saw these now and studied them, but they seemed to have no meaning.

"I went to the hospital, but they wouldn't let me in. I don't know, if they had, if I'd have seen her. I just went out again and walked up and down on the cobblestones. Jean-Claude was there."

She paused, and I wondered stupidly if I should ask her to sit down.

"I did it . . . very well," Prytania told me. "I'm glad of that. I said, 'Loving you has made me strong enough not to be loved by you.' That was right, wasn't it? That was both true and what I needed to have said."

The truth has never engendered such gentle pride. She stood against the chair, brushing her knee on its slatted back, contemplating her success, and rubbing over a nailhead the hand in which she would never get quite all the feeling back.

"He didn't even love me differently. He only loved me less. It's like those little dust devils you see in New Orleans in the parks. I got caught up in it, and I

244

mistook myself for the wind. Have you any idea how it feels to discover that?"

"I think I have," I replied, and Prytania's eyes slid from me in one languorous blink.

"You mustn't think I'm stupid. I'm not at all stupid."

I prepared some hesitant noise by way of protest that I did not think that, but she went on again, with greater effort.

"Jean-Claude must make speeches, but he doesn't always say exactly what he means. So I wanted you to know from me, because you might not know it. . . ." She stilled her hands on the chair back, searching for the words. ". . . love is its own impossibility. Not being loved is a detail."

She stopped, gestured slightly, as if to say that was the best she could do.

"Tell Kenneth that I'm sorry. He'll know it, but it's all he needs to know."

She stepped in toward me, and in perfect certainty of the degree of farewell required, she touched my hand with two unbeautiful fingers.

When she had gone I sat for some time feeling the raised letterhead of the Harrison Import-Export Co., Chicago. I thought that I might go home, might play the truant for an afternoon, with a glass of sherry and some dry book in an easier chair than this. I might have, would have, had not Papadeneau scraped in then, with so cheekily intimate an air that he might have been the only friend remaining to my old age; with his little half-bows and his obsequious gall that always says, "I'm not worth any trouble, but trouble about me all the same." He had some maudlin tale of a little orange-eyed cashier, who, though she touched him with power to the core, inspired him to the reaches of his paltry soul, yet she would not yield him so much as the focus of her eyes.

God! We are so vexed on all sides by these simpletons, these asses who will tell you, "I'm an ordinary man, no one knows his insignificance so well as I; but, look you, once I have felt the madness of the gods in me!" The Devil take them all.

New Orleans, 1961
Ghent, 1964

www.ingramcontent.com/pod-product-compliance
Lightning Source LLC
Chambersburg PA
CBHW032000050726
47590CB00006B/1987